DEATH IN A SKIP

A gripping British crime mystery full of twists

P.F. FORD

A Slater & Norman Mystery Book 8

Originally published as *The Kidney Donor*

JOFFE BOOKS

Revised edition 2024
Joffe Books, London
www.joffebooks.com

First published as *The Kidney Donor*
in Great Britain in 2016

This paperback edition was first published
in Great Britain in 2024

Cover art by Dee Dee Book Covers

ISBN: 978-1-83526-576-5

With thanks to my amazing wife, Mary — sometimes we need someone else to believe in us before we really believe in ourselves. None of this would have happened without her unfailing belief and support.

CHAPTER ONE

Former Detective Sergeant, now just plain Mr, David Slater yawned expansively as he made his weary way to baggage reclaim at Gatwick Airport. His flight back from Bangkok that should have taken sixteen hours, including a three-hour stopover in Dubai, had actually taken eight hours longer because first, some idiot had left an unattended bag in the main concourse at Dubai, and then their aircraft had developed some sort of technical problem while on the ground.

Slater had thought it somewhat ironic that so many people had complained very loudly about the bag turning out to be a false alarm, and he had wondered if perhaps they would have preferred the bag to have been the real deal. Then there had been more complaints about the technical problem with their aircraft, as if some of them would have preferred to take off with the problem unsolved. At one point, he had even pointed out to some particularly vociferous passengers, who were haranguing one of the airline staff, that had the aircraft developed a problem while they were in the air, they might not have had been in the fortunate position of being able to complain about it.

He hadn't really been surprised to find his comments fell on stony ground, and it seemed to him that for some people complaining was simply a form of pleasure, much like a hobby. He assumed these must be the same people who spent all their time writing to complain to someone, somewhere, about something . . .

Now he stood back and watched, amused, as those very same people now indignantly complained about the lack of space around the carousel. Apparently some other people from their flight were trying to secure their own bags first. How dare they? Life just wasn't fair, was it?

Slater found a relatively uncrowded space away from the carousel, leaned back against the wall, and waited. He would watch, and wait, until the crush died down. He was way too tired to fight with anyone for anything right now, and besides, he had nothing to rush home for, and there was nowhere in particular he had to be. His suitcase would still be there, going round and round, until he collected it. And, if he was honest, right now he just couldn't be arsed.

As he waited, he thought about his current position. He was now officially jobless, which was either a good thing or a bad thing, depending on his mood at the time he was considering it. On the negative side, it meant he had no visible means of support, which was just a tad worrying, but then, on the positive side, it had just enabled him to spend three weeks in Thailand, something he would never have done had he still been employed.

He had gone away on his own for some peace and solitude to celebrate his fortieth birthday. Or at least that was what he had told anyone who had asked, and that was the story he was sticking to now he was back. It was true he had travelled out on his own, and he had travelled back on his own, but what had actually happened while he was out there, and had made it necessary to extend his stay from two weeks to three, was no one's business but his. Not that there was anyone here in England who was likely to ask, except perhaps his best friend Norman Norman, who had been forced to retire from the force on the grounds of apparently being a bit too roly-poly for the demands of the job.

During his three weeks away, Slater had come to realise that apart from Norman, his only friends were his ex-colleagues, and it had occurred to him that without realising it, he had been so involved with his job he had become a loner with almost no social life. This was something he had resolved to put right. All he had to do was figure out where a single, forty-year-old man would go to meet people. This was a puzzle he had yet to solve as he felt he was probably getting a bit old for clubbing. He'd heard internet dating was a popular, modern way of meeting people, and he thought maybe he should give that a go.

He suddenly realised the chaos surrounding the baggage carousel had subsided, and he could see there was just the one solitary suitcase still trundling around. Somehow, it seemed totally appropriate that his suitcase should be going around in circles on its own, as if it was enacting a metaphor for his own life. He enjoyed a wry smile at this idea as he pushed himself away from the wall, ambled across to the carousel, and rescued the solitary suitcase.

He extended the handle on his case and, trundling the bag along behind him, headed for the exit. He was pleased to see his tactics had worked perfectly. Not only had he avoided the melee at baggage reclaim, he now had clear passage through customs. Within minutes, he was making his way out into the arrivals lounge. As he walked, he weighed up the advantages of finding a train home straight away against booking a hotel room and getting some sleep first. After all, there was no need to rush, and he was knackered.

His thoughts were interrupted by the sound of a familiar voice calling out his name.

'Hey! Dave! Over here!'

Slater looked across at the faces gathered by the barrier that held the waiting public back from the arrivals. At busy times, this would be a veritable sea of excited, anticipatory faces, but this early in the morning, the few faces he could see were bleary-eyed and looked almost resentful. All, that is, except for the beaming face of a man whose unruly mop of curly hair and faded, tatty denim jacket made him instantly recognisable.

As if he was worried Slater might have a problem spotting him, the man called out again, raised his arms, and did an enormously exaggerated pair of 'jazz hands'.

Slater was grateful for two things. First, he was grateful his friend Norman was there to meet him, and second, he was grateful it had been such an early arrival there weren't too many people around to witness his embarrassment.

CHAPTER TWO

'I wasn't expecting you to be here, Norm, but boy, am I pleased to see you,' said Slater, as Norman led him towards the car park.

'Crap journey, huh?' said Norman.

'It would have been long enough anyway without hanging around halfway,' said Slater. 'And then, on top of that, I've had to listen to people bleating about the delay. I mean would you want to take off knowing there was a technical problem? It's a safety issue. What do these people expect?'

'I wouldn't take off even if there wasn't a problem,' said Norman. 'It's not natural. Do you see any wings on my back? Of course not, and that's because we aren't supposed to fly!'

'So how come you're here anyway? I thought you were busy today.'

'That was yesterday,' said Norman. 'As it happens, your delay means you've landed this morning instead of last night. I was busy last night, but I'm free this morning, so here I am.'

'But how did you know?'

'About the delay?' asked Norman. 'Well, I used to be a police officer, and learning how to check the arrival time of a flight was one of the things I learned. You left me all the info, remember?'

Slater looked at Norman. He had obviously missed some sleep to get here so early, but now the greeting was over and the big beaming smile had faded, he appeared to have something on his mind.

'Are you okay?' he asked. 'Only you look like shite.'

Norman looked at Slater. 'Aww, shucks, Dave,' he said, coyly. 'You say the nicest things, you know that? But if you think I look bad, you'd better stay well away from any mirrors.'

'Yeah,' admitted Slater, 'but I have an excuse. I haven't slept for hours because I've been travelling. What are you doing here anyway?'

They were at the car now, and Norman popped the boot open.

'I'm your friend, right?' he said, taking Slater's suitcase and placing it inside. 'I just thought you would appreciate a lift home after a delayed flight.'

'Norm, you look like you've had bugger all sleep, and you obviously have something on your mind.'

Norman looked unhappily at Slater as they walked to opposite sides of the car and climbed inside.

'What happened to, "Hi Norm, great to see you. Thanks for coming to pick me up"?' asked Norman as he slumped into the driver's seat and began heaving at the seat belt, which seemed reluctant to accommodate his waistline.

'Of course I'm glad to see you,' said Slater. 'I already said that when I first saw you. But now I can see it in your face. Something's wrong.'

'Jeez, is it that obvious?'

'You look unhappy, and you look guilty,' said Slater. 'So why are you really here, Norm?'

Norman sighed. He started the car, reversed from the parking space, and headed for the exit ramp.

'You know I have a key to your house,' said Norman.

'Yeah, of course I do. I gave it to you.'

'And you keep another key in the kitchen drawer.'

'So, what? You lost the spare key?' asked Slater.

'Oh, it's not lost,' said Norman. 'I know exactly where it is.'

'Jesus, Norm,' said Slater, exasperated. 'This is like pulling teeth. Will you just tell me what's wrong!'

Norman sighed again. They were on the way out of Gatwick now, heading onto the M23 motorway.

'I have this friend,' he said. 'He's in trouble and needed somewhere to stay. Obviously if I had my own place, I'd have moved him in with me, but I've only got the room at the pub, and they don't have any spare rooms, and your house was empty and—'

'You've moved someone into my bloody house while I was away?' asked Slater, aghast. 'Without asking?'

'How could I ask?' said Norman, reasonably. 'You were halfway around the world. Besides, you asked me to keep an eye on your house while you were away. This is even better — there's someone there twenty-four seven looking after it.'

'I asked you to keep an eye on it and pick up the post now and then, not move a security guard into the place! Who is this bloke anyway? And what does he do? And where does he normally live?'

'Ah, well, he doesn't exactly do anything.' Norman shifted in his seat. 'He sort of doesn't have a job right now, a bit like you and me.'

'So where's he from?'

'It's a bit difficult to say,' said Norman, uncomfortably.

Slater turned sideways to look at Norman. 'Do I detect a certain amount of evasion?' he asked. 'Only considering this guy's a friend, you seem to be having a lot of difficulty answering these questions.'

'I don't know what you mean,' said Norman innocently, keeping his eyes fixed firmly on the road.

'Alright,' said Slater. 'So let's try an easy one. Where does this guy live when he's not squatting in my house?'

'He's not a squatter. I invited him to stay.'

'Yes, but you seem to have forgotten it's not your house. So where does he normally live?'

'Err, well, up until a couple of weeks ago he was living in a skip by the old printing works.'

'What?'

'He's homeless, alright?' said Norman. 'And he's in some sort of trouble, and I think someone ought to try and help him, but it seems no one gives a damn about people like him, so I thought I'd try. And I was hoping you might help me.'

'Whoa! Wait a minute,' said Slater. 'You mean to say I've got some tramp living in my house?'

'Can you hear yourself?' said Norman. 'This guy's not a tramp. He's a damned hero, who's been fighting for his country, but now he's finished doing that, he seems to have been discarded like some piece of trash.'

'Since when have you been friends with this guy?' asked Slater. 'I thought I knew all your friends. In fact, I thought I was the only friend you had.'

'I met him a few weeks ago. We just got talking and I fed him a few times. He's a good guy. He's just down on his luck, that's all.'

'You felt sorry for him so you decided to invite him to come and live in my house?'

'It wasn't like that,' said Norman. 'It's not that simple. I told you, he's in trouble and he needed somewhere to hide.'

'What sort of trouble?'

'I'm not sure exactly.'

'Are you sure he's not just giving you a load of bullshit and taking advantage of your better nature?'

Now Norman was clearly beginning to get irritated with the whole situation.

'Look, I understand you're annoyed with me right now, but you also know I'm not a complete idiot, right? If I thought the guy was full of shit, I would never have let him anywhere near your house.'

'What's he done that he needs to be in hiding?' asked Slater. 'He's not on the run from the police, is he? I mean that would be just a tad awkward, don't you think?'

'Will you hold off with the indignation? Jeez. Remind me never to come to you when I need help.'

For a moment, Slater's mouth flapped open and closed silently, but only for a moment. 'Hang on a minute,' he said. 'Let's just have a quick recap of the situation here, so we can understand just why I may appear to be a tad indignant, shall we?'

Norman looked like he was about to say something and then thought better of it.

'In case you had forgotten, I've just been away for three weeks,' continued Slater, 'to celebrate my birthday. Now, on my return, the first thing I'm greeted with is the news that there's a tramp dossing down in my house.'

'For the last time, he's not a tramp,' said Norman, testily.

'It wouldn't matter if he was a bloody prince,' said Slater, even more testily. 'The point is, you invited someone to stay at my house while I was away without even asking me first.' He raised his voice to emphasise the next bit. 'Even more to the point, I don't want some stranger living in my house!'

They drove on in stony silence, each nursing his own grievance against the other. It was Norman who eventually broke the ice.

'Look, I'm sorry. I was sure if you met the guy and spoke to him, you'd want to help him out, but obviously I was wrong. Maybe I don't know you as well as I thought.'

The comment had been designed to target Slater's better nature and it scored a bullseye. 'Now you're trying to make me sound like a complete arse,' he said, 'when you know damned well you're in the wrong for giving the guy my front door key.'

Norman nodded his head to acknowledge his guilt. 'Yeah, I know,' he said. 'And I really wouldn't have done it if I'd had any other choice. But he really is a good guy. I promise you you'll like him when you meet him. Just don't call him a tramp, right? He's just down at the moment and he needs some help. Is that a crime?'

'What's his name?' asked Slater.

'Ryan.'

'Ryan what?'

'It's just Ryan. I don't know if that's his surname or his Christian name.'

'So what trouble is he in?'

'Like I said, I'm not exactly sure,' admitted Norman. 'All I know is that his skip was set on fire and another homeless guy got roasted inside it. I get the feeling Ryan thinks he was the target.'

'The police must be involved — what do they say?'

'Yeah, they are involved, but they don't wanna be. They seem to be happy to accept the fire was an accident or some sort of prank and it was unfortunate there was a guy inside. They're calling it a tragic accident, but it doesn't look as if they're busting a gut to find out who started the fire.'

'But Ryan doesn't think it was an accident, right?' asked Slater. 'Why does he think that?'

'I'm hoping if you talk to him, you can help me find that out,' said Norman.

'You haven't forgotten we're not the police any more, have you, Norm?'

Norman grinned. 'Yeah, I know. But that means we don't have someone above us to push it to one side and pretend it never happened because the victim wasn't important enough.'

Slater inclined his head in agreement. 'Now that's a fact,' he said.

'And I know you're getting curious already,' added Norman.

Now Slater was grinning. 'And that's another fact,' he agreed.

'Anyway, last I heard you were out of work and looking for something to do. I reckon this is right up your street.'

* * *

Slater didn't think his little house looked any different from the outside but he had severe reservations about what to expect when they got inside. He decided to let Norman lead the way.

'He knows you, so you go in first,' he suggested, pointing towards the front door.

He followed Norman down the path, the suitcase rumbling along behind him as he pulled it along. Norman fished the key from his pocket and noisily opened the door.

'Ryan,' he called out, as he pushed the door open. 'It's me, Norm. I've got Dave with me. Come and say hello.'

There was no reply. Slater followed Norman into the house, still wondering what sort of mess he might find waiting for him. Once inside, he took a good look around. The lounge appeared to be spotless, so he headed for the kitchen. Meanwhile, Norman had gone upstairs, still calling Ryan's name.

'He's not here,' said a perplexed Norman a moment later, coming back down the stairs.

'There's a note in here,' called Slater, from an immaculately clean kitchen. 'It's addressed to you.'

As Norman came into the kitchen, Slater handed him an envelope.

'Are you sure this isn't some sort of joke and you've had a team of cleaners in here?' he asked, not quite able to take in just how clean his house was. 'This really isn't what I was expecting.'

'Yeah, well, I told you he was good guy,' said Norman, carefully opening the envelope. 'You were the one who seemed to think he was some sort of wild animal.'

He pulled a sheet of paper from the envelope and read it. 'Crap! He's gone,' he said, gloomily, passing the note to Slater. 'It seems he thinks it wouldn't be right for you to come home and find some stranger in your house.'

'I'm liking this guy already,' said Slater. It seemed he and Ryan were on the same page when it came to personal space and privacy.

He quickly read through the note.

'He didn't need to do that,' he said to Norman, guiltily. 'I know what I said earlier, but he didn't need to move out.'

'But where the hell's he gone?' asked Norman.

'It says here he'll see you later.' Slater peered at the note and then at Norman. 'What's that? Some sort of date?'

'Err, yeah,' said Norman, awkwardly. 'Well, no, not a date exactly. It's something I started doing when I retired. I just do two or three nights a week.'

'Look, you don't have to tell me if you don't want to,' said Slater. 'What you do with your evenings is your business.'

'It's not that I don't want you to know. I just think I'd rather show you than tell you.'

'This sounds very mysterious. Is it legal?'

'Of course it's legal, you idiot. Why don't you get your head down for a few hours and catch up on some of that beauty sleep you've obviously missed out on, and I'll come and pick you up later?'

'Will I like whatever it is I'm going to do?' asked Slater.

'That's what I want to find out,' said Norman. 'One thing's for sure, you'll enjoy the food, it's amazing. And the whole evening will be an education for both of us. In the meantime, I'm going to see if I can find Ryan. I'll pick you up around seven.'

'Do I need to get tarted up?'

'Your usual jeans and sweater will be fine,' said Norman. 'We're not going anywhere posh.'

* * *

Norman pulled the car to a halt and switched off the engine. 'Okay, we've arrived. Before we get out of the car, I have a couple of rules I would like you to observe.'

'Like what?' asked Slater.

'Like you keep an open mind, and don't go speaking without thinking.'

Slater thought about protesting, but he knew Norman was right. He did have a tendency to speak his thoughts.

'Okay, I can do that,' he said, looking out at their surroundings. 'Where is this place? Is that a church?'

'Just follow and stick with me, and you'll soon see where we are,' said Norman, opening the car door. 'I found this place a while ago. I love it here, and you will if you'll just open your mind and not rush to judge people.'

Slater didn't quite know how to respond to that, so he said nothing and stepped from the car. They were in a car park. There was a large church to the left, in complete darkness, but over to their right was what appeared to be the church hall. The curtains were drawn, but a warm welcoming light blazed from the open doorway. He had to walk quickly to catch up with Norman, who was striding purposefully towards it.

'What is this?' asked Slater as he caught up with Norman.

'Welcome to St Anne's,' said Norman as they reached the doorway.

'Why have you brought me here?' asked Slater, dubiously. 'You haven't turned all religious while I've been away, have you?'

'I suppose, in a manner of speaking,' said Norman, 'but not in the way you think of finding religion. What I've done is find something I can do that helps those less fortunate than me and makes me feel good at the same time. Just follow me, and remember, you are not here to piss anyone off.'

They were in the hall now, and Slater looked around. Long tables and chairs were laid out randomly throughout the room. At the far end was a large serving hatch, with plates piled up on a trolley to one side. He could just make out two people busily working away in the kitchen beyond the hatch. Then he caught the aroma that was drifting across the room, and his stomach began to remind him just how long it had been since he had eaten.

As he looked around, he realised there were other people in the room, too. A scruffy-looking man with wild hair wearing a tatty old suit was stood to one side, muttering away to himself. On the opposite side, what appeared to be a great coat standing up on its own turned around to reveal a grubby-faced individual who looked three sheets to the wind.

'Do you want me to throw the scruffs out?' asked Slater, quietly.

Norman turned and gave him a pitying look.

'Didn't I tell you not to rush to judge?' asked Norman. 'These people aren't scruffs, they're our guests.'

'Guests?' said Slater. 'They look like vagrants.'

'We don't call them that,' said Norman, testily. 'These people might be homeless, but that doesn't make them any less human. We all fall from grace sometimes, but some people fall harder than others, and they don't always have someone to help them get back up.'

Slater was suitably chastened. 'Since when have you cared about these people?'

'Since someone pointed out to me that, just a few short years ago, I could have ended up like this myself,' said Norman.

'It wasn't that bad, was it?' asked Slater.

Norman smiled wistfully. 'It was a close thing. I was getting pretty desperate, I can tell you. I'd lost the wife I had loved with all my heart, I'd lost my home, I had no friends, no one wanted to even work with me. I'm pretty sure if things hadn't changed for me, I would have hit rock bottom before much longer. But I got lucky, see? I had a job, and I got offered the chance to make a fresh start. Then I got even luckier and got teamed up with a guy who was prepared to give me a chance and trust me. I've never looked back.'

He turned away from Slater, but not quite quickly enough to hide the glistening in his eyes. He headed across the room towards the kitchen. 'Come over and join us when you're ready,' he called over his shoulder.

As Slater watched his friend walk easily and comfortably towards the kitchen, he realised he had been the guy Norman was talking about. He had been the one who had been prepared to partner with Norman and give him a chance to resurrect his career and regain his self-respect. He had always known Norman had been at a pretty low point back then, but he had never realised just how low that had been.

'Hey, Franky!' Norman called across to the greatcoat as he walked. 'What have I told you about coming here drunk?'

The man in the greatcoat seemed suddenly galvanised and a crooked smile broke out across his face. He raised a hand to acknowledge Norman.

'I'm sorry, Norm,' he called, cheerfully. 'It won't happen again.'

The scruffy man with the wild hair suddenly moved towards Norman and raised his hand in the air. For a moment, Slater thought he was going to slap his friend, but then he felt foolish as he realised they were simply exchanging high fives. He watched as Norman exchanged greetings with the man, hugged him, and patted him on the back. It was obvious he was totally at home here, and it was equally obvious he was hugely popular, although that didn't surprise Slater one little bit.

Slater felt distinctly out of his depth, but he was equally intrigued, so he made his way towards the kitchen area, nodding to the greatcoat and the other man, who watched him with a good degree of suspicion. As he approached the doorway, he slowed down, not sure of what to do next.

'Come on in, Dave,' called Norman, realising Slater's uncertainty.

He walked through the door and into the kitchen. A huge vat of soup bubbled away on the cooker, and he could see the oven was full to bursting point with baked potatoes. An enormous pile of vegetables was visible to one side, awaiting preparation. A man stood at a table, rapidly slicing more vegetables. Slater guessed from the dog collar he was sporting that he must be the local vicar. He had to have been in his late thirties, or early forties, but he had the youthful good looks of a teenager. An attractive young woman was stirring the soup with a huge ladle.

'Chris and Diane, meet my good friend Dave Slater,' announced Norman as Slater entered the room. 'Dave, meet my good friends Chris and Diane Moore.'

The vicar stopped slicing and wiped his hands on the apron he was wearing. He stepped forward and shook hands with Slater.

'Pleased to meet you,' he said. 'Norman's told us a lot about you.'

'He has?' asked Slater, doubtfully.

The vicar smiled at him, encouragingly. 'Oh, don't worry, it's all been good stuff so far. He must be saving the best bits for later.'

His wife had come over to shake Slater's hand as well. 'How are your taste buds?' she asked.

'I'm sorry?' said Slater, confused by the question.

'Come over here and taste this soup.' She led the way across to the cooker. 'I think it may need a bit more seasoning, but Chris has no idea.'

She dipped a spoon in the soup and offered it to him. 'Careful, it's hot,' she warned.

He took the spoon and blew on the soup before gingerly putting it to his mouth. He took a small sip. It tasted fantastic.

'What do you think?' she said. 'Too salty?'

'I'm no expert, but I think it's just right,' he said. 'Perfect, in fact.'

She blushed with pleasure and giggled. 'Aw, he can definitely come again,' she said, turning to Norman.

'That depends how useful he is,' said Norman, then he turned to Slater. 'See? I told you the food was amazing, didn't I? The deal is, you get fed, but in return you have to help out for the evening.'

'What do I have to do?'

'You can help me and Chris in here, if you like,' Diane said. 'Are you hungry?'

Behind him, Slater could hear the knife as Chris resumed his vegetable-chopping duties.

'I haven't eaten all day,' he said.

'Have a bowl of soup now to keep you going,' she said. 'We usually eat when everyone else has eaten.'

'Everyone else?' he said, as she ladled some soup into a bowl for him.

'They're starting to gather now.' Chris pointed out through the hatch.

Slater followed his finger and through the hatch he could see more people had gathered out in the hall. They stood around in ones and twos, many having the haunted look of the helpless and the hopeless.

'I feel a bit like a square peg in a round hole,' said Slater, taking the bowl of soup. 'I've never done this sort of thing before.'

'You'll be fine,' Chris said encouragingly. 'But it's probably best if you stay back here in the kitchen. They tend not to trust new faces. This way, they get to see you with a barrier to protect them.'

'I suppose a lot of them are a bit paranoid.'

'Most of them are, and those that aren't soon will be if they find out you're a policeman,' said Chris. 'It's probably best if we don't mention that in front of anyone here.'

'Ex-policeman,' said Slater. 'So I'm definitely not here on official business.'

'I didn't for one minute think you were,' said Chris, still chopping away. 'Norman called me earlier and said he had a friend who was hungry and needed a change of scenery for a few hours. Any friend of Norman's is welcome here, and if you want to help out too, well, that's a bonus for us.'

Slater looked around for Norman, but he had disappeared. Slater wasn't worried. He felt strangely humbled in this amazing place where the vicar and his wife worked every evening to feed those who couldn't afford to feed themselves.

As if she had been able to read Slater's mind, Diane nodded her head towards the hatch. 'He's out there working his magic,' she said. 'He's like the master of ceremonies, meeting and greeting everyone. He has a kind word for every single one of them, even the ones who don't trust anyone.'

Slater watched through the hatch as Norman worked the small crowd, offering a handshake here, a high five there, and the occasional hug. He managed to make them all smile, and a good number were laughing out loud at something he had said.

'He has a gift,' said Chris.

'Yeah,' said Slater. 'I know. In my experience, he always knows how to handle everyone he comes across. He was a great partner to work with.'

'He speaks very highly of you,' said Diane. 'He reckons you saved his life — first metaphorically, and then, later, literally.'

Now Slater was blushing. 'I don't think it was quite like that. It was teamwork that rescued him when he got kidnapped.'

'Maybe,' she said. 'But you were the one who gave him back his self-respect at a time when he was near the end of his tether.'

'I wasn't in a position to choose who I worked with,' said Slater. 'It was my old boss who decided that. We were just put together and had to get on with it.'

'I could say that's the way God works,' said Chris. 'And that He brings us together to help each other, but I don't suppose you're any more religious than Norman. Besides, I'm not here to preach to anyone. Let's just say the Universe works in strange ways and everything has a purpose.'

'I can go with that.' Slater swallowed the final mouthful of soup. 'That was delicious,' he said to Diane. 'Now then, what do you want me to do?'

'You'll need this.' Diane passed him an apron. 'Then you can start slicing up those French sticks. There's a bread knife in that top drawer.'

* * *

The four workers — Chris, Diane, Norman and Slater — were sitting around one of the now-vacant tables eating their own dinners. Most of the dozen or so homeless had eaten their food, offered their thanks, and headed off into the night. All that remained were a couple of stragglers who huddled around a table close to the door. Their voices could be heard as a murmuring in the background, but whatever the conversation was about, they kept their voices low enough to make sure they weren't sharing.

'So what do you think?' Diane asked Slater.

He smiled at her. 'I think if this was a restaurant you'd be packed every night.'

'It's very good of you to say so,' she said, clearly flattered by the compliment, 'but I think you know very well that's not what I meant.'

'I'm not really sure how to answer your question. Is this a typical night? I mean, I know there are supposed to be homeless people everywhere, but I hadn't realised just how many there were in a tiny place like Tinton.'

'It rather emphasises the scale of the problem, doesn't it?' said Chris. 'If it's like this here, what's it like in bigger towns and cities?'

'It's an eye-opener, that's for sure,' agreed Slater.

'I was the same when I first came here,' said Norman. 'I felt lucky it wasn't me, and at the same time guilty that it wasn't me. It's sort of overwhelming, but then Chris and Diane explained that these are just people like you and me. The only difference is they've hit hard times, and we haven't. That's when I realised it could easily have been me, and that's when I decided to help out for a couple of nights a week. The thing is, when you get to know them and talk to them, you start to realise they like a laugh and a joke like the rest of us.'

There was a brief silence, broken after a minute or so by Chris. 'I take it there's still no sign of Ryan?' he asked Norman.

'I spent hours looking for him earlier, but I can't find him anywhere. He's definitely hiding.'

'Or he's left the area,' suggested Diane.

'That's becoming more of a possibility, although he told me he felt at home around here, so I'm hoping he's just hiding out somewhere.'

'Do you know where he's from?' asked Slater. 'Is he local?'

'The problem we have with these guys,' said Chris, 'is they already feel let down and persecuted, so they don't take very kindly to people asking a lot of questions. We have to make do with what information they're prepared to volunteer. It can take weeks before some of them will even tell you their name.'

'And even then you never know for sure if it's their real name,' added Diane.

'So what do we know about why he's done a runner?' asked Slater.

'You really want to help find him?' Norman raised an eyebrow.

'I might not be a police officer any more,' said Slater, 'but I'm still a detective, right? It's what I do, and right now I'm a free agent so I can do what I want.'

Norman beamed across the table at Slater. 'You see, Diane?' he said. 'I said he'd want to help.'

'So why don't we start from the top,' said Slater. 'So far you've just told me the guy's gone missing and that you think he's in some kind of trouble. How about you give me a little detail.'

Slater looked around as the sound of chairs scraping on the floor heralded the two stragglers getting up from their table by the door. To his surprise, they were heading towards them and not towards the exit. Opposite him, Diane rose from her chair.

'It's okay,' she said to Slater. 'This is tonight's cleaning party. They're going to help with the washing-up and cleaning the kitchen. I never refuse when someone volunteers.'

She led the two men towards the kitchen, leaving Slater, Norman and Chris to talk. Slater felt a bit doubtful.

'It's okay,' explained Chris. 'Some of them don't like the idea of accepting charity. They like to give something for their dinner. We won't take their money, but they can give us a half hour to help clean up. It doesn't happen every night, so we make the most of it when we have a couple of helpers.'

Satisfied Diane was in no danger, Slater returned his focus to the missing Ryan. 'Right then,' he said. 'Tell me what you know about Ryan and why he's done a runner.'

'All I know,' said Norman, 'is everyone calls him Ryan. I don't know if that's his first name, surname, or a nickname. I *do* know he's ex-forces, and I believe he's ex-special forces, probably SAS, but I don't know that for sure. I do know he's seen action in Afghanistan and Iraq. He's been around this area for a while, and he's been coming here every night since Chris and Diane moved here and opened the kitchen.'

'That was four months ago,' added Chris.

'That's not much to go on, is it?'

'Yeah, well observed, Sherlock Holmes,' said Norman, failing to hide his irritation. 'Don't forget — this guy has been let down by his country, has the usual persecution complex, and added to that, he's also been trained not to divulge information. What do you suggest I should have done? I mean, it's not as if I knew he was going to go missing, did I?'

'Alright, Norm, easy,' said Slater. 'I didn't mean to suggest you should have interrogated the man. I get it. You like the guy and you're worried about him. I said I'll help you find him and I will, but there's no getting away from the fact we don't have much to go on, do we?'

Norman looked suitably guilty and nodded his head to acknowledge the situation.

'Alright,' said Slater. 'How long's he been missing?'

'He's been gone two weeks now.'

Slater thought this was a bit odd as Norman had expected to find Ryan in his house this morning, but he said nothing and played along with Norm. He could ask him why later.

'And what made him run? Or what do you *think* made him run?'

'He used to sleep in an old industrial skip up by the old printing works,' explained Norman. 'He told me he'd been sleeping there for weeks. Two weeks ago, someone set fire to it.'

'He was lucky he wasn't in there or he would have been roasted alive,' observed Slater, then felt slightly foolish for stating the obvious.

'The thing is, he *should* have been in there,' said Chris, 'and when it happened, we thought he had been, but Ryan wouldn't share his skip with anyone. For some reason, someone else was in there that night — a stranger — and he was the one who died, not Ryan. Our best guess is this other guy had moved in before Ryan got back there, and Ryan moved on because he didn't want to share and the other guy wouldn't leave.'

'And that's why you think Ryan believes he was the target,' said Slater. 'Which makes sense, of course, but what about the police? What do they say? Surely they're investigating, aren't they?'

Norman laughed at the mention of the police. 'Apparently it's a tragic accident. They see the fire as a prank or an unfortunate accident that couldn't have been foreseen.'

'You're joking.'

'Do I look like I'm laughing?'

'But Marion Goodnews—'

'Is the one who made the decision, I believe,' said Norman, 'ably assisted by DS Biddeford.'

'DS?' echoed Slater, in amazement. 'That happened fast, didn't it?'

'Don't ask me,' said Norman. 'The whole place seems to have gone to pot over the last month. Last I heard, they're going to close the place down soon and move everyone over to Merryton.'

'So they're actually going to do that, are they?' said Slater, sadly. 'I knew it was a possibility, but I never thought it would actually happen.'

'It's not officially announced to the big wide world yet, but it seems all the staff have been told.'

'I guess that's what they call progress,' said Chris, who had been listening to Slater and Norman.

'I think it's called ever-reducing budgets,' said Slater. 'That's what it's really all about. Anyway, we're not here to talk about Tinton Police. Where were we?'

'We got to where Ryan thinks he's the target.'

'Right. Or it could simply be the other guy was the target and his enemy had been following him. Do we know this other guy's name?'

'Biddeford wouldn't tell me anything,' said Norman. 'But I've heard Naomi Darling will be back on duty soon. I suspect she might be a bit more forthcoming when it comes to helping us.'

'She's coming back?' asked a surprised Slater. 'I thought she was being drummed out of the force for stalking and then beating up a suspect?'

'Yeah, that's what we all thought, but it turns out the boot was on the other foot. She said all along that those two guys had ambushed her, but that idiot DI Grimm was so determined to blame her, he accepted the story the other two guys had concocted and ignored her version of events. Goodnews didn't listen either, so there's no love lost between those two.'

'I didn't help her either,' admitted Slater guiltily. 'She was my partner. I should have made the effort to find out what had happened.'

'You were in hospital, remember?' said Norman. 'She had already been suspended and left town in disgust by the time you got back.'

'So how come she's coming back to work? What made Grimm listen to her?'

'She put one of the guys in hospital for a couple of weeks, but when he came out, he couldn't resist going to the pub and celebrating how he'd stitched up the bitch detective and got her suspended. The thing is, it seems he's not as popular as he thought he was, and several witnesses came forward to report what he'd done. So Goodnews had no choice but to drag him in, and a few tough questions later, he told the truth. Him and his mate ambushed Darling, but they didn't know what they were letting themselves in for.'

'So Goodnews saved her job,' said Slater.

'She could have done that from day one if she'd only listened,' said Norman. 'I think it was more like she saw a chance to leave Grimm with egg on his face, but then I always find it hard to see anything good in that woman. Anyway, we're getting off the subject again.'

'You're right,' said Slater. 'So we've got an unknown man who dies in a skip, and your mate Ryan who thinks it should have been him. Like I said, it's not much, is it? Especially when you consider Ryan's gone missing. How do we know whoever set the fire hasn't caught Ryan too?'

'We don't,' admitted Norman, 'but my hunch is he's too clever to get caught that easily. He's trained, remember? And he would have been on his guard once he knew what had happened to the guy in the skip.'

Something had become apparent to Slater, and he had to ask the question even if it might upset Norman.

'Don't take this the wrong way, Norm, but you don't actually know for sure that Ryan thinks he was meant to be the victim, do you?' asked Slater, carefully. 'I mean, it's just your hunch, right?'

'Well, yeah,' said Norm, looking uncomfortable.

'That's probably my fault,' said Chris. 'Ryan has mentioned that they might come for him once or twice before.'

'Who's they?' asked Slater.

'Ah, well that's the problem. When you're dealing with these guys who are suffering PTSD and what have you, you never know if they're telling you what's real or what's going on in their head.'

'That complicates things,' said Slater.

'You're telling me.' Chris shook his head ruefully.

'So maybe I'm wrong,' said Norman, looking Slater right in the eyes, 'but my gut says I'm right, and on that basis I feel I have to try and find out where he is and what he's running from.'

Slater met Norman's gaze for a moment before he spoke. 'Well, that's good enough for me. Your gut's never let us down before.'

'For real?'

'What did you think I was going to do, turn you down?'

'Well, no, I guess not—'

'Right then, so we need to make a start in the morning. I assume they did a PM on the victim?'

'Yeah,' said Norman. 'They just wouldn't tell me anything, and I doubt they'll be too pleased to see you.'

'I wasn't planning on going to the police,' said Slater. 'I thought I'd go and see the pathologist.'

'Ah, right. You and Eamon got on well, didn't you?'

'We still do as far as I know,' said Slater. 'We'll see just *how* well in the morning.'

CHAPTER THREE

Next morning, just after nine thirty, Slater made his way quietly through the hospital and down to the basement where the mortuary and pathology laboratory was. He smiled and nodded at a lab technician who smiled and nodded back. She obviously knew who Slater was — she had seen him down here often enough and probably assumed he was on his way to see Eamon Murphy the pathologist. She didn't ask him what he was doing or where he was going.

He stopped at the mortuary door and peered through the window to make sure there was no one around he wouldn't want to see him here. The only figure he could see was that of Murphy, leaning over a bench apparently making some notes. Even better, there didn't appear to be a body on either of the two tables, so he wouldn't have to endure the sight of bodily fluids or parts being removed, weighed and catalogued. He pushed the door open as quietly as he could and slipped through.

'You need to do something about your security, Eamon,' he said, as he approached Murphy.

The pathologist swung round, eyes wide in surprise. 'Dave Slater,' he said. 'How on earth did you get in here?'

'I just walked in,' said Slater, 'which is why you need to do something about your security. Perhaps you should start by telling everyone I'm no longer with the police force.'

Murphy looked suitably embarrassed. 'Ah, yes,' he said, sheepishly. 'I suppose maybe I was hoping you'd change your mind.'

The two men shook hands.

'It's good to see you,' said Murphy. 'You're looking well. Thailand obviously suited you. Perhaps I should head out that way.'

'I recommend it to anyone and everyone. I guarantee you'll come back feeling ten times better.'

'Is this just a social visit?' asked Murphy, 'only I'd be surprised if it was. You used to hate this place.'

Slater arranged his face into a suitable expression of guilt. 'It's not the place, Eamon, it's having to watch what you do here that I didn't like.'

'Yes, that may be so, but like I said, what are you really here for?'

'Jeez, I must be so transparent,' said Slater.

Murphy laughed. 'Totally. So what can I help you with?'

'You had a guy brought in a couple of weeks ago — got cremated in a rubbish skip.'

'You mean the one DS Biddeford described as "done like a crispy duck"?'

Slater groaned his disappointment. 'I wish you hadn't told me that, but I can't say I'm surprised.'

'You know I can't discuss this with you, don't you?' asked Murphy.

'Of course I do,' said Slater. 'But I'm told the police don't want to get involved, and I wondered how you felt about that. And of course, technically, that means it's not an active case, is it?'

'How do you think I feel?' asked Murphy. 'The guy might have been sleeping in a skip, but he was still a human being.'

'Well, that's how Norm and I feel, especially as we think he wasn't the intended victim.'

'Victim? I thought it was being classified as an unfortunate accident.'

'So I've heard. The thing is, we have good reason to believe the only accidental bit was that the wrong guy got incinerated. We think the intended victim just got lucky that night and someone else nicked his sleeping place and paid the price for it.'

'Have you told the police?' asked Murphy.

'Do you really think they're going to listen to us two black sheep? We need to make sure we can prove there's a case before we go near them.'

Murphy studied Slater's face and Slater got the distinct feeling he was weighing up whether or not to trust him.

'What do you want to know?' Murphy asked finally.

Slater grinned. 'What can you tell me?'

'I can't tell you what he looked like,' said Murphy, 'but I can tell you he was about six feet tall. Caucasian, brown eyes and brown hair, probably once very fit but now somewhat worn-out. I would suggest he was ex-special forces judging by what was left of his tattoos.'

'Special forces? Now there's a coincidence,' said Slater. 'Any idea who he was?'

'We took DNA, but the thing is, if he's a special he won't be on our database. He must be on a military one somewhere, though, if you know how to access it. We did manage to X-ray his teeth so I'm still optimistic something might come from that.'

'Anything else you can tell me?'

'There is one thing that was rather odd. He had recently had an operation to remove a kidney.'

'What, you mean he had some sort of disease?'

'I couldn't see any signs of disease,' said Murphy, 'so it could be he was a donor.'

'Wouldn't there be a record of that somewhere?' asked Slater.

'Well, yes, there should be, if it was an official donation.'

'What does that mean?'

'Well, there is no record that I can find that would relate to this man. However, bearing in mind he was living on the street, it could be he sold one,' said Murphy. 'And, of course, that's illegal, so there certainly won't be any record of that.'

* * *

Slater had spent the rest of his morning on personal business, and then a largely fruitless afternoon trying to identify the dead man. A couple of wasted hours trawling the internet soon demonstrated to him that trying to figure this out without access to the channels he would normally have used as a police officer was not going to be easy.

At one point, he had toyed with the idea of approaching his former boss, Detective Chief Inspector Marion Goodnews, but that idea was quickly discarded when he recalled how fraught their relationship had become since he had offered her his spare room one night when they'd both had a bit too much to drink.

* * *

'So how did you get on with Eamon?' asked Norman as soon as Slater stepped into his car that evening.

'Can I get in first?' asked Slater, who still had one foot on the road.

'Oooh! Sorry, Mr Grumpy,' said Norman, amiably. 'I take it someone's had a bad day.'

'I think I get to ask the first question,' said Slater. 'Last night, when we were talking with Chris about Ryan being missing, what was all that "Ryan's been missing for two weeks" stuff? I thought he was hiding out at my house?'

'Yeah, sorry about that,' said Norman. 'I should have told you earlier. Ryan doesn't trust anyone except me and a girl called Ginger. He swore me to secrecy about where he was.'

'Jeez, he really is paranoid, then?'

'So would I be if someone had tried to incinerate me,' said Norman.

'Okay, that's fair enough, I suppose he's got good reason.'

Slater was in his seat now, pulling the seat belt over his shoulder as Norman pulled away from his house.

'So anyway, about your day?' asked Norman.

'Not so much a bad day as a frustrating one,' he said, clipping the seat belt and sitting back in his seat. 'I'm so used to being able to check things on the police databases I forgot how difficult it would be to find a dead man on the outside.'

'It's not impossible,' said Norman. 'People do it all the time. You just have to know how to get into these things from the outside.'

'You mean we hack into their database?'

'What? Us? Break the law?' asked Norman, innocently. 'Our partnership won't last five minutes if we get caught breaking the law, now will it?'

'Partnership? What partnership?' said Slater. 'I wasn't aware we had a partnership.'

'Yeah, but you have to admit it would be pretty cool, don't you think? You must have thought about what you're gonna do now you're back. I mean, you've got to pay your way somehow, right? And you did say being a detective is what you do.'

Slater looked across at Norman, but he kept his eyes firmly on the road and refused to turn his head Slater's way.

'You've put some thought into this then?' asked Slater.

'Well, I told you once before I'd do it on my own, didn't I? That I'd set myself up to do a bit of security consultant work and maybe I'd get the odd detective job out of that.'

'You did mention it,' admitted Slater, 'but I didn't think you'd actually do anything about it.'

Norman grinned. 'Oh, you thought it was just talk, did you? You see the thing is, when I first talked about it, I didn't know you were going to quit your job, did I? I mean you mentioned it, but I didn't think you'd actually do anything about it. Oh, sorry, did you just say something like that about me?'

Slater laughed out loud as he turned back to face the road. 'Touché,' he said. 'You've got me there. So you were thinking about setting yourself up, but then I made myself available to join you as a partner, right?'

'Yeah, something like that,' said Norman, smiling. 'So, what do you think? We're a good team, right? It makes perfect sense. I'll even let you put your name first if you like. I can see it now — Slater and Norman, security and investigations.'

'Has it occurred to you I stopped being a detective because I'd had enough?'

'You had enough of being held back by authority, red tape and stupid rules. It had nothing to do with not wanting to be a detective any more.'

Slater raised his eyebrows. Norman glanced across at him. 'Am I right? Or am I right?' he insisted.

'Well, yeah, I suppose there is something in what you say,' conceded Slater.

'I've done some work already,' continued Norman. 'I've put out some feelers about security consultations. I even got a couple of places interested, and I've hardly started yet.'

'What places?'

'Well, there's that fancy art college on the outskirts of town. They get a lot of private funding and they'd prefer to keep everything under the public radar so I'm pretty sure we could get some work out of them. Come on, what do you say?'

'Let me think about it,' said Slater. 'Let's see what happens with this case first.'

'That sounds fair. So let's focus on this case. What did Eamon tell you?'

'Not a great deal. It seems the body was done to a turn before he got to it. He did say the guy was Caucasian, about six feet tall, with brown hair and brown eyes.'

'Oh, that narrows it down then,' said Norman. 'Only about half the male population to choose from.'

'He reckons the guy may have been special forces because of a couple of tattoos he had. He's got DNA but the guy doesn't show up anywhere. Eamon reckons that's consistent with him being special forces.'

'Crap!' said Norman, as he turned his car into the church car park. 'It's not much, is it? But then I suppose it's better than nothing.'

He pulled on the handbrake and switched off the engine.

'There was one other thing,' added Slater. 'The guy had very recently had a kidney removed.'

Norman turned to stare at Slater. 'You mean he was a donor?'

'If he was, he's not on record anywhere.'

'Isn't there a black market in body parts?'

'Eamon reckons the guy would have been super-fit once, but thinks he was in a right state now. You never know, it's possible he was desperate and he sold one.'

'Jeez, really? That doesn't bear thinking about.'

They sat in silence for a moment as they considered the possibility.

'Come on,' said Slater, finally. 'Sitting here's not going to help us find out who he is.'

* * *

The hall was filled with the soft mumbling sounds of people talking and eating. Through the hatch in the kitchen, Slater could be seen on slave duties again — not that he minded. He knew very well he didn't have Norman's easy charm with these people, and they had decided if anyone was going to start asking questions, it would be better if it was Norm, who they were all familiar with, rather than the stranger who had yet to prove himself to be trustworthy. And Slater was okay with that. He understood why they wouldn't trust him straight away.

'Do you think anyone here knew the dead guy?' he asked, as he began to work his way through an enormous pile of washing-up.

'He wasn't a regular here,' said Chris. 'We do get the odd person turning up now and then so we don't necessarily know them all, but we hadn't seen anyone new around that time. Of course, that doesn't mean he hadn't been in the area for a while, simply that he'd never been *here*.'

'So it's possible someone might have seen him out on the street?' asked Slater.

'It's always possible,' said Chris, 'but no one's mentioned anything and they all know what happened. We thought it was a good idea to warn them to keep an eye out, you know? Did you find anything out from your pathologist friend?'

'Not a great deal. It seems he was probably special forces before he hit the street. White, six feet tall, brown eyes, brown hair. Could be half the population.'

'It's a pity he couldn't tell you anything a bit more specific.'

'He did say the guy had recently had a kidney removed.'

Out of the corner of his eye, Slater thought he saw Chris do a comic book double take.

'Really? Good heavens! Was it very recent?'

'He couldn't be specific because of the state of the body, but he seemed to think it had been a matter of days, not weeks.'

'Should the poor man even have been out of hospital?'

'According to my research, a normal donor would be out of hospital in a few days, but would then take another six or eight weeks to recover,' said Slater. 'He certainly shouldn't have been out on the street fending for himself within a few days. Eamon thinks this guy's operation had been only three or four days before he died, and if we assume he was out for at least a day before the fire, it means he can only have been in hospital for two days, possibly three at most.'

'What sort of hospital would do that?' Chris sounded utterly appalled.

'Not your standard National Health Service hospital, that's for sure,' said Slater. 'The possibility has to be that this was more of a business deal.'

'You mean he sold his kidney?' said Diane. 'That's too terrible to even think about.'

'It's a pretty grim idea, isn't it? But I guess if you're desperate enough, you'll sell whatever you've got, for whatever you can get,' said Slater.

'I've heard of people selling their body parts, but I thought that was a Third World thing,' said Diane. 'I didn't think we'd ever see such a thing in a place like Tinton.'

'Even if we're right, we don't know it happened around here. Don't forget — we're only an hour from London by train.' Slater scrubbed a plate clean, his thoughts firmly on the identity of the missing man.

* * *

Out in the main hall, Norman was working the crowd as usual, offering a kind word here and a joke there, making sure everyone had enough to eat and there was plenty of water to drink. He had become adept at this particular job over the last three months, and jokingly described himself as the 'head waiter'. Tonight, he was using the full range of his interpersonal skills to win people over, and he had somehow managed to bring up the subject of strangers in town and the unfortunate skip fire with everyone he had spoken to. So far, however, he had drawn a blank. If the guy had been in town before the day he died, no one had seen him, or, at least, no one was *admitting* they had seen him.

He watched in frustration as the faster eaters began to shuffle quietly away. Already half the tables were empty. Surely someone must know something about the dead man. He ambled over to the serving hatch and peered inside at Slater.

'Any luck?' asked Slater.

'Not a sausage,' said Norman, gloomily.

'They're not stonewalling you?'

'Nah!' said Norman, confidently. 'I can't believe he could have pissed them all off that much they'd hide it from me, and I didn't get the feeling anyone was lying.'

'Oh well, I guess we'll just have to think again,' said Slater. 'There will be a way, we just haven't thought of it yet.'

There was a commotion from the main doorway and Norman swung round to see what was going on. A scruffy-looking man who could have been anything between twenty-five and forty was standing in the doorway. His shabby combat jacket and camouflage trousers had seen better days, and the worn-out army boots should have been put to rest many years ago, but despite all that, there was a strangely optimistic air about him, and the cheeky grin on his face had brought a sudden smile to Norman's.

'Doddsy's back,' he called over his shoulder to the kitchen crew, and then he set off towards the door.

'Who's Doddsy?' Slater asked Diane as he watched Norman head for the door.

'Remember the Artful Dodger?' she asked. 'Well, Doddsy is like an adult version who's still a little boy inside. He's a lovely kid, but he's a chancer who's full of stories. You never know when he's telling the truth, but there's something about him that makes it very difficult not to like him.'

'But he's homeless, right? Where did he come from?'

'He's another one who's ex-army. He'll tell you he was special forces, but we reckon he was actually just a regular, in the catering corps or something like that.'

'He's a bit late for dinner, isn't he?'

'He's been away for a couple of weeks, but he did say he'd be back today. It's okay, he can eat with us, we've got plenty for one extra.'

Slater turned his attention back to Norman, who was exchanging high fives and then a hug with the young man called Doddsy. Each seemed genuinely pleased to see the other. They walked across to the hatch and peered into the kitchen.

'Hi Di,' called Doddsy, a huge, cheeky grin on his face. 'Lookin' hot tonight, babe.'

'I suppose I should be flattered by the compliment,' she said, trying to look stern, 'but if you're expecting to be fed you'll need to mind your manners. And I would appreciate it if you didn't call me "babe".'

Doddsy's grin grew even wider. 'Gotcha, chick, message understood,' he said.

She winced. 'Or "chick",' she added, testily. 'Especially not "chick".'

'Whatever you say, babe,' agreed Doddsy, cheerfully. 'You know I love it when you talk to me like that.'

'Alright, Doddsy, that's enough,' said Chris, looking daggers. 'Just remember — we don't have to offer you food.'

Doddsy looked suitably crestfallen. 'Alright, Chris. Sorry, mate. I don't mean no harm. It's just a bit of fun.'

'Yes, but sometimes you need to know when to turn it off, as well as on.'

'Alright, mate, I'm sorry. Point taken.'

'Take Doddsy out to our table and lay an extra place for him, please, Norm,' said Diane, holding her hands up as if trying to soothe the tension.

'Sure,' said Norman. 'Come on, trouble, follow me. Dave, would you give us a hand?'

Slater dried his hands and followed Norman and Doddsy out to the main hall.

'This is my good friend Dave. Dave, this is Doddsy.'

The two men shook hands.

'So where have you been?' asked Norman, as he laid the extra place at the table.

'Been up to the barracks at Hereford for a few days, catching up with me old mates in the regiment, you know?'

'Cut the crap, Doddsy,' said Norman. 'Everyone knows you were never in the SAS and you couldn't even point to Hereford on a map, so there's no way you'd get there under your own steam.'

Doddsy raised a thumb in the air. 'I don't need no steam, nor no map, Norm,' he said, proudly. 'I just puts up the old thumb and I'm away, mate.'

'Only people aren't quite so keen to offer lifts these days, are they?' pointed out Norman. 'Exactly how many hours have you spent stood by the roadside, or walking?'

'Well, yeah, alright. I'll admit I probably walked further than I rode, but I got there in the end.'

Norman sighed, wearily. 'Okay, Doddsy, have it your own way. You know half your problem is the fact you bullshit so much, no one knows when you're actually telling the truth, don't you?'

'That's one of the things we learn in the regiment, see, how to avoid telling the enemy what they want to know.'

Norman laughed out loud at that one. 'I think you'll find that's not quite the same thing as talking a load of bollocks, Doddsy,' he said, fondly. 'What they learn is how to resist torture. And anyway we're not your enemy. Why can't you tell us the truth?'

'You ask Ryan, he'll tell you—'

'I can't ask Ryan anything,' said Norman, 'he's disappeared.'

Doddsy's cheeky grin was suddenly replaced by genuine concern. 'What do you mean he's disappeared?'

'I mean he's gone missing. We don't know where he is.'

'Have you tried his skip?'

'There is no skip. There was a fire.'

'Is he alright?' The alarm was clear in the younger man's voice.

'We don't know for sure,' said Norman. 'There was another guy in the skip that night. He died in the fire.'

'Another guy? That must have been that Morgan bloke. He was—'

'You knew that guy?' asked Slater.

'I wouldn't say I knew him, but I met him the day I left. He said his name was Morgan and he was looking for Ryan. He said they were in the same squad in the regiment.'

'What did he look like?' asked Norman. 'Only he was pretty badly burnt in the fire, you see.'

'He didn't look well,' said Doddsy. 'White as a bloody ghost he was. And stooped, like he had a bad back and it was killing him, you know? I suppose if he had been able to stand up, he would have been about the same size as me.'

Slater looked at Doddsy. He was about six feet tall.

'What about his hair, and his eyes?' asked Norman.

Doddsy squinted into the distance. 'I can't really remember,' he said eventually. 'I don't think there was anything special about him. Just sort of normal colour. Brown, I think.'

'So what did he say to you about Ryan?' asked Slater.

'You're not the filth, are you?' asked Doddsy, suspiciously. 'Only you're asking a lot of questions.'

'He's ex-police, like me,' explained Norman. 'We're just worried about Ryan and trying to find him that's all. You trust me, don't you?'

'Well, yeah, course I do.'

'Well he's my business partner, so you can trust him too,' said Norman.

This seemed to satisfy Doddsy's concerns regarding Slater.

'I was in the bus station trying to wangle a free ride when this guy calls out to me. He says he guessed I was ex-military, and that his name was Morgan, and did I know a guy called Ryan. So I says yes. Then he says he used to be in the same squad as Ryan and that he's looking for him. He looked half dead, so I told him about Ryan's skip and where to find it.'

'That's supposed to be a secret,' said Norman. 'Ryan woulda gone ape when he found the guy in there in his place.'

'Nah, mate,' said Doddsy. 'That's where you're wrong. Those guys are like brothers. Ryan would have been pissed off, but he would have seen the state that other guy was in and he would have let him have the place for the night. He wouldn't have left him to rough it the way he was.'

Slater suddenly realised the massive gulf between himself and people like Doddsy and Ryan. In Slater's world, spending the night in a skip *was* roughing it . . .

'And you're quite sure Ryan would have let the guy have his skip, just like that?' he asked.

'Sure,' said Doddsy. 'He wouldn't have been happy about it, but he would have looked after the guy. I bet he was probably going to come back next day and see he got some help. That's the sort of bloke Ryan is.'

Slater looked across at Norman.

'It adds up, doesn't it?' said Norman. 'It explains why Morgan was in the skip instead of Ryan.'

'Yeah,' agreed Slater. 'But we still have no idea if Morgan's killer followed him here, or if he was intending to kill Ryan and didn't realise Morgan was inside.'

'Did Morgan say where he'd come from?' Norman asked Doddsy.

Doddsy squinted into the distance again. 'No. I don't think so. No. I'm sure he didn't.'

'If you think of anything else, you'll let us know, right?' asked Norman. 'Just let Chris and Diane know and they can contact us if we're not here.'

'If it means finding Ryan, of course I will,' said Doddsy.

* * *

'This Doddsy is a bit of a lad, isn't he?' asked Slater, as they drove off later.

'Yeah, he's so full of bullshit it oozes from his ears, but he's harmless enough,' said Norman. 'I find there's something weirdly optimistic about him. It makes him quite likeable.'

'Unless you're the vicar, who doesn't like the way Doddsy flirts with his wife.'

'Yeah, that can get kind of awkward sometimes,' admitted Norman.

'So Doddsy and Ryan are mates?'

'That depends on who you listen to,' said Norman. 'Doddsy thinks Ryan is some sort of godlike figure because he was in the SAS. To Doddsy, that's the ultimate achievement, and he would like us all to believe he had achieved it too. Of course, he didn't and he never will. So, in a nutshell, Doddsy thinks he and Ryan are best mates because they have the SAS in common.

'Then again, if you listen to Ryan, you'll find he thinks Doddsy is a twat who lives in some sort of fantasy world and should never even have been in the regular army and would never have got anywhere near the SAS. I think Ryan only tolerates him because he feels sorry for the guy and his situation. He certainly won't be impressed if he finds out Doddsy told Morgan where his skip was!'

Slater laughed. 'I thought it was probably something like that. So one thing we know for sure — Ryan's no fool, right?'

'Yeah, but let's face it, it doesn't take a genius to see through Doddsy, does it?'

Slater grinned. 'You're right there. Oh well, at least we've got a name for our dead guy now, so let's see what tomorrow brings when we do a search for Morgan.'

CHAPTER FOUR

Next evening, it was Slater's turn to pick up Norman from home.

'Have you ever tried to get information from the military?' he asked, once Norman had his seat belt buckled and they were on their way.

Norman laughed out loud. 'Ha! I sure have. You'd have more luck trying to get milk from a bull. I'm sure they're trained in the art of obstruction.'

'You're not kidding me,' said Slater. 'It gets even worse if you're trying to find out about special forces. They won't even admit they exist, even though everyone knows they do!'

'So, should I assume we're no further forward with our background check on Morgan?' asked Norman.

'I'm afraid not. And I have no idea what more I can do.'

'Then we have no choice. I'll call Vinnie.'

Vinnie the Geek was an associate of Norman's from his days in London. A technical genius, he could get into any computer system, and out again, without detection. Much against Slater's better judgement, they had unofficially used his services before with great success. There was just one problem: Vinnie and Slater were like chalk and cheese.

'I know you two don't get on,' said Norman, 'but you'll just have to grin and bear it. If we're going to learn anything about this Morgan guy, Vinnie is our only chance.'

Slater sighed. 'He has to be a last resort solution. That's the only way I'm ever going to accept his involvement.'

'Your disapproval is noted,' said Norman with a wicked grin, 'and I'll leave him out of it for now, but as I have the casting vote, you may well be overruled at a later date.'

'How does that work?' asked Slater. 'How can you overrule me? I thought we were partners.'

'Yeah, we are, but sometimes your refusal to bend the rules can get in the way. When that happens, I have the casting vote. It's in the contract.'

'What contract?'

'Oh, did I forget to tell you about that? It's nothing to worry about, it just says that as this whole thing is my idea, any time we reach a sticking point I get my own way.'

'I don't remember signing any contract,' said Slater.

'It's notional,' said Norman. 'No signatures required.'

Slater glanced across at Norman. 'You're a scheming sod sometimes, you know that?' he said. 'And you reckon Doddsy can bullshit.'

Norman turned a huge grin Slater's way and gave him a theatrical wink. 'It's called advanced strategic planning,' he said. 'You know it makes sense.'

* * *

Norman had his back to the doors, speaking to a young couple who came most nights. They were always together and seemed to be determined to stay that way. If you listened to their conversation and ignored the fact they were both somewhat scruffy and obviously homeless, it would have been easy to confuse them with any other young couple planning a future together. Norman was just thinking what a sad state of affairs it was when he felt a tap on his shoulder. He made his excuses to the young couple and turned around.

A handsome-looking thirty-something man stood in front of him. Despite his unshaven, untidy appearance, he seemed relaxed and confident. The same couldn't be said for the figure stood next to him. Her slim, almost scrawny figure just about demonstrated her femininity, but her face was hidden behind a huge pair of dark glasses, and a hood was pulled tight around her face, making her features almost indistinguishable. She had the edgy nervousness of an addict, and was biting her fingernails. Like everyone else, Norman knew her as Ginger, and he guessed she hadn't scored recently.

It was the man he spoke to first. 'Ryan! Where have you been? We were beginning to wonder what had happened to you.'

'Relax, man,' said Ryan. 'I didn't think it would be fair to involve your mate when he doesn't even know me, so I thought it might be a good idea to get out and keep my head down for a few days, you know? I've been at Ginger's squat.'

At the mention of her name, Ginger tilted her head up towards Norman. He guessed she was acknowledging her part in keeping Ryan safe, although the shades made it impossible to know for sure.

'Well, thanks for that, Ginger,' he said.

She nodded her head, but didn't say a word. He turned his attention back to Ryan. 'We need to talk,' he said.

Ryan nodded to acknowledge the fact, and then tilted his head towards Ginger. 'Yeah, okay,' he said, taking her hand in his. 'But first we need to eat. This one hasn't eaten properly for days. She's starving.'

'Sure,' said Norman. 'Help yourselves. That's what it's all here for.' He stepped aside to let them approach the counter.

From the rear of the kitchen, behind the counter, Slater watched the couple approach. Diane had already told him Ryan had appeared, and he was curious to see for himself. He was more or less exactly as Norman had described him, but it was the woman who caught his attention. Despite the dark glasses and hood that hid most of her face, he felt there was something vaguely familiar about her. He continued watching as they reached the serving hatch, and then she suddenly seemed to realise he was there and quickly turned her head away. Feeling guilty for invading her privacy by staring at her, he returned to the sink and the pile of washing-up, but he couldn't shake off the feeling that he knew her from somewhere.

Norman waited until Ryan and Ginger had taken their food and let them settle at a table in the far corner of the hall, well away from the others, before he ambled over to the kitchen and leaned against the counter.

'Now there's a surprise,' he said, nodding his head towards the far corner.

'Diane tells me that's Ryan,' said Slater. 'Did you find out where he's been?'

'He's been hiding out with the girl. She has a squat somewhere in town. He said he needs to make sure she eats first, then we can talk.'

'Who is she?' asked Slater.

'Her name's Ginger,' said Norman. 'That's about all I can tell you. She never says anything to any of us, so that's all we know.'

'Maybe she can't talk,' suggested Slater.

'Oh, she can talk, when she wants to,' said Diane, who was cleaning up close by. 'She just doesn't want us to know anything about her, but that's often the way.'

'It's one of the unwritten rules,' explained Norman. 'We don't ask — we wait until they want to tell us.'

They became aware the hall had fallen silent. Over by the door, two big guys were taking in the scene. They both wore suits, but their menacing attitude made it quite clear they weren't your everyday businessmen.

'Uh oh,' said Norman. 'This looks like trouble.'

He pushed himself away from the counter and made towards the entrance. Slater grabbed a cloth and quickly wiped his hands as he headed after Norman.

'You'd best stay here,' he said to Diane and Chris. 'We can handle this.'

'Can I help you, gents?' asked Norman as he walked towards the two newcomers, who obviously weren't homeless.

'You can stand aside while we take a look around,' said the slightly shorter of the two, who was still a good four or five inches taller than Norman.

Norman gave him a genial smile. 'I don't think so. This is for homeless people. If you're hungry, you'll find two or three places in town where you can get something to eat.'

'Look, fatty,' said the man. 'Perhaps there's something wrong with your hearing? I said you should stand aside.'

'And he said he wasn't going to,' said Slater as he stepped into place alongside Norman. 'And I'm not going to either, so unless you intend to make both of us move . . .'

The man took a step towards Slater, but his friend wasn't so keen to get into a fight. 'Leave it, Gus,' he said. 'The boss said not to cause a scene.'

Gus stepped back reluctantly, still glaring at them, but it was clear he knew better than to argue with his colleague.

'I'll see you two another time,' he growled, before turning and following his partner from the hall.

'Yeah, sure you will,' said Norman, when they were out of earshot. 'I'll look forward to it.'

They heard a car start up out in the car park, then turned back to the hall.

'Shit!' muttered Norman.

'What?' Slater followed his gaze towards the corner of the hall.

'Ryan's gone.'

Over in the corner, they could see two empty chairs had been hastily pushed back from the table. The only sign anyone had been sitting there were the two full plates Ryan and Ginger had left behind.

'They didn't even get to eat their dinners,' said Norman.

'Maybe they're in the toilets,' suggested Slater, hurrying towards the only other door, situated not far from where they had been sitting.

'It's more likely they went past the toilets and used the fire exit,' Norman muttered, as he followed Slater and pushed his way through the door. To the left was a door into the ladies, to the right was the gents, and at the end of the short passage was a fire exit. Slater was outside, looking both ways, but in the darkness there was nothing to see.

'They have a head start,' called Norman, 'they know their way around, and they could have gone in any direction. It'll be a waste of time trying to find them.'

Slater knew Norman was right. He took one last look before he came back through the fire exit, pulling the door closed behind him.

'I think we can safely assume Ryan knows the two heavies,' he said.

'Or maybe he's just so paranoid right now, he assumes they must be after him, and didn't feel like waiting to find out for sure,' suggested Norman.

'He didn't look paranoid to me,' said Slater. 'If anything, I would have said he looked pretty cool and confident.'

'It's easy to look cool when you think you're in a safe place,' argued Norman.

'I might be stating the obvious here,' said Slater, 'but I'd suggest there's got to be a link between Morgan, the two heavies, and Ryan.'

'It's certainly beginning to look that way. Although it's anyone's guess what the connection might be.'

'Well, if we can find him, Ryan can probably tell us that.'

'Yeah, you may well be right about that. The problem is, if Ryan thinks he's being chased, he might leave the area altogether, and then we'll *never* get to find out what's going on.'

'We need to find him before he leaves then.'

'Or before those other two guys find him.'

'He said Ginger was starving, right?' asked Slater.

'Hasn't eaten for days,' Norman confirmed.

Slater looked pleased with himself. 'And where do these guys go if they want breakfast?'

Norman looked blank for a moment and then a smile filled his face as he remembered. 'Of course,' he said. 'The bakery in town!'

'Right,' said Slater. 'My guess would be that at least one of them will be there bright and early in the morning. We just need to make sure we're there too.'

They walked back into the now almost-deserted hall. It seemed the brief appearance of the two heavies had unsettled everyone enough to make them want to eat up and leave as soon as they could. Chris and Diane were just finishing setting a table for the four of them.

'No luck?' asked Chris.

'Long gone,' said Norman. 'And we'll never find them now. It's a pity we don't know where to find this squat of Ginger's.'

'Sorry, I can't help you there,' said Chris. 'I couldn't even tell you which part of town to start looking.'

'Have you any idea who those two men were?' asked Diane.

'Never seen them before,' said Slater. 'I thought I knew all the thugs around here, so maybe these two are from out of town.'

'But what were they doing here? Were they looking for Ryan?'

'That's the million-dollar question,' he said. 'Were they looking for him or, as Norm says, is he just so paranoid, he's going to run from everyone?'

'Wouldn't they have waited outside if they were looking for someone in particular?' asked Chris.

'The last thing we need is a couple of thugs hanging around trying to intimidate people,' said Diane.

'One of them said they'd been told not to cause a scene,' said Norman. 'That suggests they're working for someone, but it doesn't necessarily mean there's going to be trouble. It could be as simple as someone looking for a lost relative.'

They helped themselves to food and settled at the table.

'I've spoken to the authorities,' said Chris. 'They've asked me to bury Morgan.'

'That's a bit quick, isn't it?' asked Slater.

'They've decided on a cause of death, but they have no idea who he is, and there seems to be no family. It's as if the man didn't exist.'

'Which is suspicious in itself, isn't it?' asked Slater.

'Maybe they're hoping the sooner he's out of the way, the sooner they can forget about him,' suggested Norman.

'I agree with you,' said Chris, 'but they have insisted the corpse should be buried and not cremated. The problem is, it's going to be a pretty quiet funeral. I think he at least deserves to have a few people there to see him off. I was wondering if you two would mind coming along.'

'Count me in,' said Norman. 'Maybe we should ask some of these homeless guys, too.'

Slater had stopped eating and was staring at his plate. He was recalling the last three funerals he had attended. The first, a year or so ago, had been that of a little old man he hadn't really known, who had died alone. Norm had been there too. As he had for Ian Becks' funeral, the police forensics expert who had died in an explosion at the station just a few months ago. The third, just a few weeks ago, had also been a man he hadn't really known.

'What about you, Dave?' asked Chris.

Slater looked up and realised all eyes were on him. 'What? Oh, yeah, I'll be there,' he said.

The rest of the meal passed in a gloomy silence as Chris and Diane pondered the possibilities posed by the appearance of the two unwelcome men. Diane's face told everyone she could see nothing but problems ahead. Meanwhile, Slater was equally gloomy as he remembered that recent funeral. Norman seemed aware something was bothering Slater, but he didn't ask any questions.

When they had finished eating, Chris made his excuses and left. Apparently someone was in need of comfort as a relative quietly slipped away.

'All part of the service,' he had told them. 'Albeit not a particularly enjoyable part.'

It was shortly after ten when Slater and Norman walked Diane home, convinced her the heavies were long gone, and then climbed into Slater's car and headed for home.

* * *

'You wanna talk about it?' asked Norman once they were on the road, looking across at Slater carefully.

'About what?'

'Whatever it is that's bothering you,' said Norman. 'You've hardly said a word since Chris mentioned burying Morgan.'

'You know I hate funerals,' said Slater.

'And that's all it is?' asked Norman.

Slater grunted what Norman assumed was a yes.

'I have to say they're not exactly my favourite social function either,' Norman said, cheerfully. 'I was recalling that funeral we attended a year ago. Do you remember? That little old guy with the sister who used to walk the town like a ghost. What was her name?'

'Florence,' said Slater.

'That's her,' said Norman. 'And then of course there was poor old Becks'. Was that your last one too?'

'No,' said Slater. 'I've been to another one since then.'

'Oh, really? You kept that quiet. Who was it?'

'It was a relative I hadn't seen in a long time.'

'Were you close?'

'A long time ago, yeah,' said Slater. 'Then we sort of lost touch, until recently.'

'If you want to talk about it, you know I'm a good listener, right?'

'Yeah, I know that, Norm, but I'm not sure there's much to talk about really. It happens, doesn't it? You lose touch with people, and then years later you wish you hadn't. It's a fact of life.'

'That's true enough,' agreed Norman, 'but if you change your mind, right?'

'Sure. Thanks.'

* * *

Although it was a dual carriageway, the Tinton bypass only had street lights where the road approached the main roundabout at either end of the town, so there was a stretch about a mile and a half long that had no lights at all. They were on that stretch now, heading north towards Norman's end of town. Norman looked ahead into the night-time gloom with only the headlights to cut a path of light in front of them. There were no other lights to be seen, either behind them or coming the other way down the opposite carriageway.

He knew this road well enough to know there was a lay-by on the left somewhere here. Right on cue, he saw the kerb peel away to the left and, involuntarily, his eyes followed it into the gloom. It was right on the edge of the beam from the headlights, a few yards into the lay-by, that something caught his eye. He turned his head to try to get a better view but, of course, whatever he had seen was now in darkness. It had been the colour that had attracted his eye at first, and the apparent texture of the material. And at one end there had been something else, a different texture and a mixture of colours. He thought he should know what it was . . .

'Stop the car!' he said.

Slater hit the brakes almost immediately and the front of the car dipped as it rapidly lost speed. 'What?' he asked.

'Back there, in that lay-by. I think I saw something. Can we go back?'

'I can't reverse up a dual carriageway, Norm,' said Slater, then he thought for a moment. 'It's okay. I'll pull in up here and reverse back down the lay-by.'

He stopped the car at the far end of the lay-by and carefully reversed into it and back along its length. They both craned their necks to look through the back window. The reversing lights weren't fantastic, but they were better than nothing. They were over halfway along the length of the lay-by now, and Norman was beginning to wonder if he'd imagined it.

'Slow down,' he called suddenly. 'There! On the left.'

Slater peered into the darkness. 'Can I get past it?' he asked. 'We'll be able to see much better with the headlights.'

'I dunno,' said Norman. 'Let me get out and have a look.'

Slater stopped the car and Norman, moving with surprising speed, slipped from the car and ran back behind it. Two seconds later he was puffing back up to the passenger side.

'It's a body,' he said. 'Looks like there's been some sort of accident. If you get right over to the kerb on your side, you can easily get past. We're gonna need those headlights to see what's what.'

He slammed the door closed and ran back behind the car again. Slater turned the steering wheel over as far as he could and crept up onto the kerb on his side, then reversed back until he could see Norman, down on his knees, next to what looked like a large bundle of rags. He swung the car to his left so the lights were pointing directly at Norman and edged as close as he dared before he snapped on the handbrake and turned off the engine.

'What have we got?' he asked Norman as he sank down next to him.

'It's Doddsy,' said Norman, in dismay. 'What the hell's he doing out here?'

'Has he been hit by a car?'

'I can't tell. But he's in a bad way. His pulse is weak and his breathing's pretty ragged.'

'See what you can do for him. I'll call an ambulance,' said Slater, getting to his feet, and heading for the car.

Norman was working frantically on Doddsy, pumping his chest to try and keep his heart going. After a few seconds, Doddsy's eyes fluttered open and he coughed weakly.

'Doddsy, can you hear me?' asked Norman.

'Norm? Is that you?' whispered Doddsy, feebly.

'Yeah, it's me,' said Norman. 'What the hell happened to you?'

'I didn't see them coming. Beat the crap out of me, and then brought me all the way out here.'

'Who? Who did this?' asked Norman, relieved that he could stop pumping Doddsy's chest.

'I didn't see,' he said.

'How many?'

'I dunno. Two? Three? Took me from behind, otherwise I'd 'ave kicked their arses, wouldn't I?'

'Yeah, yeah. Sure you would,' said Norman.

Doddsy's eyelids fluttered for a second and then closed.

'You're not gonna die on me, Doddsy,' said Norman desperately, beginning another round of chest-pumping. 'You're too bloody young for that.'

He stopped for a second and patted the young man's cheek. 'Come on, come on, talk to me!' he pleaded, before beginning his frantic chest-pounding again.

Doddsy coughed once again, and his eyes opened. 'Gawd, Norm, it fuckin' hurts,' he wheezed. 'Am I gonna die?'

Norman stopped to reply, but as soon as he did, Doddsy faded again, so he quickly got back to work. 'Not if I can bloody well help it,' he panted, as he began to feel the strain from his efforts.

'Move over, Norm,' said Slater, gently, alongside him. 'Let me have a go. The ambulance is on its way.'

Norman moved gratefully aside as Slater edged into position and took over massaging the failing heart. In the distance, its sound carrying a long, long way in the dead of night, they could hear a siren.

'Stay with me, Doddsy,' said Norman. 'They're on the way. I can hear them. Come on, talk to me.'

Doddsy grimaced as he opened his eyes once more. Slater sat back, relieved.

'Tell Ryan, I never told 'em nuffink,' hissed Doddsy, this time through gritted teeth.

'Is that what they wanted to know?' asked Norman. 'Where Ryan was?'

'Tell 'im they won't find 'im because of me. I told 'em nuffink. Did I do alright?'

'Yeah, you did great, Doddsy,' said Norman, sadly.

'Will you tell 'im I made the grade?'

'Yeah, I promise I'll make sure I tell him. He'll be proud of you.'

And then they watched, helplessly, as Doddsy closed his eyes one more time and, like a candle that had just been snuffed out, his light seemed to fade and die right before their eyes. The ambulance was getting closer now, so Slater made sure he didn't stop pumping. Maybe, just maybe, they could pull off some sort of miracle.

When they arrived, the paramedics took over with cool professionalism.

But it was no use. On arrival at the hospital, Doddsy was pronounced dead.

CHAPTER FIVE

'What do you mean he was hit by a car?' asked Norman. 'He told me he had been attacked from behind by two or three men.'

'Look, Norm, I'm not trying to suggest you don't know what you're talking about,' said the newly promoted DS Steve Biddeford. 'What I'm saying is your dead guy was telling you a story. He might even have believed he was jumped by some guys, but the truth is he was as high as a bloody kite so you'd have to take anything he said with a pinch of salt. On top of that, all our forensic evidence suggests he was hit by a car at the entrance to the lay-by, and the car dragged him along to the point where you found him. It looks as if it was just another accident involving a down-and-out druggie.'

'The guy was not a druggie,' said Norman, vehemently. 'I've known him for several months, and I have never had reason to think he was taking drugs.'

Biddeford sighed and glanced at the unfamiliar surroundings of the Station Cafe. It was the day after Norman and Slater had found Doddsy in the lay-by, and despite working his arse off all day, he had been unable to find a shred of evidence to back up the story Doddsy had told Norman as he lay dying.

'I can't make a case where there isn't one, Norm,' he insisted. 'You know how it works. We've put a couple of signs up near the scene of the accident asking for any information. There's not much more we can do.'

'A couple of signs?' said Slater. 'Wow! Are you sure you can go to all that expense?'

Biddeford gave Slater a baleful glare, but Slater merely glared straight back.

'What about the fact his sleeves had been cut off?' asked Norman.

Biddeford reluctantly drew his eyes from Slater and back to Norman. 'He was off his head. Maybe he thought he was making some sort of fashion statement.'

'When you're homeless and you only have one coat and winter's coming, you don't cut your sleeves off,' said Norman, his voice strained.

'This one did,' said Biddeford.

'So, what are you really saying here? That these homeless guys just aren't worth wasting your precious time on? Is that it?'

'Give me a break. You know that's not true.'

'Do I?' asked Norman. 'What about the guy who died in the skip? I didn't see anyone busting a gut to find out what happened there.'

'The guy had a hurricane lamp in a bin full of bone-dry paper,' said Biddeford. 'He fell asleep and knocked it over.'

'Are you kidding me?' Norman let out a hollow laugh. 'Where did the lamp come from? Are you suggesting he carried it around with him all the time? Have you ever seen one of these guys carrying something like that around with him?'

'The guy had been living in the skip for weeks—'

'It's not the same guy!' Norman's voice was getting louder. 'How many times do I have to tell you? And the guy who was living there did *not* have a hurricane lamp. I know that for a fact.'

Now Biddeford was getting irritated. 'And how many times do I have to tell you I'll believe you when you bring this guy to me! How come there's a fire and the guy disappears? Tell me that.'

'I told you. His name's Ryan. The dead guy is called Morgan. It's not the same damned man!'

'So, where is this "Ryan" then?'

'He's on the run because he believes he was the intended victim.'

'No,' said Biddeford. 'He's disappeared because he was the crispy cracker we found in the skip. It's just that you won't believe it.' He turned to Slater. 'Will you tell him?'

'I think the respect you show for the victim is telling us all we need to know about how seriously you're taking this investigation,' snapped Norman, shaking his head.

Now it was Norman's turn to exchange glares with Biddeford.

'I can see where you're coming from, Steve,' said Slater, 'but it's not that simple—'

'For instance, if he's dead, how come he turned up last night?' Norman crossed his arms in front of him and glowered.

'What?' asked Biddeford.

'Ryan. He turned up last night.'

Biddeford looked doubtfully from Norman to Slater.

'He was there,' Slater said, coolly.

Biddeford sighed. He really couldn't decide if these two were just trying to waste his time and wind him up. 'So why don't you bring him to me and prove it?'

'Like I said, he *was* there,' said Slater.

'What's that supposed to mean? Where is he now?'

'We're not sure. He ran away before we got a chance to ask him to come and speak to you.'

Biddeford sat back and folded his arms across his chest. So they *were* taking the piss . . .

'We'd just got Ryan settled at a table with his meal when these two hard guys turned up in the doorway,' explained Norman.

'This would be the same two guys you reckon beat up your mate Doddsy, would it?' asked Biddeford, raising an eyebrow.

'Dave and I went over and told them to clear off, and when we looked back, he'd done a bunk out through the fire exit.'

Biddeford gave them a knowing smile. 'That's very convenient, isn't it?' Who is he really, this Ryan? The Invisible Man?'

'You think we're bullshitting, don't you?' asked Slater.

'Well, it has crossed my mind, that you two might just feel the need to waste my time. I mean first you have a guy called Ryan who's never around when you want him, and now you're asking me to believe there are two thugs who seem to have appeared from nowhere and are just as invisible as your mate Ryan. This is all a wind-up, isn't it? Just for old time's sake, you know?'

'Can you hear yourself?' asked Norman. He pointed at Slater. 'He admits he can be childish—'

'No, I don't' said Slater, indignantly.

'But he's just a bloody beginner compared to you!' continued Norman, ignoring Slater's protestations. 'When are you going to get over this stupid idea you have that we want to hold you back? We never have! We just want you to open your damned eyes and look properly at this case. Two homeless guys are dead, and at least one more seems to think his life is in danger, but all you care about is a grudge that doesn't even exist!'

'I've had enough of this.' Biddeford fixed them both with icy stares. 'I suggest you find yourselves another hobby and stop wasting my time. It was a hit-and-run, alright? We've done forensics, and we've put signs up at the scene asking for information. With no witnesses to what actually happened, that's all we can do. And I'm warning you — if you mess me around again, I'll have you charged with wasting police time.'

He stood up and marched away from their table towards the exit.

'I take it that means he's not going to pick up the bill for the coffees,' said Slater, quietly, as he watched Biddeford wrench the door open so violently it almost came off its hinges.

'How much of an arse can one guy be?' asked a very frustrated Norman. 'Did he listen to anything we said?'

'Well, I don't want to say I told you so,' said Slater.

Norman glared at him. 'So don't,' he said, but Slater carried on anyway.

'I said it would be a waste of time and that he won't listen to anything we say, simply because it's us, and my, didn't he prove me right? In any case, he doesn't have the imagination to do anything unless Goodnews tells him to.'

'Talking to her will definitely be a waste of time,' said Norman, gloomily.

'So it looks like it's down to us, then. And the first thing we need to do is find Ryan.'

With all the distraction of Doddsy's death and giving statements to the police, they'd been unable to get to the bakery that morning.

'We can start by trying the bakery tomorrow,' said Norman. 'But you agree with me, right? There is something going on here.'

'That's what we're going to find out,' said Slater, pushing his chair back. 'Come on, you've got to pay for these coffees.'

'How come I get to pay?' protested Norman, as he pushed his own chair back.

'Because it was your dumb idea to invite DS Tunnel Vision to come here and join us.'

'I suppose I have to admit to that.' Norman followed Slater towards the door. He patted his pockets. 'Err, I have no money on me. Can I borrow a fiver?'

Slater stopped in his tracks and sighed. 'You are unbelievable, you know that?' With a pained expression he paid the bill and led the way out of the cafe.

CHAPTER SIX

St Anne's wasn't the biggest of churches, but even with the dozen or so people Norman could see as he looked around before the service, it seemed a cold and unwelcoming place. As he surveyed his surroundings, he thought it was probably one of the gloomiest places he had ever been. He thought back to the last time he'd been here, when he and Slater had been two of barely a handful of mourners to see off a lonely man. At least this time there were a few more in attendance.

It would have been just himself, Slater, the vicar and his wife, but the numbers had been swelled by a handful of people who, although they didn't actually know the dead man, had identified with his situation as they were homeless themselves. Chris and Diane had made a point of inviting anyone who ate at the church hall of an evening, promising tea and sandwiches afterwards for all those who made the effort. Ten of them had decided to take advantage of the offer to attend in exchange for a free lunch, and as more than one of them had observed, 'it was something to do for a couple of hours, wasn't it?'

Knowing the majority of the homeless present were likely to get bored easily or fall asleep, Chris had chosen to keep the service short. This hadn't been difficult, as he knew next to nothing about the dead man.

To Norman's surprise, the entire congregation made the walk across the neat, tidy graveyard to a distant corner where a grave had been prepared, and they all stood in silence and watched as the vicar said a few words before the coffin was slowly lowered into the ground. It was at this point Slater had turned away and stared into the distance. Norman guessed he was thinking about the relative he had just rediscovered and then lost, and he reached across and patted his friend on the shoulder.

Then he felt a tap on his own shoulder and snapped his head around in surprise. As he did, Ryan stepped up alongside him, finger pressed to his lips.

'Shhh!' he said, nodding respectfully towards the disappearing coffin. He stood to attention as Morgan disappeared for the last time. Then, as the others hurried off for tea and sandwiches, he hung back by the grave, Norman and Slater waiting respectfully to one side while he bowed his head and seemed to say a few silent prayers.

'How did you know about the funeral?' asked Norman, when Ryan turned towards them.

'Someone told Ginger at the bakery yesterday morning and she told me,' he said. 'I've been keeping a look out to make sure there weren't any unwanted guests waiting to jump on me. I wouldn't want to cause a scene at me old mate's funeral.'

'So you *did* know him?' asked Norman.

'We spent a couple of years together,' said Ryan. 'That's why he came down here to look for me. He needed help and he didn't have anyone else to turn to. Fat lot of use I turned out to be.'

'You can't blame yourself for what happened,' said Slater. 'The police say it was an accident. He knocked over a hurricane lamp.'

'But that's a load of shit. He didn't have a lamp,' said Ryan. 'The only light he had was a torch, and he would have had a hard job starting a fire with that!'

'Yeah, that's what I told 'em,' said Norman, 'but they found a burnt-out lamp in there, and it's the easiest solution.

Anything else suggests foul play, and they don't want to go down that road if they can avoid it.'

'So you think the fire was started deliberately, and it was intended to kill someone?' asked Slater.

'It was intended to kill me,' said Ryan. 'But I let Morgan have the skip that night because he was in such a bad way.'

'What was wrong with him?' asked Norman.

'The silly bugger told me he'd had an operation of some sort. But instead of going through the National Health Service like any normal person, he'd used some bloody back-street doctor or something. He needed a hospital, but he didn't want to go to one because of what he'd done. I let him have the skip for the night because it was warm and dry. I was going to come back next morning and get an ambulance out to him. It's got to be better to be alive and have some explaining to do rather than be dead, hasn't it?'

'The pathologist reckoned he'd had a kidney removed,' said Norman. 'He thinks he might have sold one. Would Morgan do something like that?'

'Who knows,' said Ryan. 'Morgan was mental. You could trust him with your life, but he had no respect for his own body. He wouldn't put anyone else in danger, but he took all sorts of risks with himself. He was a risk junkie, you know? If he was desperate he'd probably think nothing of flogging a kidney. You can get by with one, can't you?'

'You say it should have been you in that skip and the fire was started deliberately. So why would anyone want to murder *you*?' asked Slater.

'I've pissed off a lot of people over the years. It's what you tend to do when you're in special forces. I expect someone's tracked me down and wants revenge.'

'You mean the two big guys who turned up at the church hall the other night? Who were they?'

'I don't know. I didn't wait to find out.'

'But you think they were looking for you?' asked Norman.

'My skip was just torched, and then two heavies turn up. What would you think?' asked Ryan.

Norman surveyed Ryan for a moment and then looked at Slater, who raised an eyebrow slightly. Slater couldn't help but feel Ryan wasn't telling them something.

'Where's Doddsy?' asked Ryan. 'I didn't think he'd want to miss out on a chance to bury a fellow soldier.'

'You haven't heard, then?' Norman sighed and rubbed his chin. 'He died the night before last. The police are saying it's a hit-and-run, but we found him, and he says he was jumped by two or three guys who beat the crap out of him.'

'Jesus. Why would they do that? I know he was a bit of a tit, but he was all talk. He was harmless enough.'

'He told us they were looking for you,' said Norman. 'But he said to tell you he didn't tell them anything. They won't find you through him.'

Ryan looked away and said nothing.

'How about you cut the crap,' Slater jumped in, 'and tell us why these guys are looking for you?'

'I don't know what you're talking about,' said Ryan. He turned to Norman. 'You know what a bullshitter Doddsy was, Norm. The police are probably right, and he did get hit by a car. But being Doddsy, he has to come up with a load of bollocks to make it look something it wasn't. I bet he was off his tits, wasn't he? Pissed, I expect. You know what he was like.'

'They say he'd been taking drugs, but you know he never did drugs, did he, Ryan?' asked Norman.

'Sooner or later, most people turn to drugs when they're on the street.'

'Why do you think his sleeves were removed?' asked Slater suddenly.

Ryan licked his lips and looked from Norman to Slater. 'What?'

'His sleeves.' Slater indicated the seam at the top of the sleeve of his own jacket. 'They were sliced off. His coat, sweater and shirt. Now, you tell me how that could happen in a road traffic accident?'

'I don't know. What do the police say?'

'Oh, they say Doddsy was off his head and cut them off himself,' said Norman. 'But why would he do that?'

'People do all sorts of weird things when they're off their heads,' said Ryan, shifting from one foot to another.

'Buy you don't really believe Doddsy did it, do you?' asked Slater. 'So tell me, why would someone want to hack off his sleeves?'

'I told you, I don't know.' Ryan glanced around. 'And I've got to go.'

'We can't help you if you don't tell us what's going on,' said Norman, reaching out to hold Ryan's arm.

'You can't help me anyway,' said Ryan, shrugging Norman off and stepping away from him. 'You're better off out of it.'

'Out of what?' asked Norman, as Ryan turned and started to walk away. 'We just want to help you, that's all.'

But Ryan didn't stop walking.

'Crap.' Norman turned to Slater. 'Now what do we do?'

'Well, we can't actually force him to accept our help, can we?' said Slater. 'On the other hand, I'm getting intrigued now, and I really don't have anything better to do, so how about we keep poking around and see if we can find something useful?'

'I need to eat,' said Norman.

'We just had breakfast a couple of hours ago,' said Slater.

'Yeah, I know, but I can't think on an empty stomach.'

Slater sighed. 'Okay, okay. Come on, let's go.'

As they walked away from the now-deserted grave, a small digger trundled into position and began to push soil into the grave. Within half an hour, the only evidence anyone had been buried there was a neat and tidy mound of soil.

* * *

An hour and a half later, Slater and Norman made their way back through the graveyard. They'd had to come back this way because Slater's car was in the church car park, which was at the opposite end to the pub they had walked to for lunch. Norman was grumbling as he walked.

'Will you stop complaining?' asked Slater. 'It's good exercise for you. And God knows you need to walk off some of that lunch.'

This silenced Norman temporarily, but Slater knew it wouldn't last for long. He glanced over to his left, towards the grave they had been standing at a couple of hours earlier. A single, lonely bouquet lay on top of the mound of soil. He walked on for another few steps before he realised. He stopped and turned to face the grave. Head down, still grumbling quietly to himself, Norman walked on for another four or five steps before he realised Slater had stopped.

'What's up?' he called as he turned to Slater.

Slater pointed towards the grave. 'Was that there earlier?' he asked as Norman shuffled alongside.

Norman turned his gaze to follow Slater's finger. 'You mean the flowers? I didn't see any. There weren't even any in the church. They didn't have the money to get flowers.'

'Exactly,' said Slater, heading towards the grave. 'So where did that come from?'

They walked over to the grave. The bouquet lay across the middle. Slater bent down for a closer look.

'Is there a card or a message of some sort?' asked Norman.

'There's a card.' Slater reached for the card, tucked in the wrapper. As he stood, he read the message to Norman.

'"So sorry I wasn't there for you. Love always. C."'

'I thought we didn't find any friends or family,' said Norman.

'We didn't,' said Slater. 'But we were wrong. Someone obviously loved the guy enough to feel they owed him this much.'

'It's gotta be someone local. No one outside the immediate area would have known anything about his death.'

'Even then, it wasn't exactly shouted from the rooftops, was it?' asked Slater. 'There can't be that many people who would have known.'

'I know what you're thinking, but don't get too excited,' said Norman. 'They created a computer-generated image of what he looked like and printed it in the local paper a couple of days after he died. They were hoping someone might recognise it, but no one ever came forward.'

'Maybe no one came forward,' said Slater, 'but it looks like someone recognised him. So, if I'm right, now we have to ask *why* wouldn't they come forward?'

'I think I see where you're going with this. You think it was a woman. You think he had a lover.'

'I think it's a distinct possibility.'

'But he'd only just arrived in the area. He came to find Ryan.'

'That's what Ryan told us,' said Slater. 'But what if he was wrong? What if this woman was an old flame, and Morgan came to find her? What if Ryan being here was a coincidence?'

'That's a bit of a long shot, isn't it?' Norman studied Slater intently.

'If you've got a better explanation for these flowers being here, I'd love to hear it,' said Slater. 'The man had only been here a day. We know he was in trouble. What if he'd been in touch with this old flame and she'd told him to come here so she could help him?'

'I can see it works as a theory. I'm just not sure Ryan's a coincidence. I'm sure he knows something and he's not letting on.'

'Oh for sure,' agreed Slater. 'He's definitely hiding something. But what if what he's hiding is all about why *he's* a target?'

Norman nodded slowly. 'There's no denying that's a possibility.'

'Then it's equally possible Ryan wasn't the real reason Morgan came here. What if he came here to find her, but he knew Ryan was here, and he had only sought him out because he didn't know his way around?'

'It's a "could be",' said Norman, doubtfully. 'But even if you're right and she *is* an old flame, we still have no idea who she is, or where we can find her. And we don't have the resources we used to have.'

'But we do have our wits.' Slater looked around the graveyard and then back at Norman. 'This is where we find out if we can cut it as real private detectives.'

'Okay,' said Norman, brightening. 'So let's make a start. If we assume this woman somehow knew about the funeral, it's a safe bet she didn't want to be seen or she would have turned up in time. My guess is she would have waited until everyone had gone. I'm also going to assume she has a car and would have parked in the car park, or out in the street nearby.'

'You're thinking CCTV,' said Slater. 'But we can't access it.'

'Hey, if we need to, I know a man who can. But first we have to see if there are any cameras.'

They walked back through the car park and out to the road, where Slater scanned up and down in both directions looking for cameras.

'Over there.' Norman pointed across the road. Opposite the car park was a small shop which had been closed for years until an enterprising young chef had spotted the opportunity to convert it into a small, upmarket restaurant. To prove his point, he had actually called it Upmarket.

They walked across the road and peered through the windows. It was obviously closed.

'Jeez,' said Norman. 'Have you seen the prices in this place? You'd need to take out a mortgage to eat here!'

'That's why it's called Upmarket, Norm,' said Slater. 'It's so the punters are under no illusions when they come here.'

'And it's really tiny in there,' said Norman.

'Yeah, well, I guess at those prices you don't need too many clients to make a profit.' Slater looked up at the camera. 'Do you think that camera's live?'

'It's not much use as a form of security if it's not,' said Norman.

'But will they let us take a look at the footage? There's no reason why they should, is there?'

'I think maybe I can help out with that.' Norman made a note of the telephone number. 'You just leave it with me.'

* * *

That evening, Slater had decided to take a break from the soup kitchen. Norman had said he was going to the church hall, but Slater knew there was something else on Norman's mind, although he had been unable to find out what it was. Norm had gone all mysterious when asked what exactly his plan was to get access to the restaurant's CCTV, so realising he was bashing his head against the proverbial brick wall, Slater had left him to it and made his way home. He had his own mission to accomplish tonight, and he preferred to do it alone. It was well past eight p.m. by the time he got settled to his task.

He had just got comfortable with his laptop and logged on to the website when his doorbell rang. He sighed and dragged himself reluctantly to his feet. As he did, he looked at his watch. It was half past eight. He walked across the room to his front door and wondered who could be ringing his doorbell. He certainly wasn't expecting anybody. If it was the bloody Jehovah's Witnesses . . . but it wouldn't be, would it? Not this late. He swung the door open to find an attractive young woman with a pale face and strawberry-blonde hair standing on the step.

Slater blinked at the woman on the doorstep. 'Oh,' he said. 'This is a surprise. I wasn't expecting you. In fact, I wasn't expecting anybody.'

'I'm sorry,' said Detective Chief Inspector Marion Goodnews. 'I know I should have called first. I was hoping you'd get in touch but you didn't, so I thought I'd take the initiative. I've been uhmming and ahhing about coming round, and then I finally thought if I don't do it now . . .' The words had been rushing from her, but now she stopped, looking at his face. 'If I'm disturbing you, I can leave.'

He suddenly realised the way he was standing, blocking the doorway, was giving off all the wrong vibes. To be honest, she was probably the last person he wanted to see, but no sooner had the thought crossed his mind than he felt guilty about it.

'No, not at all,' he said, backing into the house to make room for her to come in. 'I just wasn't expecting anyone. I was immersed in what I was doing.'

She swept past him, and he caught the merest trace of her familiar perfume. He couldn't help but pause to breathe it in, closing his eyes and remembering as he pushed the door closed. He turned to follow her into the house, but she was standing expectantly, face tilted up towards him, so close he could almost count the individual freckles. Her hair was tied back, but one or two of the strawberry curls had escaped and hung tantalisingly to one side of her face. He resisted the urge to reach forward and tuck it behind her ear.

'Here, let me take your coat,' he said.

She looked disappointed but turned her back so he could slip the coat, and her scarf, from her shoulders. He turned and hung it on one of the hooks behind the door, looping the scarf over a different hook.

'Go on in,' he said. 'You know the way.'

She walked forward into the tiny room and turned to face him again. He pointed to the two-seater settee. 'Take a seat. Can I get you a drink?'

'No, thanks. I'm fine,' she said, backing towards the seat and sinking into it.

'Ah, right.' Slater walked across to the armchair and sat down. He smiled at her, uncertainly, and she smiled back, equally uncertain. Her expression suggested she was wondering if she had made a mistake in coming here.

'I get the impression you're not exactly over the moon to see me,' she said.

'I just wasn't expecting anyone, that's all,' he said.

'And if someone had to come, you'd rather it wasn't me. Am I right?'

'That depends on why you're here.'

'Oh, does it make a difference? Why d'you want me to be here?'

'Jesus,' he said. 'That's a leading question, isn't it? I don't think it's up to me to answer that. You're the one who came to see me, remember?'

She smiled a sad little smile. 'Aye, I suppose you're right. So let me start again. Do you think I've come here to offer you your job back?'

'I don't think so. Your pride wouldn't allow you to do that. I suppose you might consider it if I was to come grovelling on my hands and knees, but chase after me after I resigned? No, I don't think so, do you?'

'Did you have a good holiday?'

'It was interesting,' he said. 'But I don't think that's why you're here, either.'

'So, why do you think I'm here?'

'You don't know?' Slater lifted an eyebrow.

'Oh, I know why I came here,' she said. 'But now I'm wondering why I thought it was a good idea. I feel about as welcome as a skunk.'

'Not so,' he said. 'You smell much nicer than any skunk I've ever met.'

'Now you're taking the piss.' Her shoulders slumped slightly.

'I'm sorry,' he said. 'I didn't mean it to come out like that.'

She smiled, but it was a sad, humourless little smile. 'So, humour me, and answer my question.'

Slater began to feel uncomfortable. He really didn't mean to make fun of her, but then again, he didn't want to play stupid guessing games either.

'Well, you made so much fuss after the last time you were here, I can't imagine you're looking to get drunk with me again,' he said. 'I don't know, Marion. Why *are* you here?'

'You're no' gonna make this easy for me, are you?'

He gave her a sad little smile of his own. 'What do you want me to say?'

'How about "Hi Marion, I'm really pleased to see you"?'

'But, if I'm honest, I'm not sure I *am* pleased to see you,' he said.

For the first time since she had arrived, Goodnews looked more than doubtful. Now she looked crestfallen, and her bottom lip trembled. 'Oh Christ,' she said, sadly. 'I'm making a fool of myself, aren't I?'

Now Slater was beginning to feel seriously guilty. The last thing he wanted to do was upset her, but he had to be honest, didn't he? Anyway, whose fault was it she was getting upset? He hadn't asked her to come here and put him on the spot.

'I think it may well be me who's the fool,' said Slater, 'but I've got to be honest, Marion. What happened between us was wonderful, but do I want it to go any further? I'm not sure.'

'Why not? Don't you find me attractive?'

'You know I do. I think you're beautiful, but there has to be more to it than that, doesn't there? I don't want to be competing with your job, or your ego. You know you'd have to have the last word. I want to be someone's partner, as an equal.'

'But that's just what I want,' she said. 'I don't want someone who's just going to agree with me all the time.'

Slater looked at her, and she stared back, straight into his eyes. 'But why me?' he asked. 'You could have any bloke you want. There are plenty better than me.'

'How do you define "better"?' she asked. 'Better-looking, earning more money, having a bigger house, better prospects?'

'Take your pick,' he said. 'There'll be one hell of a long list. Mr Perfect must be in there somewhere.'

'But I don't want perfect. That's one of the things I like about you. You're not perfect, and you know you're not. You have faults and sometimes they get the better of you, but that's my whole point. Don't you see? You don't pretend to be anything you're not. With you it's a case of what you see is what you get. How can anything be better than that?'

Slater felt rather embarrassed by her frankness, and was struggling to know how to respond. 'This is all a bit sudden, isn't it? I mean you've always done your best to keep a distance between us, and now you're asking me to—'

'I'm not asking to move in with you,' she said. 'I just thought maybe we could go out together now and then. We've only ever worked together. Why can't we spend some time together as people, instead of colleagues? You never know, we might get to know each other and like what we find. After that, who knows what could happen?'

'Oh, we know what could happen. What could happen is we end up in bed, and then you make my life a misery afterwards because you're terrified someone might find out.'

'But I was your boss before, for God's sake,' she argued. 'That wouldn't happen now, would it? It wouldn't matter what anyone said.'

'Yeah, but . . .' he began, and then realised he couldn't actually think of a 'but'.

'But, what?' she asked. 'Look, if you've got some problem with me being your girl, please tell me. It took a lot of courage for me to come here like this. At least if you're going to turn me down, give me a decent reason I can understand and I'll get out from under your feet.'

'Don't say that,' he said. 'You're not "under my feet" at all. It's just come as a bit of a shock, and I already had a bloody big one in Thailand. To be honest, I don't know if I'm coming or going when it comes to my life.'

'Why? What happened in Thailand?' she asked.

'You don't want to know,' he said. 'It's family stuff, a bit complicated.'

'Actually, I *would* like to know,' she said. 'Have you got any wine?'

'I got a couple of bottles of red from duty-free on the way home,' he said. 'I don't know what it's like.'

'I'm sure it'll be fine. Why don't I go and find two glasses and we open one, and you can tell me all about your family stuff.'

Slater didn't know what to say to that idea. His head was trying to think of a reason to say no, but in his heart he knew there really wasn't one. He knew how hard it must have been for her to come here, and he admired her for that. He looked across at her beautiful green eyes, which were staring intently at him, willing him to make up his mind and put her out of her misery.

'Or I can put my coat on and go home,' she said. 'Your choice.'

'Can you remember where the glasses are?'

'Oh yes. And where you keep your wine.'

For the first time since she had arrived, she relaxed, and the change was clear to see, the strain in her face being replaced by a warm, glowing smile. She headed for the kitchen.

Slater watched her walk away from him, then rose from his chair and walked across to his laptop, sitting on the tiny table. The browser was open, still showing the website sign-up form he had just started filling in. He moved the mouse and clicked it to close the browser, prodded the button to shut down the laptop, and then flipped the lid down. Maybe he didn't need to join that dating site after all. At least, not tonight.

CHAPTER SEVEN

It was lunchtime next day when Slater met up with Norman, in the pub where he lived. They were at the bar waiting to be served when Norman proudly produced a couple of still photos.

'So how exactly did you get your hands on these?' asked Slater. 'Please don't tell me you used your pet hacker?'

Norman hated it when Slater referred to his old friend Vinnie the Geek as a hacker. As far as he was concerned, Vinnie had come a long way in the time he had known him and was something of a genius when it came to computers. Yes, it was true, Vinnie could get in and out of most systems undetected, but he didn't do anything malicious with his skills and only used them for good purposes. He could have used them for bad, but he was making millions online through a legitimate business. Why would he risk losing that?

'I didn't need to use anyone else,' said Norman, proudly. 'This is all my own work.'

'You mean he's trained you to hack systems?' asked Slater, dubiously.

'Look, you cynic, I didn't need to hack anything. I just went into the restaurant and asked them if I could take a look at their security. The CCTV is obviously a part of that, so they let me test it to make sure it all worked properly.'

'What? You just showed up on the off-chance?' asked Slater. 'I thought they were closed during the day.'

'Yeah, but they're open every night,' said Norman. 'So I called in there last night, gave them my card—' he tossed a business card onto the table — 'and offered them a free survey.'

Slater picked up the card and looked at the inscription which read *S & N, Investigations & Security.*

'You've used my address,' complained Slater.

'I can hardly use the pub's name and address, can I?' said Norman. 'What sort of message would that send out? We want to be taken seriously, don't we?'

Slater looked at the card again. He was quietly impressed with Norman's work, but he knew he could get some winding-up mileage out of this if he tried.

'S & N?' he asked. 'It's not very imaginative, is it?'

'Hey, I'm sorry I'm not a marketing whizz kid,' said Norman, testily. 'It might not be beautiful, but it does what it says on the tin, right? It was good enough to get me an appointment this morning, and that's all I wanted it to do.'

Now Slater was wearing a wide grin. 'Easy, tiger. I'm only teasing. It was good thinking, and it was a damned sight more constructive than what I did last night.' He reached for the photos and looked at them closely. 'And you think this is the car driven by the woman who left the flowers at the grave yesterday?'

'That's the only car that went anywhere near that church car park between the time we left the grave and when we got back after lunch. Of course, if she was on foot, or came from the other direction, it won't be any help, but we must be due a break somewhere, so maybe this is it.'

'How are we going to trace the number?'

'I've got that covered, too,' said Norman. 'Naomi Darling's back at work. I called in a favour.'

Slater smiled at Norman's apparent ability to be owed favours by all and sundry. 'Are you sure you actually need me in this partnership? Only you seem to be managing just fine on your own.'

'Someone's gotta drive the car when I get tired,' said Norman, with a cheeky grin.

'And I suppose I'm also quite handy for buying lunch.'

'Now you're talking,' said Norman. 'That's the best idea you've had so far.'

* * *

'So, how come Naomi's willing to help us out?' asked Slater, when they were settled at a table eating their lunch. 'Doesn't she have the same view as Biddeford?'

'She hates his guts,' said Norman. 'She wouldn't agree with him if he said black was black.'

'No change there, then,' said Slater. 'So making him DS hasn't changed his attitude?'

'According to her, he's even worse now,' said Norman. 'Before, he just regarded her as a possible conquest. Now he knows he's not going to get inside her knickers, and he's above her in the pecking order, he just treats her like some sort of lackey.'

'I bet she'll make him regret that before he's finished.'

'Oh, for sure,' agreed Norman. 'But it doesn't end there. She has no time for Goodnews either.'

Slater made sure he showed no reaction when Norman mentioned Goodnews. There was no love lost between the two, and he wasn't sure exactly how Norm would react if he knew she had been at his house last night. He said a silent prayer Norman hadn't arranged to come to his house first thing this morning, that really would have been an interesting start to the day — for all three of them.

'Oh, really?' he said, non-committally, 'but I thought it was Goodnews who got her fast-tracked.'

'Yeah, that's right, but it was also Goodnews who dropped her like a hot potato when the accusation about beating that guy up first surfaced. Naomi feels that as DCI, Goodnews should have supported her, but she didn't listen to her side of the story at all. Instead, she hung her out to dry. It seems all she cared about was what the chief constable would say when he found her recommendation had gone bad.'

'I feel bad about that,' said Slater, guiltily. 'I should have done more.'

'Yeah, you should have,' agreed Norman. 'But don't worry, Naomi doesn't have it in for you, at least not as much as the other two. She did say you were in hospital at the time because of her, so you had reason not to want to help.'

'It wasn't that I didn't want to help,' said Slater. 'She was gone before I got back, and I didn't know where she was.'

'You have to admit that sounds pretty lame. I mean, you *are* a detective, aren't you?'

Slater was stung by Norman's comment, but he had to admit it was true — it wouldn't have been that hard to track her down if only he had tried.

'Yeah, but to be fair, one of my mates did get murdered,' he said, defensively, 'and that rather grabbed my attention and became my priority.'

'It's okay, she understands that. And she doesn't hate you. She has more than enough of that for the other two.'

'Has she asked for a transfer?' asked Slater. 'If it's that bad, she'd be better out of it.'

'It's worse than that. She's gonna quit,' said Norman. 'She's just biding her time, although I'm not sure what for.'

'I hope she's not planning some sort of revenge,' said Slater.

'I wouldn't be surprised, and you have to admit, it would be poetic justice,' said Norman. 'In the meantime, she said if there's anything she can do to help, I should let her know. She's gonna call me later with an address to go with that number plate.'

Not for the first time, Slater was in awe of the way Norman got on so well with someone he himself should have known better. He had worked with Naomi, yet he knew hardly anything about her. Norman was more of a passing acquaintance, yet he seemed to know her like an old friend. *How did that work?*

His thoughts were interrupted by a ring tone. Norman grabbed the phone from his pocket and put it to his ear.

'Yo,' he said.

Slater watched his friend's facial animations as he embarked on a short conversation. Of course, Slater could only hear Norman's half of the conversation so he had to guess at the responses from the other end.

'Oh, right. Wow! That was quick.'

Slater guessed it must be Naomi Darling.

'Just make sure you don't get caught. We don't want you getting into trouble because you're helping us. Yeah, I suppose there is that. Can you text it to me? That's brilliant! I owe you one, right? Yeah, I'll tell him. Speak soon. Take care.'

Norman cut the call and placed the phone down on the table.

'That was Naomi. She's gonna text me the address. How quick was that?'

'Pretty impressive,' said Slater. 'But she's taking a big risk.'

'I told her that. She said she doesn't give a shit. If they sack her it'll save her writing out a resignation letter.'

Slater didn't quite know what to say to that, so he took a sip of his shandy. 'So what did she ask you to tell me?' he asked.

'She said to tell you she still hasn't told anyone what really happened that night she slept with you.'

Slater almost sprayed shandy everywhere. 'She didn't bloody sleep with me,' he spluttered, red-faced.

Norman grinned at his friend's discomfort. 'Surely that depends on how you want to define "sleep with".'

'She told you?' asked Slater, aghast.

'She told me you were too drunk to stand up,' said Norman with a huge grin. 'And that when she put you to bed, you didn't even get excited when she undressed you.'

'Jesus, who else knows?'

'Aw, come on,' said Norman, shaking his head. 'Do you really think I'm going to go blabbing about it? Don't worry, your secret's safe with me. She swore me to secrecy, and I promise you she won't tell another soul.'

'How can you be so sure?'

'Oh come on, get real. If she told anyone, how many would believe nothing happened? Not many, right? So look at it from her point of view. Do you really think a good-looking young woman like her is going to admit she shared a bed with an old guy like you? How desperate would she need to be? She has her pride, you know.'

Slater was about to argue the case for men his age, but then the phone on the table pinged to announce the arrival of a text message, distracting Norman's attention from the conversation. It was just enough of a distraction to give Slater the chance to think better of continuing the argument. Second thoughts told him he would be playing right into Norman's hands and setting himself up for more humiliation.

Norman looked at the phone, and then passed it over to Slater. 'D'you know this name and address?'

Slater took the phone and read the message. 'The name doesn't mean anything to me, but Malvern Gardens rings a bell,' he said, thinking hard. 'I feel I should know it. I've got a feeling it's one of the roads on that big estate to the east of town. It's all great big new houses with huge gardens.'

'So we know this Clara Sterling isn't short of cash then,' said Norman. 'You don't get to buy one of those houses for less than a million. Should we go up there now?'

'Don't you want to finish your lunch first?'

'Well, yes, obviously.' Norman rolled his eyes. 'I didn't mean we should drop everything and rush off straight away.'

* * *

Norman eased the car along the road and turned right into Malvern Gardens.

'Just look at these houses,' he said, as they drove slowly down the road. 'Who the hell can afford to buy these places?'

'Certainly not Mr Average,' said Slater. 'So, I guess that means it must be millionaires.'

'They would have to be, wouldn't they?'

The house they were looking for was called Silver Birches, but if they thought there would be a clue in the name, they were mistaken. There were silver birch trees everywhere.

'I should have known that would be too easy,' muttered Norman.

There was a driveway up ahead on the left. They could see a pair of double gates were open inwards, but there seemed to be no sign of a house name anywhere.

'I bet they've got a nameplate up inside the drive,' said Norman. 'How is anyone supposed to be able to see that?'

He was just about to crawl past the gates so Slater could have a good look up the drive, when a chauffeur-driven Jaguar suddenly emerged at speed and swung right across the front of them. Norman slammed on the brakes, stopping just inches away from the other car's doors. The chauffeur had been equally sharp on the brakes, and a collision was narrowly avoided.

Norman wound down his window and gave the other driver a vividly coloured piece of his mind, but the abuse was wasted as the driver studiously ignored him, managing to avoid eye contact as he eased the Jaguar slowly and carefully around the front of their car. As the Jaguar came alongside, the chauffeur stopped so his passenger, a smartly dressed man in his early sixties, could wind his window down and speak to Norman from the back seat.

'Well, well, well,' he said, genially, 'if it isn't PC Wide-Arse Norman, the fattest copper on the force. I thought I recognised you.'

From alongside Norman, Slater got the distinct feeling these two had a past, and from the way Norman had stiffened and almost swelled in size, he guessed they weren't exactly the best of mates.

'Stan Coulter?' said Norman in undisguised disgust. 'I thought there was a funny smell. What are you doing here? Are you out on parole?'

'Ha! You cheeky fat lump,' sneered Coulter. 'What do you mean, "out on parole"? I'm a law-abiding businessman.'

'Yeah, sure you are. And I'm auditioning for Stick Man. What you mean is they haven't managed to put you away yet.'

'I can't help it if the Metropolitan Police mistakenly think I'm some sort of criminal,' said Coulter. 'My solicitor thinks it's a disgrace the way they keep harassing me. We're seriously considering a law suit. I'll be happy to include your name on the credits if you're going to start hassling me for visiting a friend.'

'You have a friend?' said Norman. 'Really? Are they simple, or are they just stupid?'

Coulter grinned and winked at Norman. 'Actually, she's more than just a friend, if you get my drift. Nudge, nudge, wink, wink.'

'What does she do with her guide dog when you're being friends?' asked Norman, straight-faced.

Slater sniggered and then tried to disguise the sound with a cough, but despite the fact it wasn't exactly an oblique reference, it was obviously way too subtle for Coulter and sailed harmlessly over his head.

'She doesn't have a guide dog,' he said, confused. 'Why on earth would she need a guide dog?'

'Don't worry about it,' said Norman. 'It would take far too long to explain it to someone like you. So what are you doing in this part of the world anyway? It's a bit of a long way from your comfort zone, isn't it?'

'I'm minding my own business,' said Coulter, venomously. 'You should try it some time.'

'The thing is, it's like when you have a busted drain,' explained Norman. 'Once you see that first turd floating your way, you just know you need to investigate and find out what's going on.'

Slater wondered if this insult was going to fly over Coulter's head too, but he needn't have worried. He could tell by the way the other man's eyes had narrowed that Norman had scored a direct hit.

'There's only one turd around here,' hissed Coulter, angrily, 'and you're it, sitting in that shit-heap of a car.

What's with that anyway? Can't the village plod around here afford to buy decent cars?'

Coulter obviously thought he was still in the police force, and Norman didn't seem to see any need to put him straight. It might suit their purposes better this way anyway, Slater thought.

'You should have something better to do than go around picking on people like me,' continued Coulter, climbing onto his favourite soap box. 'There's enough real scumbags in this country. Why don't you go and pick on some of them? My son didn't fight in Afghanistan so you lot could pick on his old dad. No, he fought so we could keep our freedom, and I'm buggered if some fat, cowardly slug of a man like you is going to besmirch his memory.'

Coulter had become increasingly animated as he was speaking, his face a fiery red, his eyes bulging. It was as if he couldn't stop himself.

'It's a bloody sin that my younger son's dying too,' he said. 'What did he ever do to anyone? Why should he d—'

The chauffeur coughed loudly, and Coulter suddenly stopped speaking. 'Anyway, I have my rights,' he said, finally. 'And I haven't done anything wrong. Do you understand?'

Norman stared impassively at Coulter, but said nothing. Slater wasn't sure Coulter himself had understood what he had been ranting about, but Norman obviously recognised there was no point in arguing with the man once he started going on about his rights.

'Like I said, I came to see my friend—' Coulter was off again — 'and as far as I'm aware, there's no law against a man having a bit on the side, is there? So, just piss off and leave me alone. Drive on, chauffeur.'

The driver slipped the car into gear and it began to move forward, rapidly gaining speed as it purred away down the road.

Norman sat in silence for a moment, and it was Slater who spoke first. 'You could have introduced me to your friend.'

'You wouldn't like him,' said Norman. 'He's a complete arsehole.'

Slater laughed. 'Really? I would never have guessed. He seemed so likeable.'

'He's a total shit, and if he's involved with some woman down here, she must be either stupid, desperate, or caught in some sort of trap.'

'He sounds like a real charmer.'

'Oh, he is. You name it, he's done it. He must have covered the whole spectrum in his time.'

He had put the car in gear now and began to edge forward.

'Silver Birches,' said Slater, looking up the drive to their left.

'What?'

'The house. Silver Birches. This is it. It's where your friend Coulter has just come from. It looks like our Mrs Sterling must be his bit on the side.'

'Oh, crap,' said Norman. 'I wonder if that means she's desperate or caught in one of Coulter's traps.'

'Or stupid,' said Slater, 'you forgot stupid.'

* * *

'Good afternoon,' said Norman. 'Are you Mrs Clara Sterling?'

The tall, slender woman who had opened the door eyed them nervously. She was expensively and elegantly dressed. Slater guessed she was mid-forties, but what struck him most was the expression on her face. She looked distinctly rattled, and it would have been no surprise if she had slammed the door in their faces.

'Who are you? What do you want?' she asked.

'My name's Norman Norman, and this is my colleague Dave Slater. We're investigating the identity of a man who was recently found dead in Tinton.'

'Man? What man?' she said. 'Are you the police? Don't you have to show me some identification?'

'We're not the police,' said Norman, handing her one of his newly printed business cards.

She scanned the card quickly. 'Well, if you're not the police, I don't have to talk to you, do I?'

'No, you don't have to, ma'am,' said Norman, 'but we were hoping you might, because we know almost nothing about the dead man. However, we have reason to believe you knew him, in which case you could maybe fill in some of the blanks for us.'

She looked uncertainly from Norman's face to Slater's and then back to Norman. 'I don't know what you're talking about. I have nothing to say,' she said, taking a step back, ready to close the door.

'Why did you leave flowers on his grave?' asked Slater, before she had time to close it.

Now she paused, confused, her eyes darting back and forth. She licked her lips nervously. 'You're not the police. I don't have to talk to you.'

'We could call them if you'd prefer to talk to them,' said Slater. 'I'm sure they'd be interested in what you know.'

'Or perhaps we could talk to your husband,' said Norman, 'about that nice Mr Coulter.'

Her face changed quickly from nervous defiance to blind panic. 'Who?'

'He was just leaving as we arrived,' said Norman.

'Oh, Mr Coulter. Yes, he was here to talk business.'

'Business?' said Slater. 'I suppose that's one way of putting it, but that's not quite how he described your meeting.'

'Of course, it's up to you who you choose to have as a friend,' said Norman, 'but I don't think your husband would be too impressed if I was to explain to him just what sort of man Coulter really is. You see, we go back a long way, and I can assure you he's a bad man, a really bad man.'

Her face had flushed a deep shade of red.

'I'm sorry, Mrs Sterling. What you do in the privacy of your own house is your business, but I'm afraid a man like Coulter likes to think he can impress other men by bragging about his conquests. If you don't mind me saying, he's batting way above his average with you, so in his head that's something he has to shout about, especially to someone like me.'

Now the colour had drained from her face and she had turned a ghostly shade of white.

'Oh my God,' she said, quietly. She sagged against the door.

'Here,' said Norman stepping forward to take her arm. 'You need to sit down.'

He helped her inside the house, following her directions in answer to his 'Where should we go?'.

While Norman helped Clara Sterling into a small sitting room, Slater stepped through an open door into the kitchen, opening cupboards until he found a glass and fetched her some water. He handed the water to her and then stepped back to give her some space. She sipped the water and within a minute, she seemed to regain some of her composure.

'How did you know it was me who left the flowers?' she asked.

'There's a CCTV camera just across the road from the car park,' explained Norman. 'It got a great shot of your car's registration number.'

'I suppose there's no point in denying it then, is there?'

'Not really,' said Norman, gently.

'You're not in any trouble,' said Slater. 'We know you had nothing to do with his death. It's just that we know very little about him, or where he came from, or what he's doing here. The thing is, the police are happy to accept his death was an accident, but we think they're wrong.'

'We're hoping you can help us,' said Norman.

'What do you want to know?'

'At the moment we know next to nothing, so anything you can tell us will be a big help,' said Slater.

'Eight years ago, we lived just outside Hereford,' she began.

'Where the SAS is based,' added Norman.

'Yes, that's right. My husband's a doctor, in private practice. I used to work part-time in the public library. Morgan used to come into the library, that's how we met.'

'He was a bookworm?' asked Slater. 'That seems at odds with being an SAS action man.'

'Doesn't quite fit the image, does it? But just because a man fights for a living, it doesn't mean he's too stupid to read. I'll admit it did surprise me, though. I suppose it made him intriguing, as if being in the SAS wasn't intriguing enough.'

'You became friends?' asked Norman.

'We had a common interest in historical fiction. He asked me to recommend some books, then we had lunch together, and before I knew it we were lovers. It was crazy, I know, but it was a bit like being on a runaway train. I just couldn't stop it.'

'But you did in the end?' prompted Norman.

'Had to,' she said. 'My husband found out.'

'How did he react?' asked Slater.

She sighed. 'How do you think? Let's just say I was given an ultimatum that I couldn't turn down. I told Morgan it was over, quit my job at the library, and didn't see him again.'

'And that was it?' asked Norman.

'I heard he went off to Afghanistan not long after, but once I left the library, I lost touch with what was going on. I suppose I did it deliberately, but the temptation was always there in the background. Then, a year ago, my husband was offered the opportunity to come and work here. He said it would be a chance for a fresh start, so we moved. After that it really was impossible to find out anything about Morgan, so I tried to forget it had ever happened. I focused on repairing my marriage and trying to be a better wife.'

Slater was struggling to see how having an affair with Coulter could possibly fit in with the idea of being a better wife, but he managed to suppress the desire to ask the question.

'Do you have any idea why Morgan would have come to Tinton?' asked Norman.

'Oh yes,' she said. 'He was looking for me.'

'But I thought that was all over, years ago,' said Slater.

'He called me about a month ago, right out of the blue. I couldn't believe it. God only knows how he found where we were living. He said he was completely messed up. He wanted to come and see me. He said I was the only person he felt he could trust.'

'Why? What had happened?' asked Norman.

'What he told me was a bit sketchy, to say the least, but I think something terrible happened. I suppose it's more or less inevitable in his line of work. They spend ages on psychological tests before they join up, but in the end it doesn't matter how much psychological profiling they do, you never know for sure what might push someone over the edge. It appears whatever happened this time was enough to push him past his breaking point.

'When I spoke to him he didn't sound anything like the old Morgan I knew. It was as if he'd lost all his confidence. He sounded a hundred years old, but he wasn't even forty. He kept saying he was going to try to make amends, whatever that meant.'

She looked even more drained now, and her eyes were filling with tears. 'He said he would call again when he arrived in Tinton. I waited and waited but he didn't call, and then the next thing I know there's one of those computer images in the local newspaper and a headline above it asking "Do you know this man"?'

'But you didn't come forward?' asked Norman.

'It might not have been him,' she said, unconvincingly, 'and I had to think of my husband. I didn't want to drag that up all over again.'

This time, Slater couldn't help himself. 'Of course not. Not when everything is obviously going so well between you.'

Clara Sterling glared at him. 'Don't judge what you don't understand,' she snapped.

Norman shot him an uncharacteristic angry glance. It was enough to stop his retort before it left his mouth.

'Leaving the flowers was taking a risk,' said Norman, clearly trying to draw her attention away from Slater and his judgemental comment. 'Anyone could have seen you.'

'I was careful. I made sure the service was long over and no one was around. I didn't spot the CCTV in the church car park.'

'There isn't any there,' said Norman. 'You were caught on a camera at the front of the restaurant just across the road.'

'Ha! Well, that's just typical of my luck,' she said, defeat heavy in her voice.

'Going back to what Morgan told you about trying to make amends,' said Slater, carefully. 'Do you have any idea what that might have meant? Did he mean he had to come to Tinton to do whatever it was?'

'I haven't a clue. All he said was, "I'm going to do my best to make amends". He said it several times, but he didn't go into any details about what exactly that meant.'

'Well, if he was coming to see you, at least now we have a reason for him coming here,' said Norman. 'Up until now, it had seemed like a random decision, but this makes a bit more sense. I just wish we knew what had happened that he needed to make amends for.'

'I'm sorry,' she said. 'I've told you all I can. I really don't think I can help you any further.'

Slater looked across at Norman, who nodded his head and began to rise from his chair.

'Thank you very much,' said Slater, getting to his feet. 'You've been very helpful. I must apologise for any offence I may have caused. You're quite right, I shouldn't judge without knowing all the facts.'

'I should give up on the grovelling sincerity, Mr Slater,' she said. 'It really doesn't suit you, and I don't believe it any more than you do.'

His face reddened, but he chose not to comment. He knew she was right.

* * *

'What did you make of that?' asked Slater, as Norman drove the car away from her house.

'What did I make of what?' asked Norman. 'You trying to piss her off? She could easily have called a halt right there and then and thrown us out. Did you think of that?'

'I'm sorry. I couldn't help myself. I mean, she knows we know about Coulter and yet she comes out with all that bollocks about repairing her marriage, and how she had to think of her husband . . .'

'I know. I was there,' said Norman. 'But we have to keep our opinions to ourselves, don't we? Jeez, how long have you been doing this?'

'Alright, alright, I was in the wrong,' admitted Slater. 'I'm sorry. It won't happen again. I just hate people being so bloody hypocritical.'

At this point, Slater would normally have gone off into a sulk, but that was before. Now he was a different person — he was determined to make sure it didn't happen.

'Anyway,' he said, taking a deep breath, 'As I said, what did you think?'

'I think that woman's a terrible hypocrite,' said Norman, with a wicked grin.

Slater gave him a sideways look and caught the grin. 'Yeah, right,' he said, grinning himself.

'I think she knows more than she's letting on,' said Norman, 'but I'm not sure what about. Does that make sense?'

'That's exactly what I was thinking. I'm sure she's telling the truth about Morgan, so I wonder what it is she's not telling us about?'

'It could be anything,' said Norman. 'But we know Coulter's around, and that's enough to make me think I should put all my money on him.'

'You think he's blackmailing her?'

'I certainly wouldn't put it past him. The thing is, do we want to know? I mean, we could waste a lot of time poking around only to find she actually wants to be his bit on the side.'

'Nah,' said Slater. 'She's way too classy to choose to be with a creep like him. She could do so much better if she wanted.'

'Maybe she likes a bit of rough,' said Norman. 'Let's face it, there must even be a woman somewhere who would even go for a guy like you.'

'Oh, don't you worry,' said Slater, rising easily to the bait, 'I've got them knocking on my door, mate.'

'Oh really?' said Norman, glancing across at Slater. 'Now that is interesting. Are you going to tell me who these women are?'

Slater blushed, guiltily.

'Jeez, you really have? Why would you be embarrassed about that? Oh no, it's not a married woman, is it? And you've just been complaining about hypocrites . . .'

'No, it's not a bloody married woman,' said Slater, testily, 'and I am not a hypocrite. Now can we get back to this case?'

'Ooh,' said Norman, obviously enjoying playing Slater, as usual. 'I wonder — if I push one more button, do you think it will give us lift-off?'

'I'm not going to give you the satisfaction,' said Slater. 'I know what you're trying to do, and I'm not playing your game. Now, can we get back to the subject that's really interesting?'

'But this *is* interesting,' said Norman.

'Trust me, it's not.'

Norman glanced across at Slater and gave him a calculated look before nodding. 'But we're no further forward, are we? I mean, we've got two murders and no motive for either of them. Apart from them both being homeless, the only connection seems to be one was in the SAS and the other was an SAS wannabee, if that is a connection.'

'I still don't get why Doddsy's sleeves had been cut off. That seems to be a bit unnecessary, especially if it was a hit-and-run. Why would the driver get out of the car and remove the guy's sleeves?'

'But it wasn't a hit-and-run in the strictest sense, was it? Okay, the guy was run down, but it didn't look like an accident to me, especially if you believe some of what Doddsy said. It was more like someone used their car to knock him down, and then when he was lying in the road, they questioned him and cut off his sleeves.'

'Yeah, but why the sleeves? There were no marks on his arms, so it's not as if they were cutting him or anything.'

'Maybe they were looking to see if he shoots up,' suggested Norman. 'Biddeford said he was high as a kite, right? Maybe they injected him.'

'You spoke to Doddsy before he died,' said Slater. 'Did he sound as if he was off his head?'

'He did come out with all that crap about three guys jumping on him from nowhere,' recalled Norman, 'but then he always embroidered everything with an amount of exaggeration.'

'So that wasn't unusual, then?'

'Very normal, now I come to think about it. He did smell of booze, but that wasn't unusual either.'

'We need to find out if he really *was* high,' said Slater.

'You're the one who knows the pathologist.'

'Yeah, I do, but I wonder how many times I can get away with asking him before he says no or gets in the shit.'

'The police aren't interested in this case, are they? So why would they care if you speak to Eamon?'

'I just don't want to push him too far.'

'So ask him,' said Norman. 'Be honest. I have no more desire to screw up his position than you do, but he can help us with this.'

'Alright,' said Slater. 'I'll check with him in the morning.'

'And I'll see if I can find out what Coulter's up to. Maybe if I can find out what he was ranting about earlier it might help.'

'You mean about his son being in Afghanistan?' said Slater. 'You think his son was SAS? You don't have to be one of those guys to get sent there, you know. There can't be many people in the forces who haven't been sent there.'

'Yeah, I know,' said Norman. 'It's probably just a coincidence, but it's worth a shot. I think I still have one friend in the Met who might be able to help me out.'

'Okay, let's meet up at my place around lunchtime.'

CHAPTER EIGHT

It was just after midday when Norman arrived at Slater's house. He had gone through Slater's kitchen cupboards, and to his dismay, found nothing worth eating, so, at his insistence, they were now in his favourite pub. And, at his insistence, they had finished lunch before they got down to business.

'Did Eamon come up with anything interesting?' he asked Slater.

'He says Doddsy had booze in his system, but not a great deal, and he definitely wasn't off his head on any drugs, unless there's some new undetectable drug they've never seen before.'

'So Steve Biddeford gave us a load of bullshit about that,' said Norman, thoughtfully. 'Why would he do that?'

'Because he doesn't want to waste his time on trivialities like homeless people,' suggested Slater, grimly. 'Perhaps he thinks they're a waste of space, and a waste of his time.'

'Jeez, you really think so?'

'I'm afraid he's never had much time for anyone he regards as lower class.'

'Do you think Goodnews knows about this?'

'How would I know?' asked Slater, evasively. 'What makes you think I've spoken to her?'

Norman looked at Slater thoughtfully. 'Nothing. I wasn't suggesting you've been discussing the case with her, it's just that you know how she works. Would she take his word for it? Or would she check all the reports herself?'

'Up until a couple of months ago, she would have made the time to read those reports,' said Slater. 'But now she's under so much pressure from above, I don't know. Last time I spoke to her she said her job was on the line. That should mean she's being extra careful.'

'Yeah, but then again, she's never *been* under real pressure before, has she? Suppose she's cracking under the strain and struggling to cope with it all?'

'You think?'

'Hell, who knows what strange decisions she might make in those circumstances.' Norman shrugged. 'Maybe Biddeford's taking advantage of the situation to pull the wool over her eyes because it's a case he doesn't want to have to deal with.'

'D'you think he'd do that? She's just got him promoted. What about loyalty?'

'Aw come on, Dave. You, of all people, should know his only loyalty is to himself. It's as if you look at him through rose-tinted glasses. Maybe you need to take them off for once and take a look at the real Steve Biddeford.'

'You really think he's that bad?'

'I think you always give him the benefit of the doubt because you trained him,' said Norman.

'I didn't train him to be like that,' said Slater.

'I know you didn't, but he's no longer under your influence. Now he's been let off the leash, his true colours are really showing.'

'So what do you suggest we do?'

'About Biddeford? Nothing,' said Norman. 'Who's gonna listen to us? I suggest we solve this case ourselves, then maybe we can take the evidence to Goodnews. He's her problem, let her sort him out.'

Slater could see his life suddenly getting a whole lot more complicated than he wanted it to be. There was just no way he could keep her a secret from Norm much longer, and somehow he couldn't see her taking too kindly to him and Norm interfering in her investigations. It was going to be a nightmare.

'Are you okay?' asked Norman. 'You look like you found a fiver and lost a twenty.'

'Err, yeah. I'm just a bit disappointed about Steve, that's all,' said Slater, hurriedly, unable to think of anything better to say.

'It's not your fault. Like I said, let Goodnews deal with the problem. She deserves it.' He smiled happily, clearly enjoying the thought of Goodnews having to deal with problems.

'Yeah, right,' said Slater, unhappily. He wondered how he was going to sort this mess out. At the moment, Norm knew nothing about his relationship with Marion Goodnews, and she knew nothing about him working with Norm. One thing was sure: he was going to have to put a lot of thought into how he broached the subject with either of them.

'Did you manage to get hold of your friend in the Met?' he asked, glad to have something else to think about.

'Yes, I did,' said Norman.

'Did he have any info about Coulter?'

'Oh, it was a very enlightening conversation. I'm not exactly sure how it helps us, but I'm sure he's involved somehow. We just have to figure out how.'

'Let's hear it then.'

'First, a little background on Coulter,' said Norman. 'He's sixty-two years old, born in North London. His father was a well-known thug who used to run his own gang until he got too big for his boots and bit off more than he could chew. He took part in an armed bank raid, in the middle of the day. A woman customer in the bank took a shotgun blast at close range. She died on the spot. Every witness testified Coulter pulled the trigger. Even the other members of the gang who were caught all agreed Coulter was the shooter. In fact, it turned out he was the only one with a gun!'

'So he got put away,' said Slater.

'For life. He was fifty-five then, and it happened thirty-five years ago, so in his case it really *was* life. He died inside, ten years ago.'

'So what happened to young Stanley?' asked Slater.

'He was twenty-seven when his old man got put away. He was part of the gang, but on the periphery. It seems no one thought he was really interested in being a serious criminal, but as soon as his father was out of the way, he showed them what they had been missing. It turns out he was a much nastier bastard than his father ever was, and he had no trouble taking over.

'Up until then, they'd been pretty small-time, but Stan had been studying what made real money and how to hide the truth. He introduced some much subtler crimes and the gang began to make serious money. He even managed to make it look, from the outside, as if they're legit, and that's why he claims to be a legitimate businessman right now, even though he knows I know he isn't.'

'What about the personal stuff, like his own family?'

'He has three sons,' said Norman. 'The oldest is his right-hand man. He oversees the day-to-day running of the business. Son number two is the one who disowned the family when he finally realised just how bent they are. He joined the army, and later the SAS. He died in Afghanistan just over a year ago.'

'Now that's interesting.' Slater leaned forward.

'Isn't it?' agreed Norman. 'It has to be more than a coincidence that the SAS keeps cropping up, don't you think?'

'Must be. But how?'

'Yeah, that's the problem,' said Norman. 'But at least I think we may be starting to make some progress.'

'What about son number three?' asked Slater.

'Apparently he's in a pretty bad way. Some sort of illness. The word is he's in a private hospital or nursing home down this way somewhere, and Stan Coulter spends a lot of time down here.'

'So visiting Clara Sterling isn't so far out of his comfort zone, after all?'

'It looks that way.'

'Do we know what's wrong with the sick son?'

'No,' said Norman. 'All my source knows is that he's very sick, and rumour has it the condition could be terminal.'

'So, one son dead, and another possibly dying,' said Slater. 'That could make a man like Stan Coulter pretty angry and pretty desperate.'

'Yeah, I agree, but what would be the point in murdering homeless people? How is that going to help his sick son?'

'Morgan had a kidney missing,' said Slater. 'What if it was used as a replacement?'

'Huh?'

'What if this younger Coulter has failing kidneys and needs a transplant?'

'But you can't just take someone off the street, chop out one of their kidneys, and hope it works as a replacement,' said Norman. 'Even a thug like Coulter would know you need to have a tissue match for a transplant to work.'

'Yeah, you're probably right,' said Slater. 'It's a stupid idea.'

'I wouldn't go that far. It's certainly a bit of an obscure idea, but it wouldn't do any harm to find the kid and see what's really wrong with him. If nothing else, it might tell us a bit more about what Coulter's up to.'

'And that might enable us to rule Coulter in or out as a suspect,' added Slater. 'It's going to be very time-consuming, though. There are private hospitals and nursing homes all over the shop.'

'Yeah,' said Norman. 'That's true, but if there was someone who knew how to do this stuff, and was willing . . .'

Slater looked at him, suspiciously. 'Why do I get the feeling you already have someone in mind?'

Norman looked sheepish. 'It's just an idea. It would help us, and I think it would help this person if they had something constructive to do.'

'Are you going to tell me who this person is? Do I get to meet them first?'

Norman looked uncomfortable.

'What aren't you telling me, Norm?'

'I can promise you, you will not have a problem with this person,' he assured Slater.

'So do I know them? What's their name? Why is it a big secret?'

'Please, you have to trust my judgement on this,' said Norman. 'Let me go and ask this afternoon. Maybe I'm wrong and they won't want to know. But I think I'm right, and if I handle it right . . .'

Slater sat back in his seat and studied Norman. He was definitely up to something. Why wasn't he telling? Then he remembered he wasn't exactly telling Norman everything right now, was he?

'Okay,' he said, finally. 'Of course I trust your judgement. Just don't keep it a secret for too long, right? We are supposed to be partners.'

'I've been going to tell you, but I want to make sure I was right and that this other person was okay with it,' said Norman, looking much happier now. 'I'll go now. The sooner we get started, the better.' He stood, ready to go.

'That's okay,' said Slater, looking up at him. 'We don't have to share everything all the time. You tell me when you're ready.'

He reached for what was left of his drink and began to raise it from the table.

'That sounds fair enough.' Norman took a step towards the door and patted Slater's shoulder as he passed. 'And you can tell me about you and Goodnews when you're ready.'

Slater was still sitting like a statue, drink halfway to his mouth, as Norman pushed his way through the doors and out into the hazy afternoon sunshine.

* * *

Norman parked the car on the road outside and looked up at the house. Detached, with four bedrooms, it looked like any other on the estate, except where the others tended to have assorted kids' stuff strewn across the driveway, the small front garden and driveway of this house were neat and tidy, all evidence of the three children who lived here, such as bikes, skateboards, etc. stowed away in the garage, out of sight. But apart from that, to all intents and purposes, it was just like all the other houses. It was only the occupants, and what had happened to them, that made this house different.

Norman always felt a little awkward about coming here, and he had never discussed it with anyone, not even Slater. It wasn't that he didn't want Slater to know, it was simply that he had never really come to terms with what had happened and didn't really know if he could share it easily. Even though he knew what had happened hadn't been his fault, he still felt guilty to think a family had been shattered because of something from his past. As a result, a husband and father was now in prison, and three children were still trying to understand why.

He knocked on the door and waited. He heard someone on the other side of the door, and he knew he was being scrutinised through the spyhole. Finally, he heard the familiar sounds of the door being unbolted, and it opened to reveal the face of a woman in her sixties. Convinced it was him and that he was alone, she smiled.

'Hi, Jean,' he said. 'How are you today?'

'I'm fine. Come on in.'

A kindly soul, with wispy white hair, Jean Jessop was the mother of the owner of this house — Jane Jolly. Since Jane's husband had kidnapped Norman and subsequently been incarcerated himself at Her Majesty's pleasure, Jean had been living here, helping to look after the children and gather up the pieces that her daughter's former life had become.

'How is she today?' asked Norman. 'Still moving on up?'

'Oh yes,' replied Jean. 'I think she's nearly there now. I even saw her smile this morning.'

'That's something that's been missing for a long time. She was known for that cheery smile.'

'Come through,' said Jean, heading for the kitchen. 'I'll put the kettle on.'

It was half term, and one of the children, ten-year-old Billy, was in the kitchen. It was a long kitchen, with a dining table at the far end. The boy was drawing something on a white pad and looked around as Norman followed his grandmother into the room. He smiled in recognition and Norman beamed back at him.

'Hi Billy,' said Norman. 'How are you today?'

'Hi,' said the boy. 'I'm fine, thank you.'

'No school today, huh?' asked Norman, walking across to the table.

'Yeah, it's really cool. School should be like this all the time.'

'I used to think like that. But you gotta learn, and the only place to do that is at school. It's just one of those things you have to do.'

'Yeah, I suppose so,' agreed the boy reluctantly.

'Here's your tea,' said Jean, bringing two cups of tea over to the table. She placed them on the table, drew a chair out, and sat down.

Billy Jolly was studying Norman intently.

'Billy, why don't you go and play?' asked Jean. 'I have some questions I need to ask Mr Norman.'

The boy's lower lip protruded briefly, and he looked disappointed. 'But I wanted to ask Mr Norman a question.'

Jean looked at Norman.

'It's okay, Jean,' he said, nodding his assent. Then, turning to Billy, he said, 'Fire away, Billy. What do you want to know?'

'Mr Norman, is it your fault my daddy's in prison?'

Norman's mouth flapped open and shut. Jean looked appalled. Billy looked from one to the other, clearly baffled as to what he'd done wrong.

'Billy Jolly! Really, what a thing to say. Perhaps you should go to your room.'

'No, it's okay,' said Norman, quickly recovering his composure. 'It's a fair question. I think if I was ten, I'd want to understand what had happened.'

He pulled out a chair and sat next to Billy, who was looking up at him with wide eyes. He sat so he was facing the boy and looked him straight in the eye.

'It wasn't my fault, and it wasn't your dad's fault,' he began. 'Your daddy made a mistake because a bad man persuaded him to believe something that wasn't true.'

'You mean about you and Mum?' asked the boy.

Norman had forgotten about the ability children had to ask the most direct questions without any qualms, and he was briefly lost for words.

'Me and your mum used to work together, and we became friends,' he explained. 'You have friends you've made at school, right?'

Billy nodded.

'Well, that's the same sort of thing,' said Norman. 'We still *are* friends — that's why I come round here now and then to see if she's okay. But the bad man told your daddy I was going to take Mummy away, even though that was never going to happen.'

'So why did Daddy think it was going to happen?'

'Because the bad man was very convincing. Sometimes, someone will find out what you're really scared of, and then they keep telling you it's going to happen. If they do it enough, you start to believe it. That's what the bad man did to your dad.'

'Is Daddy a bad man? Mum thinks he is.'

'I don't think so,' said Norman, sadly. 'It's just that the bad man wanted to hurt me, and he made your daddy think bad things.'

'Is that why he took you prisoner?'

'Yeah, that's why he took me prisoner. But he didn't hurt me. If he really was a bad man, I'm sure he would have hurt me.'

The boy considered this.

'Does that make sense, Billy?'

'Yes, I think so. Thank you, Mr Norman.'

'I tell you what,' said Norman. 'You and me, we're friends, right?'

The boy nodded.

'Well, in that case, I don't think you need to keep calling me Mr Norman. I think it would be good if you call me Norm, like all my other friends, don't you?'

A big grin split the boy's face. 'Really? Oh, wow, that's so cool!' He beamed from ear to ear.

'Go and play now, Billy, I want to talk to Norm,' said Jean.

'Okay, Granny.'

Norman held up his hand and exchanged a high five with Billy as he climbed down from the table and headed for the door.

'He's a great little boy,' he said to Jean when Billy had gone.

'I'm so sorry,' she said, embarrassed. 'I don't know where that came from.'

'There's no need to apologise. He's a bright kid, and he wants to understand. It's better he's asking questions than bottling it all up inside. He deserves some answers. I'll talk to him any time.'

Jean didn't look convinced.

'Where is Jane, anyway?' asked Norman.

'Counselling session,' said Jean. 'But I think this will be the last one. She thinks she's gone as far as she can with it. What she wants to do now is make herself useful and have something else to think about. You do still want her to work for you, don't you?'

'That's what I came to see her about,' he said. 'We've got this case we're working on, and we could do with some help. It's going to be mostly stuff she can do online.'

'It's just what she needs,' said Jean. 'It's stuff she knows how to do, and it'll break her in gently and get her back into some sort of routine.'

'The thing is, Jean, I can't guarantee there'll be more work after this. I'm pretty sure Dave's going to join me, but we have no way of knowing how much work we can get, or how much we can pay her.'

'I understand that, and so does Jane. Even if it only lasts a couple of weeks, it'll be a start.'

'And you're sure she's up for it?' asked Norman.

'She can't wait,' said Jean.

'Alright. Tell her I'll be here at nine in the morning. And if there's any problem with that, or anything else, you call me, right? You have my number.'

He stood and made ready to go. Jean walked him to the front door.

'I can't tell you what a help you've been through all this,' she said at the door. 'I don't know if I could have got her through it without your help.'

'Sure you would have,' said Norman. 'You're her mum, that's what mums do.'

'But after what happened to you . . .' she said, and Norman could see she was getting teary-eyed.

'It was *because* of what happened to me that I had to help,' said Norman. 'I felt like it was my fault, and anyway, Jane's my friend. It's no trouble. She would have done the same for me.'

He reached out and pulled Jean to him and gave her a big hug.

'I have to go now,' he said, 'before you get me started . . .'

'Thank you,' she said.

CHAPTER NINE

Slater and Norman had agreed they would be on church hall duties that night. Slater was driving, and he had made sure he had been running late. This meant they didn't really have time to speak to each other until they joined Chris and Diane at their table for dinner after all the 'guests' had eaten their own meals and headed off to their respective roosts. Slater figured, quite correctly, that Norman wouldn't bring up the subject of his relationship with Goodnews in front of Chris and Diane.

'How are your investigations going?' asked Chris.

'Pretty slow, to be honest,' said Norman. 'We still have no idea where Ryan is. We thought he was hanging out with Ginger and that if we found her, she would lead us back to him, but there's been no sign of either of them.'

'We haven't seen them here either, I'm afraid,' said Chris. 'Do you think they've left town?'

'That has to be a possibility.' Slater heaved a sigh. 'But then, that might not be such a bad thing. Admittedly it won't help us find out what Ryan knows, but maybe it will keep him out of trouble while we follow up one or two other leads.'

'So you are making some progress?'

'It's a long shot,' said Norman. 'There's this gangster guy who comes from London. It seems he's spending a lot of time down this way.'

'A gangster? That sounds very dramatic, like something off the TV,' said Chris. 'Does this man have a name?'

'His name's Stan Coulter. He's a nasty piece of work, but then we can't see any reason why he would want to bump off a couple of homeless guys in Tinton, so like I said, it's probably a long shot and could well be a waste of time. We'll know a bit more tomorrow.'

'What's happening tomorrow?' asked Diane.

'We have a new helper doing some research for us. She's very good. If there's anything to find, I'm sure she'll find it.'

'She?' asked Diane. Norman didn't reply so she looked at Slater.

'It's Norm's mystery woman,' he said. 'I believe her name might be Jane.'

Norman looked at Slater in surprise.

'What?' said Slater. 'You think you can read me, but I can't read you? It didn't take a lot of working out really, did it?'

Diane looked from Slater to Norman and back. 'You sly old devil, Norm,' she said. 'You've never mentioned this mystery woman before. So, come on, do tell.'

Norman looked uncomfortable. Slater thought about telling the story for him, but then realised maybe Norman didn't want to share it with Chris and Diane.

'It's not what you think,' said Norman. 'Jane used to work with us. She had some problems and left the force, but she's much better now and she needs to feel useful. I thought maybe we could help her out for a while.'

'What happened to her?' asked Diane. 'Is it anything I can help with?'

Norman sighed. 'Okay. This goes no further, right?'

Diane nodded.

'Of course,' said Chris.

Norman took a deep breath. 'Like I said, we used to work together — Dave, Jane and me. She's a great girl, Jane, always happy and smiling, you know? The sort you can't help but like. We used to have some real laughs back then but we always got the job done, too. Anyway, there was a guy from my past. He thought I had framed him years ago, and he wanted to get his own back. He convinced Jane's husband we were having an affair. Then he suggested it would be a good idea to kidnap me and hold me prisoner until he could get down here. The idea was Jane's husband would hold me prisoner, and then when the other guy got here he was going to finish me off. Only this man here—' Norman pointed at Slater — 'found me first.'

'Wow!' said Diane. 'So when you say he saved your life, he really did! You two have such dull lives, don't you?'

Norman looked decidedly unhappy. 'The thing is, Jane didn't deal very well with her husband turning into a kidnapper and murderer's accomplice,' he said, sadly. 'She had a breakdown and had to leave the force.'

There was a brief silence.

'I'm sorry,' said Diane. 'I can see how upset you are. Now I wish I hadn't asked.'

'No, its fine. It'll probably do me good to bring it out into the open. I don't usually talk about it at all.'

'So she's alright now, is she?'

'Her mother thinks so. Apparently she's finished her counselling sessions, and she tells me she's raring to get started.'

'Well, that's a good thing,' said Diane.

'Yeah,' said Norman. 'We just need to be careful we don't push her too hard, so for now it's just going to be online research.'

* * *

'You kept that quiet about you and Jane,' said Slater.

They were in his car, driving away from the church hall.

'And that's exactly why I kept it quiet,' said Norman, irritably. 'You immediately assume there's a "Me and Jane" situation, when there isn't. She's just a friend. I feel responsible for what happened and I've been trying to help her get herself back together. It would be the same if she was a he. The fact she's a woman is neither here nor there.'

'Okay, Norm, keep your hair on. Actually, I wasn't assuming anything. If you recall, I was heavily involved with the situation, and I understand why you would want to help, although there's no way you should feel responsible. It wasn't your fault.'

'Yeah? Well, you try telling my conscience that,' said Norman.

'Jeez, I knew it had affected you, but I didn't realise you were feeling that bad about it,' said Slater.

'That's why I feel I have to help her out. You do get it, don't you?'

'Of course I do, and if it helps, I think it's a great idea. I just hope you haven't promised her this is going to be a permanent job.'

'I wish,' said Norman. 'That would be great, wouldn't it? The old team back together.'

Slater took a quick glance across at Norman, who caught the look.

'No, I didn't promise her a job. She knows it's probably just a one-off, but she still wants to do it. She's ready to start rebuilding. I said I'd see her first thing tomorrow to let her know what we have and what we want her to check out.'

'D'you want me to come?' asked Slater.

'I thought we'd save that for when she's done her stuff. She can report back to both of us. One step at a time,' said Norman, looking across for approval of his plan.

'That makes sense.' Slater swung the car past three exits of the next roundabout, and then headed for the centre of town and the pub where Norman lived.

'So, how did you figure out about me and Goodnews?' he asked, having decided to raise the subject himself and get it out in the open.

'Don't you know I'm a detective, trained to observe? She left her silk scarf hanging behind your front door. I thought I recognised it, and then when I got a whiff of the perfume, I figured it had to be hers. That stuff's expensive. I don't know anyone else who can afford it.'

Slater quietly cursed himself. He was the one who had hung the scarf separately from the coat. She had grabbed the coat when she rushed from the house next morning, but she must have missed the scarf. A nagging thought occurred to him. She had said she was going to come over again. Was it tomorrow night, or the night after? He hoped to God it hadn't been tonight or he was going to be in real trouble.

'I was going to tell you—' he began.

'You don't have to tell me anything,' said Norman, quite reasonably. 'Who you go out with is none of my business, and you certainly don't need my permission.'

'Yeah, but I know you don't like her.'

'I don't have to like her. I'm not the one sleeping with her.' He turned his head to look at Slater. 'You are sleeping with her, right?'

Briefly, Slater thought about taking the opportunity he had just been given to lie and say she had just called round to speak to him, but he quickly dismissed the idea.

'Why do I feel guilty about this?' he asked, unhappily.

'I don't know,' said Norman. 'Perhaps it's because your secret's out, although I don't understand why you thought you needed to keep it a secret. Maybe it's because you were making oblique references to her instead of coming right out with it. I'm assuming she's the woman you were referring to? The one who's been knocking at your door wanting to have sex with you?'

Now Slater felt even more guilty, and embarrassed too. He *had* said that, hadn't he? And she deserved better than that. In glorious technicolour, a short movie played in his head showing, yet again, his amazing ability to morph from a normal bloke into a complete arse with no effort on his part whatsoever. Then Norman's voice interrupted his thoughts.

'If she makes you happy that's all that matters. What I think is irrelevant,' he continued. 'She does make you happy, right?'

Now this was a question Slater hadn't considered. Did she make him happy? He supposed she did, although he hadn't really given it much thought. He wasn't even sure they were really in a proper relationship. Did spending the night with someone more than once constitute being in a relationship? Or did it just mean they'd had sex twice?

'What's the matter?' asked Norman, interrupting his thoughts. 'Was that question too difficult?'

'Err, well, no, of course not,' began Slater, but the sentence fizzled out because he didn't really know how to finish it.

There was an awkward silence which was eventually broken by Norman.

'I don't want to piss you off, but can I speak frankly?'

'Go ahead.'

'I may be wrong,' said Norman, carefully, 'and, let's be honest, I'm not really in any position to offer relationship advice—'

'You're my mate,' said Slater, interrupting him. 'That's good enough for you to have an opinion, but will you stop beating about the bush and get to the point.'

Norman sighed. 'Okay, it's been obvious to everyone since the day Goodnews arrived on the scene that there is a very powerful sexual attraction between the two of you.'

'Yeah,' said Slater, grumpily, 'so you've said before. I think it's bollocks myself.'

'I should point out I'm not the only person who thinks this. When I say it's been obvious to everyone, I mean *everyone*.'

'Is there a point to this?'

'Now don't start getting shitty.' Norman waggled a finger at Slater. 'You agreed I could speak frankly.'

'Okay,' said Slater, guiltily. 'You're right, I did. So speak frankly.'

'What I'm trying to say is it seems to me you two have finally got to the point where your physical attraction to each other has been fulfilled, right?'

Slater went to open his mouth, but Norman beat him to it.

'It's okay, I don't need to hear any gory details. Your face is telling me I'm right. My point is this: if there's nothing more to this relationship than lust, it won't last, and you know it won't.'

'What makes you say it won't last?' asked Slater as he slowed the car and pulled up outside the pub.

'When I asked you if she made you happy, you couldn't answer,' said Norman, unbuckling his seat belt and reaching for the door handle. 'Now, if this was the real deal and, say, you were in love with her, you'd be floating on cloud nine. You'd be so happy you'd be shouting from the rooftops, and yet you're not even sure how you feel.'

He opened the door, climbed out, then turned and looked at Slater.

'So what do I do?' asked Slater.

'That's for you to decide,' said Norman, 'but I suggest you think about what you really want. Meanwhile, I'll catch up with you in the morning after I've been to see Jane.'

He swung the car door shut, turned on his heel, and walked around the pub to the back door. Slater sat in the car and watched him until he turned the corner and was out of sight, then he slowly headed off homewards.

As he drove, he thought about what Norman had said, and about Marion Goodnews. He thought about their relationship. Was it really all about lust, or was there more to it than that? If he was honest about it, he knew Norman was right about one thing — he *had* fancied the pants off her from day one. Having said that, she had been the one who had manoeuvred them into a sexual relationship. So what did that mean? Was he being used? Or was he using her? Did it matter? After all, they were both consenting adults, weren't they? But it was the next thought that stayed with him longest. *If it was all about sex, was that really what he wanted?*

He suddenly realised he had arrived outside his own house and slipped the car into his parking space.

As he pulled the handbrake on and switched the engine off, he glanced towards his house. He was just in time to see a shadowy figure rush away from his front door. He flung his car door open to give chase, but the figure had a head start and was off like a shot, tearing across the front lawns of the other houses. By the time Slater turned the first corner, the person he had been chasing was nowhere to be seen.

He stopped and looked around. There were plenty of hiding places here, assuming whoever it was hadn't just kept on running. He would need help to search the area, and previously he would have been able to make a call and ask for backup, but, of course, backup was a luxury he could no longer call upon. He swore quietly to himself and headed back to his house.

As he walked back, he thought about the fleeing figure he had seen and tried to recall as much detail as he could. He hadn't been able to see too much in the dim light, but whoever it was had been small and slim, and as fast as a whippet. He couldn't be certain, but he was pretty sure it had been a woman and not a man. Hopefully he had disturbed her before she had managed to break in or do any damage.

A quick survey of his front door revealed nothing untoward, so he unlocked it, pushed it open, and switched on a light for a better view. There was no damage that he could see. It was only when he was on the inside, pushing the door closed, that he noticed a scruffy piece of paper hanging from his letterbox. Just a tiny corner had become caught in the flap, but it was enough to keep it from falling to the floor. He carefully prised the flap of the letterbox open, removed the piece of paper, and unfolded it. A note had been written on it in neat, round, yet slightly wobbly handwriting.

Ryan will be at the bakery around 6 a.m. You need to speak to him before he does something stupid.

He was sure he would have noticed the note if it had been there earlier, so he assumed this must have been the reason for the visitor he had disturbed, but if they were just delivering a note, why run away? Why not just tell him? He assumed it must have been one of the homeless community; when he thought about it, he realised he wasn't fully trusted yet, so not wanting to speak seemed to make sense.

He thought of Ginger. She was supposedly hiding Ryan, so she would know of his movements and his intentions. But how would she know where he lived? Norm made no secret of the fact he lived in a pub in town, but Slater was sure he hadn't mentioned where he lived to anyone. In any case, wasn't Norman's place in town easier to get to? So why not leave the note there? It would surely be a lot more convenient than coming all the way out here.

He continued to puzzle over the who and the why as he dialled Norman's number and told him what had been waiting for him at home. They decided it would be risky if Slater went alone as Ryan hardly knew him and was unlikely to want to talk to him. It would be much better if they were both there. Slater could leave his car at the pub and they could make the short walk to the bakery from there.

CHAPTER TEN

'So tell me again why I thought I needed to get up at this ungodly hour,' said Norman, grumpily.

'Because Ryan is unlikely to speak to me on my own,' said Slater, 'and if it's any consolation, I had to get up even earlier.'

They were making the short walk to the bakery, but they had decided to go the long way round so they wouldn't be spotted marching the length of the High Street.

'I hope you didn't have to disturb anyone in the process,' said Norman.

Slater glared at him sharply. 'Can we not do this now? Shouldn't we be focused on finding Ryan and learning what he knows?'

Norman held up his hands in surrender. 'I'm sorry. That was a cheap shot, and I apologise for speaking without thinking.'

Slater grunted in acceptance of the apology.

'So tell me again what happened when you got home last night.'

'I disturbed someone at my front door. I gave chase but she had too much of a start. I lost her almost straight away. When I got indoors, this note was caught in the letterbox.'

He handed Norman a thin, clear plastic bag. The note was inside.

'You seem very sure it was a "she" you were chasing and not a "he",' Norman remarked as he studied the note under a street lamp.

'She ran like a girl,' said Slater, 'and she was built like a girl. She was skinny, and probably undernourished, but definitely a girl. And the clothes were definitely those of someone down on their luck, you know what I mean?'

'You think she wrote this note, too?'

'I'm no expert, but I'd say that was a girl's handwriting, wouldn't you?'

'Yeah,' said Norman. 'It has that sort of careful roundness to it that a lot of girls have, but it's managing to be a bit erratic at the same time. Does that bring anyone to mind?'

'I don't follow,' said Slater.

'You don't really know Ginger, do you?'

Slater thought that actually he was sure he *did* know Ginger, but he still hadn't figured out where from, so he kept that to himself for now.

'She's never actually spoken to me,' he admitted, 'and she seems to keep her face turned away from me all the time.'

'Yeah, she is pretty evasive,' said Norman, 'and secretive. She doesn't really speak to anyone, but from what I've been told by some of the others, she's like that handwriting — well-rounded, yet somehow erratic at the same time.'

'She was the person I thought most likely to have pushed the note through my door,' said Slater, 'if only because she's hiding Ryan, so she would be likely to know what his plans are.'

'I think you're probably right about that,' agreed Norman. 'I wonder what she means when she says he might do something stupid.'

'D'you think he's likely to do a runner when he sees us? Only I don't fancy giving chase this morning.'

'I'm hoping I can play it right and he won't do that. To be honest, we can't stop him if he does decide to go. I just hope he'll talk to us first.'

'How much are you going to tell him?'

'As little as possible,' said Norman. 'I'm not sure how paranoid he is, and I don't want to be stoking it up. I'll tell him we're after Stan Coulter and anything he can tell us about his son Bobby might help. We'll leave it at that and see what he's prepared to say. I can always add a bit more if it's needed.'

They walked a bit further, in silence, before Slater spoke.

'About Ginger,' he said. 'I'm sure I know her from somewhere, but I can't figure out where. I was thinking about asking her next time I see her. What do you think?'

'I think you should be careful you don't scare her away,' warned Norman. 'The best policy with these people is to be friendly but don't be pushy. You start asking questions they're likely to clam up and tell you nothing, but if you take your time and let them come to you, you'll find they'll open up, but only when they're good and ready. So, unless you're in a hurry, I should wait and see.'

'Okay,' said Slater. 'You're probably right.'

The bakery was just around the next corner, about thirty yards along the street. They turned the corner and stopped. In the light seeping through the windows from the inside of the shop, they could see half a dozen people huddled together against the early morning chill. Ryan was one of them.

'Let's wait back here,' said Norman, quietly. 'Let him get his food, and we'll catch him on the way back.'

From their vantage point they watched the half dozen suddenly turn and step towards the shop door. Someone must be opening up. Slater and Norman waited patiently as each person came away from the shop clutching a bag in one hand and a cup of hot coffee in the other. The bags were filled with a hot pasty, a couple of filled rolls, and maybe a cake or two. The last one to leave was Ryan.

As he stepped from the shop doorway and turned towards them, Norman stepped forward. Ryan stopped dead in his tracks. He was about ten yards from them.

'Ryan, it's me. You know I don't want to hurt you. I just want to talk. There are things you know that we need to know. Just give us ten minutes and you can be on your way.'

'What do you want to know?' asked Ryan, looking poised for either flight or fight.

Slater hoped he wasn't going to run because he didn't fancy his chances of catching the other man in a race. Then again, he certainly didn't want to get into a fight against someone with Ryan's background. He might be homeless, but he still looked pretty fit from where Slater was standing, and there seemed little doubt he could easily outrun him or beat the crap out of him, depending on whichever alternative took his fancy.

Getting a good hiding wasn't something Slater relished at any time of the day, and it was a particularly unattractive proposition at this time of the morning. And, of course, there was no point in relying on Norman to help. In his own words he 'didn't do running' and hadn't done for many years. It was the big disadvantage of having him as a partner, and Slater knew from experience that all Norman was likely to do was sit back and watch should it come to a chase. He realised Norman was speaking to Ryan again.

'We're investigating a guy who had a son out in Afghanistan at about the time you were out there. We think you might have known him. We'd appreciate some background about that son if you know anything.'

'Who was he?' asked Ryan.

'Bobby Coulter. Ring any bells?'

The change in Ryan's face was only momentary, but they both saw it. There was no doubt Ryan knew, or rather he *had* known, Bobby Coulter. His stance had changed now and he was no longer poised for action. Slater breathed a quiet sigh of relief.

'Yeah, I knew him. Bobby, me and Morgan. We were working together.'

'We can't talk out here,' said Norman.

'Let's go to the Station Cafe,' said Ryan. 'It's about the only place open this early. You can buy me breakfast.'

'Crap,' said Norman quietly to Slater, as he patted his pockets. 'I didn't bring any money. I don't suppose you—'

'Now there's a surprise,' said Slater, his voice heavy with sarcasm. 'I suppose you'll be wanting to eat breakfast as well.'

'I should hope so,' said Norman. 'After all, it was your idea to drag me out of bed at this God-awful hour!'

'Yeah, right, of course it's all my fault,' said Slater. 'I suppose I'm doing all the driving today, too, am I?'

Norman yawned expansively and grinned. 'Well, now you come to mention it, I am a bit weary.'

'Don't push it, Norm, don't push it.'

* * *

'So that's how you knew Bobby Coulter?' asked Norman. 'You served together?'

They were sitting around a corner table of the Station Cafe eating their fried breakfasts. Ryan had insisted on sitting right in the corner with his back to the wall. He said it was his habit nowadays wherever he was — if anyone was after him he wanted to be able to see them coming. As if to confirm his paranoia, he had hardly taken his eyes from the door all the time they had been there.

'Yeah,' he said. 'Bobby and me, we were a team. We worked together, played together, and drank together. We were like brothers. I mean literally. We even had the same blood group and everything. If either of us were wounded, we were each other's blood transfusion. We could have swapped organs, that's how closely matched we were.'

'What about Morgan? Where did he come into it?' asked Norman.

'We needed a three-man team for our last operation, so he was sent with us.'

'What happened to Bobby?'

'Sniper,' said Ryan, sadly. 'He must have been watching us from behind, about half a mile back, up in the hills. Blew Bobby's bloody head clean off his shoulders. Death had never bothered me before that. I've killed plenty of people and seen plenty of dead bodies, but when it's your best mate . . .' His voice trailed away to silence and although he was still staring at the door, he was looking into the past. For a moment, Slater, who had elected to stay silent throughout, thought the super-tough Ryan was going to burst into tears.

'Did Morgan blame himself for what happened?' asked Norman.

Ryan tore his eyes from the door and back into the present. He flashed a look at Norman. 'What?'

'Someone told us Morgan felt responsible for what happened.'

'He bloody should have,' said Ryan, angrily. 'He was supposed to be watching our backs. We knew there were likely to be snipers — that's why we needed the third man. That's all he had to do: watch out for snipers.'

'Do you know why Morgan came here?' asked Norman.

'Yeah. He was looking for me.' Ryan's gaze returned to the door.

'Why? Why was he looking for you?'

'Because he was in some sort of trouble, and he thought I would help him out.'

'What trouble was he in?'

'I dunno, we never got that far. I knew he'd had some sort of operation and he was in a bad way. I was going to get an ambulance out to him next day, but someone beat me to it and turned him into a crispy cracker.'

His face split into a slightly disturbing, crazy grin, and Slater winced as he wondered just how damaged inside Ryan really was.

'So what can you tell us about Bobby?' asked Norman.

'He was a good bloke. One of the best I ever knew.'

'Did you ever meet his family?'

'No way,' said Ryan. 'He wouldn't even discuss them with anyone, except once when we got pinned down by the enemy and we thought we were going to die. There was just the two of us. He told me he was ashamed of his family. He told me they were gangsters. Any other time I might have thought he was joking, but this was like confessional time, you know? He said he'd left home at sixteen, joined the army, and never been back in almost twenty years. You'd have to be seriously hacked off with them to stay away that long, wouldn't you?'

'So you don't know anything about the rest of his family?'

'All I know is he's got two brothers. The older one's a chip off the old block, part of the gang, you know? Then there's a younger brother. Bobby was hoping he was going to turn out to be a good 'un, but he thought it was probably wishful thinking on his part.'

'Did he say anything about the younger boy being sick?'

Ryan thought for a moment. 'I don't remember him saying anything like that,' he said, 'but he did say his dad was a real shit, I remember that.'

'He's right about that,' agreed Norman.

Ryan looked quickly at the clock on the wall above the door. 'I have to go now.' He held up the bag of goodies from the bakery. 'I should get these to Ginger, she'll be starving.'

Norman slid one of his business cards across the table. 'If you think of anything else, would you give me a call?'

Ryan looked at the card and then slipped it into his coat pocket.

'Thanks for sparing us the time,' said Norman. 'You've been a great help.'

'We all know I haven't really, Norm,' he said, as he got to his feet. 'I've told you near enough bugger all, and you know it.'

He shuffled around the table, squeezed past Norman and headed for the door.

Norm looked distinctly ruffled. 'See you around,' he called.

Ryan stopped and turned. There was a determined look on his face. 'That will depend on whether I've still got what it takes,' he said, before spinning on his heels and heading through the door.

'What was that all about?' asked Slater as the door banged closed behind the departing Ryan.

'I haven't a clue,' said Norman, 'but I don't like the sound of it.'

'He knows what's going on here, doesn't he?'

'He certainly knows a damned sight more than we do.'

'Did we learn anything?'

'We know he feels Morgan let his mate get his head blown off, but we're none the wiser about what trouble Morgan was in or why he died. If anything, Ryan's put himself forward as a potential suspect in Morgan's murder. He's certainly got a good motive.'

'What did we learn about Coulter's family?' asked Slater, going on to answer the question himself. 'Sod all we didn't already know.'

'So, basically, you got me up early for nothing,' said Norman, rolling his eyes dramatically. 'I hope you're not going to make a habit of this.'

'It's not even seven yet,' said Slater, dismayed. 'Oh well, now we're awake, we might as well make sure we agree about what we do actually know.'

'I suppose it won't do any harm,' agreed Norman. 'Okay, so we know Morgan and Doddsy are dead.'

'I can't argue with that, but what do we know about *why* they're both dead?'

'In Morgan's case, we now know he was held responsible for the death of Bobby Coulter, so at least we have revenge as a motive for Stan Coulter having him bumped off.'

'It's also a motive for Ryan bumping him off,' pointed out Slater.

'Ryan's a soldier,' said Norman. 'I think that makes him more likely to view Bobby's death in a different way. I don't think he would have murdered Morgan for revenge. I actually believe him when he said he was going to call an ambulance the next day.'

'But he is a trained killer,' argued Slater, playing devil's advocate.

'But even so, I don't see it.'

'You're probably right, but we shouldn't rule it out completely.'

'And then there's Doddsy,' said Norman. 'Why would anyone want to bump him off? Is there a connection? If so, what the hell is it?'

'They were both in the forces,' said Slater. 'Maybe we just have someone who hates soldiers?'

'Or maybe it's a bit more specific than that,' suggested Norman. 'Morgan was SAS, and Doddsy loved to tell everyone he was. Perhaps someone with a grudge against the SAS believed him. Maybe Coulter heard about him and figured he had to be involved with Bobby's death.'

Slater pulled a face. 'It's possible, I suppose, especially if those two heavies we met were Coulter's and reported back to him.'

'And don't forget — Doddsy told me to tell Ryan he hadn't told them anything that would lead them to him,' said Norman.

'And Ryan made a run for it the night they turned up,' added Slater. 'So how about if this *is* really all about Ryan? What if someone's trying to find him, knows he's ex-SAS, but doesn't know what he looks like?'

'You mean Coulter?'

'There were two other guys in that team with Bobby Coulter,' said Slater. 'If Stan Coulter knew Morgan was one, he could just as easily know Ryan was the other.'

Norman looked appalled at the idea. 'What? And he's murdering anyone he thinks might be ex-SAS just to cover all the bases and make sure?'

'Either that or some mystery person is just bumping off anyone who's ex-services,' said Slater. 'Either way, it works for me.'

'We're leaning towards Coulter aren't we?'

'It looks that way.'

'D'you think that's because I don't like him?'

'That could be a factor,' said Slater. 'Or, it could be because, so far, he's the only suspect we have who appears to have any real sort of motive for both murders.'

Norman sighed. 'This is making my head ache. It's these early starts, they're not good for me. I think I'm going to head off home for a shower and a shave, see if I can't make myself a bit more human before I go and see Jane.'

'You really think a shower and a shave is all it will take?' asked Slater.

Norman gave him a look, but it was obviously too early for him to think of a smart answer.

'D'you think she's going to be alright?' asked Slater.

'I think she'll be just fine,' Norman assured him, 'as long as we treat her like we always did and don't make a lot of fuss about what happened.'

CHAPTER ELEVEN

'So what's the big deal?' asked Slater, as he climbed into Norman's car a couple of hours later.

'Jane's come up with something already. It was brilliant,' said Norman, a huge grin on his face. 'I'd barely finished telling her all about the case and what we were looking for. She just did a Google search and up it came. I would never have found it so easily. I would have been searching for Stan Coulter, but not Jane. She went straight in for Stanley Coulter, and up it came.'

Slater had to give Norman ten out of ten for enthusiasm, and he was obviously delighted for Jane, but he had yet to reveal anything about where they were going — or why.

'Up what came?' he asked patiently.

'Heston Park,' said Norman.

'What's Heston Park?' asked Slater.

'It's a private hospital and nursing home,' said Norman.

Slater waited, and waited.

'How about you give me a little more?' he suggested. 'Like why this place is relevant? Or where is it? Maybe I can start to get as excited as you obviously are if I can understand why we need to be flying straight over there.'

'Oh, right,' said Norman. 'Sorry, I got a bit carried away. I think it was seeing Jane looking all business-like again after all this time.'

Slater looked across at him. 'Are you *sure* you two are just friends?'

Norman blushed what Slater thought was a nicely incriminating shade of crimson, but he kept his eyes glued to the road and didn't so much as glance at his passenger.

'I'm just pleased for her, that's all,' he said, quietly. 'I mean, if you'd seen how low she was, you'd understand what a big step this is.'

Yeah, right, thought Slater, cynically, but he chose not to push the matter any further.

'So what did she find?' he asked.

'At first glance, you could be forgiven for thinking our Stanley might have turned into something of a philanthropist,' explained Norman, 'because, according to the internet, he's been donating a lot of money to Heston Park.'

'That's good of him,' said Slater, 'but people like him aren't naturally charitable, so what's the real reason?'

'When you start to dig around, it turns out his son, Terry, is a patient.'

Like a dog that had just heard its quarry in the distance, Slater's ears suddenly seemed to tune Norman in so well he heard nothing but his colleague's voice.

'Now I'm interested,' he said. 'Would this be the younger son? The one we think is long-term sick?'

'You got it in one,' said Norman.

'Does it say what's wrong with him?'

'Nope. We're going to have to find that out, but they do terminal care at this place, so I'm thinking it's nothing minor.'

'Do you really think it needs two of us to find that out?'

'I dunno,' admitted Norman, looking inordinately pleased with himself, 'but that's not the only reason I thought we should go down there.'

'So, what else did Jane find?' asked Slater, patiently playing the game.

'There was a photograph that will really interest you. It seems Coulter has become a massive hit with the powers-that-be at this hospital, and he's become pretty influential, so much so that he even gets to recommend, and then welcome, new members of staff.'

'Recommend staff?' spluttered Slater in amazement. 'What the hell does he know about medicine?'

'You'd like to think that would be part of the criteria when they're selecting new staff, wouldn't you?' said Norman, 'And let's hope that was how it was in this case. But I guess it's okay because we know this guy's a doctor.'

'We do?' said Slater. 'You mean we know him?'

Norman kept glancing at Slater as he drove onwards. Slater could sense he was preparing for a dramatic reveal.

'We haven't actually met him,' Norman said, 'but we do know of him. We met his wife the other day.'

Slater was lagging way behind Norman's train of thought and hadn't yet managed to join the dots that were being so carefully placed in front of him.

Norman sighed in frustration. 'The doctor's name is Fabian Sterling!'

It took a second or two, but then the penny dropped.

'Sterling?' said Slater. 'You mean Clara Sterling's husband? Are you sure?'

'Well, if it's not her husband it's got to be one hell of a coincidence,' said Norman, 'because she's in the photograph.'

'Okay, so that's no coincidence, then,' agreed Slater. 'But isn't he some sort of fancy surgeon or something? Why would a guy like that want to move to some piddly little private hospital? I thought when these guys went private they shared their services around for maximum financial benefit.'

'According to the story that went with the photo, Heston Park is planning to open a surgical unit. Fabian Sterling is going to set up and head that unit.'

'Can they do that just because they want to?' asked Slater.

Norman shrugged. 'Beats me,' he said. 'Maybe you have to start with something simple, like removing warts, and then build up to complex stuff.'

'What sort of surgeon is he? Some sort of specialist?'

'In the article it says he's a general surgeon. Now I'm not sure, but if we assume it does what it says on the tin, I guess it means he can do all sorts of stuff but nothing too complicated or specialised.'

'I suppose that makes sense,' said Slater. 'Start simple, build up a reputation, and then expand.'

He thought for a few moments. 'Is it just me, or can you smell something?'

'You mean like a rat?' asked Norman.

'Yeah, something like that,' said Slater, 'but a great big bugger of a rat, you know? We've got Coulter bonking Clara, and then employing and welcoming her husband to a hospital that he's only funding because of his son's illness.'

'We don't know if he was bonking her back then. Maybe they met when they had this welcome shindig.'

'Christ,' said Slater. 'If they met before that . . . If they met before her old man got the job—'

'It suggests a long-term plan on Coulter's part,' finished Norman.

'We need to find that out. We'll have to pay Clara another visit.'

'Well, I had nothing planned for this afternoon anyway,' said Norman.

* * *

They pulled off the road and onto the drive that approached Heston Park. At first glance, it looked like just another grandiose house that had been standing for two or three hundred years, but as they followed the signs around the back to the car park, a huge modern extension was revealed, attached to the rear of the main house.

'How are we going to play this?' asked Slater, as Norman pulled into a vacant parking space. 'First we need to find out where Terry Coulter is, then we need to try and find out what's wrong with him.'

Norman turned to him and offered a huge, theatrically exaggerated wink. 'Have no fear, I have a plan. I took a gander at the place online. It seems they have a reception desk which just has one lady watching it. How about if you go in just ahead of me with a bouquet of flowers for Terry Coulter. If we're really lucky, they'll show you to his room, but if not, you can create a diversion and maybe I can sneak in, or have a look at the register and see which room he's in.'

Slater looked at him and raised an eyebrow. 'How long did it take you to think of that?'

'It must have taken me all of five seconds,' admitted Norman.

'That'll explain all the gaping great holes in it, then.'

'We can improvise. Come on, it's just one lady on the desk. How hard can it be?'

Slater wrinkled his nose slightly.

'Have you got a better idea?' asked Norman, challengingly.

Slater sighed. 'No, I haven't. But I don't have a bouquet either.'

'No problem,' said Norman, opening his door. 'They have a small shop inside. It'll probably be a rip-off, but that's okay, you can claim it as expenses and take it back out of the petty cash tin.'

'Petty cash tin?' said Slater. 'We have a petty cash tin? I thought that was my wallet!'

'Will you quit complaining?' said Norman, climbing from the car. 'Anyone would think you were getting a rough deal here.'

'But I *am* getting a rough deal. I'm not getting paid, and I seem to be shelling out for anything and everything. I'm not a bottomless pit, you know. I quit my job, I didn't win the damned lottery.'

Norman looked up at the sky and rolled his eyes. 'And, of course,' he muttered to himself, 'I *did* win the lottery when I chose to have Moaning Minnie as my partner.'

'What was that?' asked Slater, climbing from the car.

'Nothing,' said Norman, innocently. 'I was just saying it would be good if we *did* win the lottery.'

Slater knew bullshit when he heard it and glowered at him.

They walked over to the doors and pushed their way into the reception area. The seat behind the desk was empty, but they could see a formidable-looking lady talking on the telephone in the office behind it. Slater peeled off towards the small shop across the hallway. The formidable lady impatiently acknowledged Norman with a gesture that suggested he would have to wait until she was free to deal with him. He thought maybe he would be able to sneak a look at the register, but she didn't take her eyes off him for one second, and he stood feeling, as he often had done as a small boy, as though he was waiting to be dealt with by the headmistress.

A couple of minutes later, Slater reappeared, carrying one of the smallest bouquets Norman had ever seen. He couldn't help but notice Slater's ashen face, but then he would have been pretty shocked himself if he had just had to lay out twenty pounds for a handful of limp flowers wrapped in cheap tissue paper.

As he caught Norman's eye, Slater indicated the flowers and mouthed his disapproval. 'Twenty bloody quid for this crap!'

Before Norman could respond, a strident voice echoed through the reception area. 'Now then, how can I help you?'

To Slater's surprise, Norman, still the schoolboy in his head, recoiled in terror, actually flinching at the sound of her voice, so he stepped forward, holding his bouquet by way of explanation.

'I'm from the florists,' he said, boldly. 'I've got to deliver this bouquet to Terry Coulter. If you'll just show me the way, I'll take them to his room.'

'I don't think so,' said the lady, drawing herself up, ready for battle. 'No self-respecting florist would send out flowers in that state. You've just bought those from our shop. And anyway, this gentleman was here before you.' She indicated Norman with a wave of her hand, and now he had regained his composure, he was ready to play his part with theatrical gusto.

'Yes,' he said, looking down his nose at Slater. 'There's a queue here, you know. Who do you think you are, barging in like that?'

Slater couldn't quite believe his ears and was sorely tempted to tell Norman *exactly* who he thought he was, but with a huge effort, he managed to keep control and continue to play his own part.

He looked apprehensively at the lady again. The name on the badge pinned to her formidable left breast said *Meryl Battle*, and she was clearly more than willing to live up to her name.

'No, I'm delivering them,' argued Slater, half-heartedly, for he already knew this was one Battle he wasn't going to get the better of, no matter what he did.

'Right,' she snapped. 'If you're going to continue with this cock-and-bull story, there's an easy way to prove I'm right. How about we go over to the shop?' She indicated the limp flowers in Slater's hand. 'We'll soon see where you got those pathetic things from.'

She marched out from behind her desk, breasts proudly to the fore, cleaving their way towards the shop like the prow of a battleship parting the waves, almost daring anyone to try and stop her. As she passed Slater, she pointed a finger at him. 'Come along,' she snapped. 'They're not exactly rushed off their feet, so I'm sure they will be able to remember both customers they've served this morning.'

Slater stood his ground, looking helplessly at Norman, until Meryl swung around and glared at him.

'Well, come along. Don't just stand there.'

Reluctantly, he followed in her wake, now feeling every inch the same terrified schoolboy that Norman had felt just a few short minutes before.

* * *

For his part, Norman had been deeply impressed as he watched Slater keep his cool and resist the temptation to tell him where he could get off, especially after he himself had sided with Meryl. That impression moved up a further notch as he then watched Slater follow meekly along behind the awesome Ms Battle into a situation that could only end in a humiliating defeat. And to think he'd had to fork out twenty quid for the privilege! This was really taking one for the team. He must make sure to remember to tell his partner what a great guy he was.

In the meantime, he leaned across the reception desk and peered at the register. It was a simple handwritten affair, where the visitors just filled in their name, who they were going to visit, which room number, time in and time out. He was pleased it was so simple — it made it so much easier to have a quick scan through. He was looking for the name 'Coulter' and he found it just one page back. Obviously Stan had been here yesterday afternoon to see Terry in Room 36. *Perfect.*

He looked over his shoulder at the shop. He could see through the door that Slater was continuing to play his part in creating a diversion to perfection and was currently being given a severe bollocking by the now triumphant Meryl Battle. He could see from Slater's body language that she certainly seemed to know how to humiliate someone who had dared to try and pull the wool over her eyes, and as Norman watched, he quietly congratulated himself on his decision to volunteer his partner to carry out that part of the plan.

The two shop assistants had their attention glued to Meryl and her victim, and there wasn't another soul anywhere in sight, so he replaced the register where he'd found it, sauntered quietly away from the desk, and headed along the corridor, following the signs that indicated Room 36 would be found deeper inside the building.

What had happened was nothing like he had expected but, to be fair, as plans went it had been worse than flimsy, so any result that hadn't got them both thrown out had to be regarded as a good one. In Norman's eyes, it was definitely a case of so far so good, although he had a feeling Slater's opinion might not exactly concur with his own.

* * *

As he walked, red-faced, away from the shop, back out through the doors and towards the car park, Slater was quietly raging to himself as he realised he had not only been lectured like a naughty schoolboy, but he had just wasted twenty pounds. In his haste to get away, he'd left the bouquet on the counter in the shop, so he didn't even have the crappy bloody flowers as some sort of compensation for his humiliation. This was a pity — not because he wanted the flowers for any aesthetic purpose, but because all the while he had endured listening to Meryl Battle lecturing him, he had been planning exactly what he was going to do with them when he got hold of Norman . . .

The sky had filled with dark, heavy clouds since they had arrived and now, as he emerged into the open, there was a blinding flash followed by an ominous rumbling from the sky, and it began to rain — great big drops that hit the ground with a series of resounding splats.

'Oh, terrific!' Slater broke into a trot. 'This just gets better and better.'

He made it back to the car, grabbed the passenger door handle, and yanked it open. Or at least, he *tried* to yank it open, but it was locked. He looked up at the black sky in despair.

'Even the bloody weather's on her side,' he muttered. 'I bet she wears a pointy hat and rides to work on a bloody broomstick!'

As if to prove his point and further mock his plight, the rain now changed up a gear from 'cats and dogs' to 'stair-rods' and was further embellished by the addition of some of the largest hailstones Slater had ever seen. He didn't often use expletives, but as the rain began to penetrate through to his skin, he thought this was probably one of those occasions where their use was fully justified.

* * *

Blissfully unaware of his partner's problems out in the pouring rain, Norman was getting close to his quarry. Having discovered visiting was allowed any time after ten a.m., he had planned on bluffing his way past any staff who challenged him on the pretext he was visiting his cousin Terry Coulter in Room 36. But he needn't have worried. He had already seen several members of staff as he walked down the thickly carpeted corridors, but as yet he had received nothing but warm, friendly smiles from every one of them.

The rooms were spaced along either side of the wide main corridor that seemed to run the length of the building with an occasional turn to the left or right. He was in the thirties now, odd numbers on the left and even numbers on the right. Number 36 must be just around the next corner. He looked up and down the corridor to make sure no one was watching and then stopped before peering cautiously around the corner, but the corridor was deserted. He could see the door that must open into Terry Coulter's room just a short way ahead on the right.

He strode confidently around the corner and up to the door, stopping just long enough to make sure it bore the number 36. He was momentarily unsure if he should knock or just walk straight in, but settled on a combination of the two, pushing the door open as he knocked quietly. Cautiously, he poked his head around the door and took in the quiet hum and beep of machinery. Terry Coulter lay sleeping under the covers of the bed, an array of tubes and wires attached to him in various places. He looked pale and emaciated, almost ghost-like, and Norman quickly realised he was looking at a young man who probably wasn't going to be around for many more days. As Norman approached the bed, it also became clear there was unlikely to be any chance of having a conversation with the poor kid, and he stood there awkwardly, not quite sure what he should do next.

His thoughts were interrupted by the sound of the door opening behind him, and he swung round to see who was there.

'Oh! Sorry.' It was a young nurse. 'I didn't realise he was due a visitor this morning.'

Norman gave her a disarming smile. 'Don't mind me,' he said. 'I'm his second cousin, Norman. To be honest, we're not exactly close, but I was in the area and, well, calling in to see him seemed the right thing to do.'

He gave the patient what he thought was a warm, familial look.

'Yes, it's a pity he's not awake,' said the nurse, following Norman's gaze. 'But I'm afraid he's like this most of the time now.'

'If you have something to do, and I'm in the way I can come back,' suggested Norman, hoping she wouldn't accept his offer.

'No, you're alright. I'm not here for any special reason. I look in whenever I'm passing, just to make sure he's okay.'

'I haven't seen him in years,' said Norman. 'He certainly didn't look this bad last time I saw him.'

'No. He's gone downhill quite quickly, I'm afraid.'

'What exactly is wrong with him? His parents told us some long fancy medical term, but quite honestly I didn't understand. I can't even remember what it was now. What is it in layman's terms?'

'What, end-stage kidney disease?' she asked. 'I would have thought it was pretty self-explanatory. Basically, it means his kidneys have stopped working.'

'I thought they could use a machine to cope with that,' said Norman.

'You mean dialysis? That works for some, but in his case he's beyond that, and just to make matters worse he's now developed cancer. The only thing that will save him is a kidney transplant, and there's no certainty that would work.'

'Is that why he's here?' asked Norman.

The nurse looked suspiciously at him. 'No, we don't do that sort of stuff here. He's here because the last one failed and there's no hope for another.'

'He's already had one?' asked Norman.

'He was taken to a hospital up in London somewhere because they thought they had a donor. They had him all prepared and ready to go and then at the last minute it turned out the donor wasn't a close enough tissue match to be worth the risk.'

'So he's come here to die?'

The nurse was beginning to look concerned with Norman's questions. 'Are you sure you're family? Only you don't seem to know much about his situation. Perhaps I'd better call security.'

At the mention of the word security, Norman began to edge slowly towards the door.

'Like I said, I'm a distant relation and we haven't really seen each other for years. Our parents fell out, that's why we haven't been in contact. Anyway, it doesn't look as if I'm going to be able to share old experiences with him, does it?'

He was close enough to the door now to feel the handle pressing in his back. He reached behind and pulled the door open. 'Maybe I should just leave you to it,' he said stepping through the door. 'I'm sure you have plenty to do.'

He turned and walked away as fast as he could, trying, but failing, to look as if he was in no great hurry. He realised he was heading away from the front desk and deeper into the building, but he figured there had to be at least one exit at the rear of the building, and anyway, the prospect of having to negotiate the fearsome Meryl Battle was more than enough to convince him he didn't want to head for the front door.

* * *

As Norman stealthily emerged from a fire exit he had stumbled upon, he was surprised by several things. First of all, he could see his car across the car park, which was quite unexpected as he had twice had to dodge along corridors unexpectedly to avoid oncoming staff. As a result of this he had completely lost his bearings, so coming out less than sixty yards from his car was definitely a bonus.

The second surprise was that it appeared to have been raining while he was inside, and judging from the size of the puddles and the amount of water just lying on the ground, it must have been some downpour, yet now the sky was almost devoid of clouds and the sun was doing its best to warm the ground and dry it out. So he'd missed getting wet. Now *that* was another bonus.

The third surprise was more of dawning realisation that he hadn't actually seen any sign of a security guard. He knew he had been on camera, and would have been quite easy to track, so why weren't they out here waiting for him, or surrounding his car? He supposed this could be viewed as a further bonus, but something told him otherwise.

He had his final surprise when he got to his car and found Slater wasn't waiting for him. As he unlocked the car and swung the driver's door open, he wondered where his partner had got to. He should be here waiting so they could get away, especially now their cover had been blown. Had Slater made his way out on his own? Would he be waiting out on the road?

Norman started the engine as he contemplated what he should do. Then something caught his eye. There was a small shelter at the far end of the car park, near a staff entrance. It was there for the benefit of those smokers who just couldn't resist. A small figure seemed to be waving at him. He peered at it. Was it his partner? It could be, but there was something different about him. The figure emerged from the shelter and moved out into the open. Now Norman could see properly. It *was* Slater.

He gunned the throttle and shot across the car park, screeching to a halt by the figure that had been gesturing to him, fully expecting him to jump inside so they could speed off and make good their escape. But instead of running, Slater waddled awkwardly, and uncomfortably, around to the passenger side of the car, and as he did, Norman realised what was different about him. He was soaking wet.

'What happened to you?' asked Norman as Slater lowered himself gingerly into the passenger seat.

Slater didn't say anything, but the way he turned and glowered at Norman should have been more than enough warning. However, elated by his success, and stoked up with adrenaline, Norman completely missed the signs.

'Hey,' he said, in alarm, 'you're not going to make my seat all wet, are you? Only the upholstery doesn't take too kindly to it, and it's a bugger to dry out.'

'You don't say,' said Slater, menacingly. 'Well, it just so happens I don't take too kindly to being all wet either.'

'So what happened?' asked Norman, refusing to be intimidated by the icy atmosphere that suddenly seemed to have filled the inside of the car. 'I thought you'd be waiting by the car.'

'Yeah, well, I would have been in it if some moron hadn't locked the bloody thing.'

'Of course I locked it. Would you leave your car unlocked in a public car park?'

'But how was I supposed to get in it and wait if it was locked?'

'Did I know you were going to be taking an early bath?' asked Norman, quite reasonably. 'You need to get used to the fact you're no longer in the police force. You might walk off and leave a police car unlocked, but you don't do that with a private car. If you do, there's a damned good chance it'll be gone by the time you get back.'

Slater realised Norman had a point, but even so . . .

'I got bloody soaked,' he said. 'That old witch in there arranged for a sudden downpour just as I got out to the car park. And when I got to the car, she made hailstones. Big as sodding golf balls they were.'

'She was pretty scary, wasn't she?' agreed Norman.

'I bet she has a black cat and cooks on a cauldron.'

'You've got to admit, she's pretty good on that desk, though,' said Norman, putting the car into gear and pulling away. 'She frightened the crap out of me, so I hate to think how you felt.'

'Humiliated, mostly,' said Slater, his bad mood seemingly fading as he began to warm up. 'The thing is, I knew she was right, so I couldn't even answer back.'

'She probably woulda given you a backhander if you had,' said Norman, with a rueful grin. 'She reminded me of my old headmistress. You only had to step even slightly out of line and you'd get a slap around the head, and you wouldn't see it coming either. It was a wonder some of the kids at my school still had heads.'

He shot a quick glance at Slater as he drove. He was smiling, so it looked as if the storm that had been brewing inside him had been averted, at least for the time being.

'Come on,' he said. 'Let's get you home and into some dry clothes before you catch pneumonia. I'll tell you what I found out on the way.'

'Best idea you've had so far today,' said Slater. 'About locking the car — d'you seriously think someone would want to steal this old heap?'

'Hey, you can mock,' said Norman, 'but I don't hear you protesting when it's my fuel we're using.'

'Yeah, about that. How come my wallet has become the petty cash tin? I had to pay twenty quid for that poxy bunch of dead flowers. Twenty bloody quid!'

'Yeah, well, I tend not to carry cash around,' said Norman, knowing it was a lame excuse.

'You don't say,' said Slater, his voice heavy with sarcasm. 'I've never noticed.'

'But it's not as if you're hard up.'

Slater sighed. 'Norm,' he said, clearly trying his best to be patient, 'I'm not joking. I might still have a few quid left in my bank account, but I've just quit my job, and I have zero income right now. You, on the other hand, have a nice big pension payment coming in every month. Do I need to go on?'

Norman bobbed his head, and was honest enough to blush guiltily. 'I guess, when you put it like that . . . I tell you what we need to do. When we set this business up properly, we'll do all legal stuff and get it set up so we have equal shares and we share all the costs. How does that sound?'

'When we set what business up properly?' asked Slater.

'S & N Investigations & Security,' said Norman, as if it was obvious. 'This is like a test case.'

'There's just one problem, though,' said Slater. 'Or am I the only one of us that can see it?'

'What problem?' asked Norman, as he negotiated the car park exit, and set off along the driveway.

'Well, as you don't seem to have noticed, I feel I should point out something I consider to be fairly important. This may well be a test case, but it's a test case we're not being paid for. Apparently this isn't a problem for you, but it raises one or two questions for me, such as how do I pay my mortgage? And how do I eat?'

'Ah, right,' said Norman, realising this wasn't something he could joke his way through. 'I see what you mean. But obviously we'd charge for our services once we were an official business.'

Slater looked across at Norman. 'I admire your optimism, Norm, but do you really think we can get enough work around here?'

'Sure we can,' said Norman. 'Okay, it might take a while to get established, but . . . What the hell's this?'

Slater snapped his head back to the front as Norman slowed the car. Up ahead, a familiar-looking Jaguar was parked across the main driveway that led to the main road. A man in a chauffeur's uniform stood on the right, watching them approach.

'That's Coulter's driver,' said Norman. 'What does he think he's doing?'

'Well, his car's pointing the wrong way if he's taking old Stanley to see his son,' said Slater.

'I don't see him anywhere,' said Norman, glancing at Slater. 'Am I the only one getting a bad feeling about this?'

'Oh, I'm with you. Somehow I don't see this having a happy ending, but there's only one way to find out. You'd better wind your window down and ask him.'

As Norman's window whirred its way down, the chauffeur stepped forward. 'Good morning, sir,' he said.

'Okay, you can cut the crap,' said Norman, looking up at him. 'What's going on?'

'Mr Coulter would like you to join him for coffee,' said the chauffeur.

'We're busy,' said Norman, 'maybe some other time.'

'He'll be most disappointed, and he really doesn't take kindly to being disappointed.'

'What does he want?' asked Slater, leaning forward to see the chauffeur's face.

'At the moment he just wants a quiet chat. If I were you, I'd accept his offer.'

'What do you think?' Slater asked Norman. 'It might save us a lot of time in the long run. I mean, what's the worst that could happen?'

'He could murder us?' Norman meant to say it under his breath, but it came out much louder than he intended, and the chauffeur picked up on it straight away.

'I have been told to assure you Mr Coulter only wishes to talk to you,' he said.

'Okay,' said Norman, wearily. 'Where is he?'

The chauffeur indicated an open gate just before the Jaguar on the right. 'If you drive through the gate, you'll see his house at the top of the drive.'

'His house?' asked Norman, quietly, as he drove through the gate. 'He has a house here?'

Up ahead, about sixty yards away, they could see what Slater guessed must once have been the coach house and stables, only now it had been converted into a rather good-looking residence. Behind them, the chauffeur was following in the Jaguar, and Norman realised there was no way back.

'I hope I'm not going to regret this,' he said. 'It feels like a trap.'

'Relax,' said Slater. 'We'll be fine.'

'You think?'

'If he wanted to do us any harm he could do it anywhere, couldn't he? And there's no way he could have known we were going to turn up here today, so I don't see how he could have had time to plan a murder and arrange to dispose of our bodies.'

There were parked up in front of the house now, and Norman swung his door open. 'If that was supposed to reassure me,' he said as he climbed from the car, 'I'm afraid you failed miserably.'

'That's what I like to hear,' said Slater, climbing from the passenger side. 'A nice positive attitude.'

'This way, gentlemen,' said the chauffeur, indicating a path that led around to the side of the building. 'Mr Coulter is waiting in the garden.'

CHAPTER TWELVE

'How nice to see you two boys again! Do come and have a seat.'

Coulter, looking every inch the English gentleman in his immaculate white shirt, cream trousers and panama hat, was sitting on one of three easy chairs arranged around a table set upon a small patio area at the back of the house. A cream parasol kept the table and chairs in the shade. He looked genuinely pleased to see them.

'Oh dear, Norm, your friend looks a little damp,' he observed, as they walked over to join him.

'I got caught in the thunderstorm,' said Slater. 'I was just going home to change.'

Coulter beamed his best smile in Slater's direction. 'Yes, I'm sorry about the delay,' he said, 'but I won't keep you long. You can always put your chair in the sun if you're cold.'

'Don't worry. I'm getting used to it now.'

'I don't know your name, do I?' asked Coulter, pleasantly. He looked distastefully at Norman. 'I think Fat Norman has forgotten his manners and failed to introduce us.'

'Dave Slater,' said Slater, but he didn't offer to shake hands.

'I'm Stan Coulter, but I'm sure Norman's already told you that.'

They took the two empty chairs. They had been arranged so they were opposite Coulter and were both smaller and lower than his chair so he could look down on them. They were also given a clear view of two familiar-looking, besuited heavies hovering in the background, about ten yards behind Coulter. They both wore stereotypical aviator shades.

'Coffee? Or would you prefer tea?' asked Coulter.

'I'll pass,' said Norman.

'Coffee for me,' said Slater, affably. He had decided that whatever was going to happen, there was no point in trying to rile Coulter just yet. He was going to go with the flow and see how it panned out, and besides, he genuinely fancied a cup of coffee.

Coulter made a big show of pouring Slater's coffee and handed it over to him. He pushed a plate of biscuits in his direction, and then poured another cup of coffee for himself. He lifted the cup from its saucer and sat back in his chair.

'Isn't this nice?' he said.

'Okay,' said Norman, 'so you've had your fun and hijacked us . . .'

'Hijacked?' said Coulter, sounding horrified at the idea. 'I didn't hijack anyone. I merely invited two acquaintances in for coffee. What's wrong with that?'

'Yeah, whatever,' said Norman, wearily. 'So, why are we here?'

'Now that's funny,' said Coulter, his voice no longer quite so friendly. 'That's exactly what I was going to ask you.'

'We're here because your chauffeur gave us no choice,' said Norman.

Coulter looked at Norman as if he was a bad smell that had just drifted under his nose. He shook his head, sighed, and placed his cup carefully back on its saucer.

'Tut, tut, tut, Norman,' he said, patiently. 'If you're really determined to try my patience, this little chat could turn into something that takes a lot longer, and I don't think your friend Dave here would be too pleased if that happens. I mean sitting there in wet clothes? He could end up catching a chill—' his voice suddenly changed from affable patience to serious threat — 'or something a whole lot worse could happen to both of you.'

There was brief standoff where Coulter and Norman glared at each other, but no one said anything until Coulter spoke again, his voice once again full of patience.

'Now then, let's start again, shall we? What were you doing in my son's bedroom?'

Norman glanced in Slater's direction.

'Don't look at him for a bloody answer,' snapped Coulter. 'I know he was your diversion to get past the receptionist, but you were the one who was found in my boy's room. I want to know why.'

Despite their rather precarious situation, Slater found himself thinking it was actually a perfectly reasonable question for Coulter to ask. After all, he was the sick guy's father. He just hoped Norman was going to see it the same way, or he was pretty sure things could soon get nasty, and he hadn't finished his coffee yet.

'We heard he was ill, and I wanted to know what was wrong with him,' said Norman.

'So why didn't you ask me, if you were so concerned?' asked Coulter.

Slater had to admit this was another perfectly reasonable question.

'I figured I wasn't likely to get the truth out of you about any of it,' said Norman.

'About any of what?' asked Coulter. 'My boy's sick, that's all there is to it. You make it sound like you've discovered I'm involved in some huge conspiracy.'

'I'm not sure exactly what you're involved in, but one thing's for sure — it won't be anything good.'

'I'm sure I don't know what you mean,' said Coulter, innocently.

'So how about all that money you've been pouring into this hospital?' asked Norman.

'They've taken very good care of my son,' said Coulter, indignantly. 'He could easily be dead by now if it wasn't for the way they've looked after him, so yes, I've shown my appreciation by investing money that will allow them to become even better. What's wrong with that?'

'What about this house? How has this happened?'

'You think you've got it all worked out, don't you?' said Coulter. 'But it's not my house, dickhead. It belongs to the hospital. I wanted to be near my son, they had an empty property, so I rent it for as long as I need it. It's a win-win for both of us.'

'And what about Clara Sterling and her husband Fabian?' persisted Norman. 'That's all a bit cosy, isn't it?'

Coulter smiled genially. 'Now, I have to admit that's a bit embarrassing, but like I said before, there's no law against a man having a bit on the side. It just happens to be the case that her husband, Fabian, is a brilliant surgeon and we need one at this hospital.'

Slater could see Norman was getting wound up by the way Coulter always had a seemingly innocent answer to all his questions, so he decided to step in.

'Look, we really are sorry about your son, Mr Coulter, we wouldn't wish that sort of situation on any family, and you're no different. What exactly is his prognosis?'

Now Coulter looked genuinely sad. 'His kidneys are as good as useless,' he said, 'and to make matters worse, he's now got a tumour growing in one.'

'Jesus,' said Slater. 'Can't they remove that one?'

'They might have to,' said Coulter. 'The problem is he's so ill he might not survive the surgery.'

'Is there no hope at all?'

'The only hope is a transplant, but somehow he's managed to get himself a rare blood type and it's almost impossible to find a donor who would be a good enough tissue match to make it worth the risk. We've all been tested, but none of us are a good enough match. We even thought we had a donor a couple of weeks ago, but it turned out he wasn't a match after all. The real bugger is he had a brother who was the same blood group, but he was a soldier — got killed in Afghanistan, God rest him.'

'Now that's interesting,' said Norman. 'A guy turned up dead in Tinton recently. He had just had a kidney removed.'

Coulter briefly looked shocked but managed to keep his composure. 'What are you suggesting? Do you think you can just go around hacking out people's kidneys and hope they'll be a good fit? It doesn't work like that, you ignorant prick.'

'Oh, I know that,' said Norman, 'but I'm not a father with a dying son.'

'Are you suggesting I took one of his kidneys and then killed him? Why would I kill someone who had donated a kidney to my son?'

'How about because it didn't match?' asked Norman. 'I mean, that would be really frustrating for you.'

'It would be worse than frustrating, but killing the guy wouldn't help my son, would it?'

'So, does the name Morgan mean anything to you?' asked Norman.

It was obvious it did, and Norman sat back, clearly waiting for Coulter to splutter and deny it all.

'Christ! He's dead? What happened?' said Coulter, incredulous.

'Someone set fire to the skip he was sleeping in,' said Slater.

'You mean he was homeless? Ex-services, and he was homeless? How the hell does that happen?'

'You know who he is, you know he was ex-services, but you don't know how he died?' said Norman. 'I find that hard to believe.'

'Why would I kill the guy?'

'Why not, if you thought he'd let you down?' asked Norman.

Coulter looked as though he was struggling to decide how much he should tell them. 'Look, I'll tell you what happened,' he said. 'But I swear I didn't kill him.'

'Go on then,' said Slater. 'What did happen?'

'This guy contacted me. He said his name was Morgan—'

'Christian name?' interrupted Norman.

'He just said his name was Morgan. He said he had been there when my other son, Bobby, got killed in Afghanistan. He said he felt responsible for Bobby's death, and he knew nothing could bring him back, but he'd heard Terry was sick. He offered to donate a kidney to make up for what had happened to Bobby.'

'If he was responsible for Bobby's death, you've got another reason for wanting him dead,' said Norman.

Coulter looked at him as if he were completely stupid. 'Don't be an idiot. If I was going to hold anyone responsible, I'd start with the people who sent him out there, not the poor sods who were sent out there to fight alongside him.'

'We think his kidney was taken against his will,' said Norman.

'He donated it,' said Coulter. 'I can assure you. He signed a consent form and everything.'

'Why wasn't he tested before the kidney was removed?' asked Slater. 'Isn't that how it normally works?'

'I don't know about that,' said Coulter. 'You'd have to ask the surgeon who removed it.'

'I will,' said Slater. 'What's his name?'

Coulter opened his mouth to speak and then clamped it shut. After a moment, he spoke again. 'Oh no,' he said. 'I don't have to tell you anything, and I'm not going to. You're not even the police, are you? Just two nosey busybodies. I can't afford to have you going upsetting the people who might be able to save my son's life.'

'Where was this?' asked Norman. 'Which hospital?'

'I just told you, I'm not saying, and what does it matter?' said Coulter. 'It wouldn't have worked whichever hospital it was in. The guy didn't match, and that's all there is to it.'

'D'you know a guy called Doddsy?' asked Slater, deciding this might be a good time to change direction.

Coulter seemed thrown by the sudden change in trajectory. 'I don't think I do,' he said, looking genuinely puzzled. 'Is there any reason why I should?'

'He's another homeless ex-services guy who was found dead recently,' said Norman.

'What is this, some sort of witch hunt?' asked Coulter, the patience that had been present earlier now completely gone. 'Do you really think I've got nothing better to do than go around bumping off homeless people?'

'Not just homeless people, but homeless ex-soldiers,' said Norman.

'Let me tell you something,' said Coulter. 'I think it's a sin that these people are homeless. If they've been prepared to fight for this country, they should be treated like heroes, not dumped on the scrapheap. I actually donate to put a roof over these people's heads. Why would I do that if I wanted to kill them?'

There was an uncomfortable silence as Slater and Norman considered what little they had learned so far, and how they weren't likely to learn any more even if they continued all day.

'I think it's time you left,' said Coulter, then he turned to call over his shoulder. 'Gus, see these two out to their car. Make sure they go straight there, and say nothing.'

'Okay, boss,' said one of the two heavies, and he stepped forward to escort Slater and Norman back to the front of the house. Slater thought about challenging the guy about the night at the church hall, but then thought better of it.

* * *

'You got that, right?' said Norman when they were back in the car, pulling away from the house.

'You mean the two heavies, one called Gus? Yeah, big coincidence, huh? One minute they're shaking down the church hall, and now they turn up here.'

'But, of course, these deaths have got nothing to do with Coulter. I mean him being here with his two goons, and people dying, they're not connected, right?'

'Certainly not,' said Slater, cynically. 'The guy's obviously a model citizen, who just happens to feel the need to surround himself with hired muscle. Nothing suspicious about that whatsoever.'

'He's right in the middle of all this, I just know it.'

'You've certainly got it in for him, Norm.'

'What? You think it's too much?'

'I think maybe you've been waiting a long time for revenge and you see this as your chance. Perhaps you're just a tad over-zealous, you know?'

'Yeah, maybe,' said Norman grimly, but he kept his eyes firmly on the road, and it was clear to Slater this subject was closed, at least for now. He decided to change the subject as Norman headed back towards Tinton, ready to tackle Clara Sterling again.

'So tell me,' he asked, 'if you had a son who needed a kidney transplant, would you have him staying fifty miles from the place where the most specialised hospitals are, or would you have him as close to those hospitals as possible?'

'According to Coulter, he keeps his son out here because the care is great, and so is the environment,' said Norman.

'Yeah, but there must be plenty of places like that up in London. They can't all be shit, can they?'

'But if the boy's terminal . . .'

'You would still want to give him the best chance,' argued Slater. 'You'd only bring him out here when you knew there was no other option.'

'Maybe Coulter does know that, but he doesn't want to admit it,' said Norman.

'So why did he think Morgan's kidney was worth a chance?'

'Ah, I see what you mean. They must have dragged the poor kid all the way up there for nothing. Just making the journey, when he's already so weak, would really take it out of him.'

'But what if they could do the transplant where he is?' said Slater. 'Instead of taking the boy to the transplant, bring the transplant to him. Wouldn't that be a much better solution?'

'But you're forgetting they don't do surgery at Heston Park yet,' Norman pointed out. 'That's why they brought in Fabian Sterling to set things up, remember? And, anyway, they have to keep records and things.'

'Yeah, right,' said Slater. 'But do you think if someone like Coulter is involved, worrying about keeping records is likely to be a top priority?'

Norman laughed. 'Coulter's not a surgeon!'

'No, but he has the purse strings, and his friend Fabian Sterling is a surgeon.'

Slater had planted the seed in Norman's head, and he decided to leave it at that, and say nothing more for the time being. However, Norman's curiosity was obviously getting the better of him. He took a sideways glance at Slater in the passenger seat next to him.

'You mean you think Morgan's kidney was taken from him at Heston Park and they were going to do the transplant there? But how could they with no surgical facilities?'

'Maybe there are no surgical facilities, officially,' said Slater, 'but Sterling's been here for a year. How long would it take to get a theatre set up and running? Perhaps it is ready, but it's not yet public knowledge. Perhaps they're running trials or something.'

'Jesus, d'you really think they could do that?' asked Norman. 'But surely it can't be that easy. This stuff is all regulated, isn't it?'

'You know very well, Norm, regulation only works if everyone complies and follows the rules. Now, we know Coulter's a man who has spent his entire life not following the rules. What if Fabian Sterling feels the same way? Or what if he owes a debt of gratitude towards Coulter for giving him this opportunity? And what if this debt of gratitude is sufficient to make him want to turn his back on the rules and regulations he would normally have to follow?'

Norman glanced at Slater again. He was obviously getting excited by the idea.

'It's just an idea,' said Slater.

'How about if Coulter's got something on Sterling?' suggested Norman. 'Blackmail's always been high on his list of hobbies. I wouldn't put it past him to have Sterling by the short and curlies. Maybe he's in so deep he feels he has no choice.'

'So you like my idea, then?' asked Slater, with an infectious grin that Norman mirrored immediately.

'I've heard more unlikely theories that turned into reality,' said Norman. 'But, even though it explains Morgan's kidney going missing, it doesn't really explain why he was murdered.'

'Unless it was to keep him quiet,' said Slater. 'If they're operating unofficially and they thought he might spill the beans, it makes perfect sense.'

'Okay, I can buy that,' agreed Norman, 'but there's still a big hole in your theory. What about Doddsy? Where does he fit in with all this? Or are you suggesting his death was unrelated?'

'I haven't worked that one out yet,' admitted Slater. 'I'm sure the poor bugger fits in there somewhere, I just don't see where.'

They were on the upmarket estate where the Sterlings lived now.

'Okay,' said Norman. 'Let's put this theory on the back-burner while we see what Clara has to say. Maybe she can shed some light on her husband's relationship with Coulter. And then, after that, I think we need to see if we can find a way to speak to Fabian himself.'

* * *

It would be fair to say Clara Sterling was less than impressed to find Slater and Norman on her doorstep again.

'What on earth do you want now?' she asked, impatiently.

'We have just a few more questions, ma'am. We won't take up much of your time,' promised Norman.

She sighed and rolled her eyes. 'Is this about my private life?'

'Err, well . . .' began Norman.

'I thought so,' she snarled, stepping back to make room to slam the door. 'Well, you can just clear off. What I do in my own time is up to me. Now go away or I'll call the police.'

'We know what your husband's up to,' said Slater, as she reached for the door.

She stopped and looked at him in surprise. 'What do you mean by that?'

'We know what he's doing at Heston Park,' said Slater.

'Yes, he's setting up a surgical unit,' she said. 'It's not a secret.'

'But did you know he's already operating before it's officially open?' asked Slater. 'Now that *is* a secret, isn't it?'

'And we know Coulter's involved,' added Norman.

Now her curiosity had got the better of her. 'If what you say is true, you know more than I do,' she said, 'but then he never discusses his work with me. Even so, I can't believe he would do anything like that. It would be unethical.'

'He doesn't even tell you about the operations he performs?' asked Slater, genuinely amazed anyone could keep quiet about such things.

She rolled her eyes and looked to the heavens. 'I don't know what you think he does,' she said, 'but I can assure you hearing about minor operations gets a bit boring after twenty years. That's why he doesn't tell me — he knows I get bored hearing it.'

'What sort of surgeon is your husband?' asked Norman.

'I believe the official job description is general surgeon, but he'd be a below average one.'

'So he wouldn't carry out an operation like, say, a kidney transplant?' suggested Norman.

She snorted a short, derisive, laugh. 'Ha! Only in his dreams. He's certainly vain enough to aspire to such lofty heights, and he's happy for people to think he's that good, but in reality he's nowhere near good enough to be trusted with anything so complex.'

'So he's not very good, then?' asked Slater.

'Let's put it this way,' she said. 'If I ever chopped off one of my fingers, I'd rather go to a seamstress to have it sewn back on than let my husband anywhere near it.'

'If he's so bad, how on earth did he come to land this job at Heston Park?' asked Norman.

'I've been asking myself the same question for over a year. You'll have to ask him yourself.'

'You know Coulter got him the job, don't you?' asked Norman.

'Yes, of course I know.'

'Why would Coulter want to employ your husband?'

'Maybe he felt sorry for him, I don't know.'

'Why would he feel sorry for him?'

She glanced away, unable to maintain eye contact. 'Why do you think?' she said, guiltily.

'Mrs Sterling,' said Norman, 'men like Stan Coulter don't know how to feel sorry for another human being. It's not in their DNA. All they know about is how to exploit people. It sounds to me like he's put your husband in that position so he can manipulate him. Can you think of any reason this might be the case?'

As she listened to Norman's opinion of Coulter and his motives, she seemed to change from fierce defender of her own rights to become almost childlike, even managing a sulky pout before she spoke.

'Stanley's really not like that,' she said, softly. 'He's very charming. He knows how to make a woman feel like a woman.'

'Oh, he's a charmer, alright,' said Norman. 'I bet he could charm the knickers off a nun, but charming? I don't think so. Trust me, he's a people-user, nothing more, nothing less.'

Suddenly her face contorted into a snarl and her eyes seemed to glow with hatred that she directed straight at Norman. 'How dare you talk about him like that?' she yelled.

'He's just a poor man who's lost one son and has another near death, and all you can do is stand there making accusations when you know nothing about him, or me.'

'I know he's using you, and I can assure you he's almost certainly using your husband, too.'

'Right. That's it,' she screeched. 'Get out of here. Go on, get away, or I will call the police. In fact, I'm going to do it right now!'

She turned on her heel, pausing just long enough to slam the door as hard as she could. Slater and Norman stood looking at the now closed door.

'I suppose that means the interview's over,' said Slater, with a rueful grin.

'D'you think she will call the cops?' asked Norman.

'I doubt it, but maybe we'd better get out of here, just in case.'

They turned together, giggling like schoolboys, pushing and shoving as they broke into a run for the car. Inevitably, Slater won the race to the car, but it was a hollow victory as Norman was driving and had the keys in his pocket.

'Lunch?' asked Norman as he started the car.

Slater looked at his watch. It was almost four in the afternoon. 'Late lunch,' he corrected Norman.

Norman looked at his own watch. 'Jeez, is that the time? No wonder my stomach keeps telling me my throat's been cut.'

'Is that what that noise is?' asked Slater. 'I thought it was the thunderstorm heading back this way.'

Norman ignored the reference to his gurgling belly. 'Now I understand why I can't think straight,' he said. 'I never can when I'm deprived of food.'

'Deprived?' echoed Slater. 'Maybe you need to look that word up in the dictionary when you get home.'

'But it's a bit late for lunch, don't you think?' asked Norman, oblivious to the sarcasm Slater was sending his way. 'I mean, I wouldn't want to spoil my dinner.'

Slater rolled his eyes. 'Good Lord, no, of course not,' he said. 'Perish the thought.'

'I tell you what,' said Norman. 'How about we just have a snack, something light to fill the gap until later?'

'Really? You? Something light?'

'Oh yeah,' said Norman, almost drooling at the thought, 'and I know just the place to get it.'

'Now there's a surprise.' Slater had a feeling he knew exactly where they were going.

Five minutes later, his suspicions were confirmed when Norman pulled off the bypass into a lay-by where a mobile burger bar was parked.

* * *

'How does two double cheeseburgers with fries constitute a light snack?' asked Slater, incredulously, as he watched Norman struggle to get two hands around the burger.

'Look, it's just a couple of small rolls,' said Norman. 'You've got the same.'

'I've got a ham roll,' protested Slater. 'How is that the same?'

'A roll's a roll, isn't it?'

'Except I have one that's about three inches in diameter,' said Slater, removing the top from his roll to survey its contents, 'with a couple of pieces of lettuce, two slices of tomato and a wafer thin slice of ham. You, on the other hand, have two huge baps, each one filled with two greasy burgers and a slice of synthetic cheese.'

'And lettuce,' said Norman. 'Don't forget the lettuce. See, at the end of the day, we both have the same thing — meat and salad. It's just that my meat is cooked and yours isn't.'

'They're nothing like the same!' said Slater, incredulously. 'Each one of yours is so big you need two bloody hands to pick it up!'

'You're just splitting hairs.'

'Splitting hairs? You have enough calories there to feed a small army! And you really intend to eat dinner later?'

He had to wait for Norman to finish chewing before he got a reply.

'Too right, I do,' said Norman, indignantly. 'I gotta keep my strength up!'

'You're going to need it to cart all that excess weight around,' said Slater.

'I think you'll find such comments are considered very unPC, these days.'

'Don't you ever think about your heart?'

'Never,' said Norman. 'Why would I? You don't think about taking your car in for repairs all the time, do you? Of course not, you wait until it breaks down, and then you worry about getting it repaired.'

'But what if your car stops and never starts again,' said Slater. 'What do you do then?'

Norman took another huge mouthful while he considered this new concept and chewed thoughtfully. When he finally realised he didn't actually have a smart answer, he decided to change the focus of the conversation.

'If this is supposed to be some new, positive, grown-up outlook on life,' he said, 'I think you may have a problem with the idea of what "being positive" really is. It sounds to me like you're still as negative as you ever were.'

Slater was completely wrong-footed for a moment, and he struggled to know how to respond. Then Norman's mobile phone started to burble away in his pocket, and the chance was gone.

'Yo,' said Norman, into his phone. 'Oh, hi, Jane.' He put his double cheese burger down so he could devote his full attention to the conversation.

Slater was impressed that Jane Jolly could have such an effect on his partner, and began to feel a little uncomfortable, as if he were inadvertently eavesdropping on a private conversation. He got up from the wooden picnic table where they were seated and walked up and down, ostensibly to stretch his legs. He waited until Norman had finished his call before he re-joined him.

'That was Jane,' said Norman, stuffing another huge bite from one of his burgers into his mouth.

Slater smiled. 'Yeah, I thought it might be.'

Norman gave him a look. 'What?'

'Nothing,' said Slater. 'I was just impressed to see you put the food to one side while you spoke to her. That one little gesture speaks volumes about how you feel about her.'

Norman took another huge mouthful.

'There, you see?' said Slater. 'I rest my case. You don't stop eating when you're talking to me, but you do when Jane's on the phone. I suppose at least now I know where I stand.'

'Yeah, whatever,' said Norman, disdainfully, and carried on eating.

'It was a private call, was it?' asked Slater.

'What?'

'Well? Are you going to tell me what she said, or shall I guess?'

'Oh right, of course, sorry,' said Norman. 'She's been looking into Fabian Sterling. It turns out maybe he's not such a crap surgeon as his wife makes out. There was a time when he was riding high and had a bright future, then he had a patient die on the operating table.'

'Ah,' said Slater. 'I suppose that doesn't look good on the old CV if you're a surgeon. Was it his fault?'

'He claimed it was unforeseen and could have happened to the best of them. His detractors claimed he was negligent and insisted there should be an inquiry. He was cleared of negligence eventually, but it took a long fight to clear his name. In the meantime, while all that was going on, he was shunted into a siding, career-wise, and even though he was cleared, the best he could hope for after that was general stuff. But even then it looks as if no one was prepared to really trust him.'

'So, it didn't quite finish him,' said Slater, 'but it effectively put the brakes on any further progress.'

'Exactly.'

'So there's a man who will, almost certainly, be filled with resentment.'

'A perfect target for a people-user like Coulter,' said Norman. 'If he was offered a chance to start afresh, away from the regulations that have been holding him back, and also offered lots of dosh on top of that, what's he going to do?'

'And we know Coulter was already bonking Clara,' added Slater, 'so maybe he knew all about Fabian wanting to up sticks and make a fresh start, which was another lever he could use.'

'I reckon he planned to trap Fabian all along,' said Norman. 'He wouldn't want his son to wait in a queue for a transplant like everyone else, he'd want to find a way to jump the queue. What better way than having your own pet surgeon, and then buying a surgical theatre in a private hospital to carry out the operation? I wouldn't be at all surprised if he found out about Fabian, and then used his wife to find out all he needed to know.'

'We definitely need to speak to Fabian — and soon,' said Slater, 'but if he knows we're coming, he'll just avoid us.'

'Yeah, we need some sort of plan. Got any ideas?'

'Let me think on it,' said Slater.

'So what do you reckon?' asked Norman. 'Did Jane do good on her first day back?'

'Considering she's only doing a couple of hours at a time, yeah, I think she did. Did she say anything else?'

'Yeah, there was one more thing. Apparently her mother's so concerned she's looking in on her and peering over her shoulder every five minutes which is driving her mad. So she said can she come and work from your house? I said you wouldn't mind. It's only for a couple of hours in the mornings, and we'll probably be out anyway.'

Slater immediately felt indignant that Norman was inviting people to come and work from his house, but instead of saying the first thing that came into his head, he stopped and considered. It *was* only for a couple of hours a day, and it wasn't as if she was a stranger, was it?

'Yeah, okay,' he said. 'When does she want to start?'

'I told her tomorrow at ten,' said Norman. 'I said I'd leave a key under the doormat if we're not there.'

Slater laughed out loud.

'Now what?' asked Norman.

'Oh nothing much. There's just a certain irony about this expert security consultant leaving a key under the doormat.'

CHAPTER THIRTEEN

It was just gone seven thirty and already it was dark. Slater always found the gloom outside that accompanied nightfall rather depressing, so he had just finished doing a tour of his little house, closing all the curtains and turning on one or two lamps. His house might be small, but with the right lighting, small soon became cosy, and choosing lamps for that purpose had been the one piece of interior design he had put some serious thought into.

He had refused Norman's offer to attend to the homeless at the church hall tonight. Sometimes he just wanted to spend some time on his own, and tonight was one of those occasions. As he settled into his favourite armchair and pointed the remote control at the TV, he thought having an evening to himself in a nice, warm, cosy house, watching football on the TV and enjoying a beer or two, was just about as good as it gets. And then his doorbell rang.

He sighed and cursed quietly. Briefly, he sat where he was, determined to ignore whoever it was in the hope that maybe they would go away and leave him in peace, but another more persistent ring told him it wasn't going to happen. He climbed reluctantly to his feet and took the half dozen or so strides to reach his front door. He paused to remove the frown from his face and then opened the door.

A small, scrawny figure wearing baggy jeans and a hoodie stood on his step. She had her back to him and seemed to be looking for someone who had perhaps followed her.

'Err, hello?' he said. 'Can I help you?'

She had her hood up, and as she turned to face him, he could see her face was hidden behind a huge pair of sunglasses, but even so he knew who she was. A pair of training shoes that were well past their best completed her ensemble. She stared at him from behind the huge dark lenses, but didn't seem to know what to say.

Slater wondered what on earth she was doing here. 'It's Ginger, isn't it?' he asked.

'Yes, that's right,' she said.

He remembered back to the night in the church hall when he had first seen her. He had been quite sure he knew her from somewhere, and now she spoke, he knew he was right. He felt he should know that voice but, annoyingly, he still couldn't quite place her.

'Can I come in?' she said. 'I need to talk to you.'

His head suddenly began to fill with questions. Although he felt he knew the voice, they had not actually spoken the night he had first seen her, so why would she think he was someone she should talk to? How had she known where to find him? What did she want?

'Is it important?' he asked, stupidly.

'I wouldn't be here if it wasn't,' she said, nervously turning to look up and down the road again. 'Can I come in?'

Slater didn't think she posed any sort of threat, and she seemed genuinely concerned about something or someone that might be out there in the dark, so he stepped back and swung the door open for her.

'Come on in,' he said.

As she walked past him into the house, he had a bizarre feeling that he could only describe as déjà vu, and it crossed his mind that this situation was getting weirder by the minute. But he was intrigued now, and all thoughts of watching a football match on TV were long gone.

She took just a couple of paces into the house and then turned to face him.

'Who's after you?' he asked. 'Only you looked as if you were expecting a pack of hounds to come swarming around the corner at any moment.'

'What? No, I didn't,' she said.

He decided not to argue with her. 'D'you really need to keep the hood up? And it's not exactly brilliant sunshine in here, so you could probably lose the shades too.'

'I'd rather not,' she said, and again he felt he knew the voice, which seemed to be much more well-educated than he would have expected from someone living on the street.

'Why, what have you got to hide? I'm not in the police force any more. I'm not going to arrest you.'

'Yes, I heard about that,' she said. 'Did you get kicked out?'

'I thought you wanted to talk to me, not question me. What difference does it make why I left the police force?'

'I'm just curious,' she said. 'You were like me, quite good at ruffling feathers. I wondered if maybe you ruffled too many and they turned on you, too.'

'Who are you?' he asked. 'And how come you know so much about me?'

She didn't answer, and he got the feeling she was waiting for him to make the next move. He took a step forward, and as he gently reached forward to remove her sunglasses, she reached up and slipped the hood back from her head. She was much thinner than he remembered, and her fine, red hair, which used to flow down over her shoulders, had been cropped short and dyed black, but even so, now he could see her face properly, there was no doubt who she was.

The last time he had seen her was at the end of a case she had urged him to take a couple of years ago. It had involved finding out what had happened to Ruth Thornhill, a supposedly God-fearing young woman who had turned out to have been living a double life. Jenny Radstock, the scruffy young woman before him, had been instrumental in persuading him to take the case. Back then she had been a high-flying young barrister. He stared at her in stunned silence, more and more questions filling his head. It was a good few seconds before he spoke.

'Jenny Radstock? Good God! What's happened to you?'

'It's a long story,' she said, embarrassed.

'But you were doing so well,' said Slater. He indicated her clothes, 'It wasn't even a couple of years ago. How can you have been reduced to this so quickly?'

'What happened to me isn't important,' she said. 'And, anyway, I didn't come here to talk about me. I've got some information about Ryan, and you need to do something about it before it's too late.'

'How can what happened to you not be important? Look at you!' he said.

'Never mind about me,' she said, urgently. 'Ryan's planning something and you need to stop him.'

'What's he planning?'

'I'm not sure, but I think he's going after whoever killed Morgan and Doddsy.'

'You mean he knows who it is?' asked Slater.

'He thinks he does,' she said. 'He's talking like he's going off to war. I'm worried he'll be the next one to get killed. The thing is, he's got the training to make him think he can take on anyone. If he doesn't get killed, he might just kill the other man.'

'Jesus, Jenny, who is he going after? Who did he say it was?'

'He didn't say. He just said there was something he had to do and that it was risky, but if all goes well he'd be back in a few days. He said he wanted to make sure no one else dies.'

'So he knows why people are dying? Why the bloody hell didn't he tell me and Norm?'

'I don't know.' She was becoming increasingly agitated. 'He said he was the only one who could stop it. Perhaps he didn't want you to get involved.'

'Bloody hell,' said Slater. 'Did he tell you what he was planning, or where he was going?'

'He said he was going in the morning, that's why I sneaked out to tell you. He thinks I've gone to the church hall for dinner.'

'Has he ever told you anything about his time in the SAS?' asked Slater. 'We know something happened involving him and Morgan, the guy who died in the skip, and another guy called Bobby Coulter. Has he ever mentioned anything about that?'

'No,' she said. 'I didn't even know he had been in the SAS until I saw the tattoos on his arms one day. He's got a regimental crest on one and this weird thing on the other arm, up here.' She tapped her biceps to indicate where the tattoos had been.

'What sort of weird thing?'

'Well, it's not really weird. Once he told me what it was it made perfect sense.'

'What was it?'

'His blood group. Apparently lots of them have it tattooed on their arms. Just in case they lose their tags.'

'His blood group?' echoed Slater. 'They have their blood group tattooed on their arms?'

'That's what he told me,' she said.

Slater rushed across to his mobile phone, found Norman's number, and hit the call button.

'Yo,' said the familiar voice in his ear.

'Norm?' Slater was rushing his words. 'How soon can you get away? I know where Ryan is. We need to get to him tonight. He's going after Coulter tomorrow.'

'Wait, wait, slow down,' said Norman, patiently. 'How do you know where he is, and why d'you think he's going after Coulter?'

'Ginger came round to my house—'

'Ginger?' cried Norman. 'How does Ginger know where you live?'

'Never mind that now,' said Slater. 'The thing is, he has his blood group tattooed on his upper arm. Now, didn't he say he was so close to Bobby Coulter they even had the same blood group?'

'That's right,' agreed Norman. 'He said they were like brothers. You think Coulter knows that?'

'It makes sense,' said Slater. 'Remember Doddsy had his sleeves cut off? Maybe someone was looking to see if he had a blood group tattoo. I can think of one very good reason why you'd want to know that, can't you?'

'Shit!' said Norman. 'You think Coulter's looking to take someone's kidneys for his son, and he's trying to make sure it's the right one?'

'It all adds up, doesn't it?'

'We'd better find him quick,' said Norman. 'Maybe Coulter's plan was to bump people off and draw Ryan to him.'

'If he did, it's worked a treat.'

'Did Ginger say where he is?'

Slater looked around to make sure she was still there, but he needn't have worried. She was watching anxiously as he made the call.

'I'll ask her,' he said. 'How soon can you get away?'

'You find out where he is. I'll explain to Chris and Diane and then come and pick you up. I'll be no more than twenty minutes.'

'Right,' said Slater, but Norman had already cut the call. He put the phone down and turned to Ginger.

'So where's Ryan now, Jenny? You have a squat, don't you? Is he there?'

She grimaced. 'My "squat" is what you would remember as my old house. It's been repossessed, but at the moment it's empty, so I'm living there under cover of darkness. There's no electricity or any of the normal mod cons, but at least it's dry.'

'Jesus,' said Slater. 'How the hell—'

'Please don't ask me to explain it all now,' she said, sadly. 'Just go and stop Ryan before he does something really stupid and gets himself killed.'

'How do we get in?'

'The board over the window by the back door. There's a spring clip holds the board in place. You'll see a hole. Just put your finger through and pull.'

'Are you and he—'

'No, we are not,' she said, firmly. 'It's a survival thing. We just look out for each other. That's all there is to it.'

He looked her up and down. She certainly looked as though a good bath wouldn't do her any harm.

'When was the last time you had a decent night's sleep? Or at least had somewhere warm to sleep, without lying awake wondering if someone was going to come along and evict you?' he asked.

She shrugged her shoulders.

'What about a hot bath and a hot meal?'

She shrugged again. Back at the time of the Ruth Thornhill case, he had felt she had manipulated and outmanoeuvred him but, at the same time, she had helped him resurrect his career and, if he was being honest, he had liked her from the first time he had met her despite any misgivings he might have had.

'Right, here's what I think you should do,' he said. 'Norm's going to pick me up in about fifteen minutes, and then we're going to find Ryan.'

'He won't be happy about me telling you where to find him,' she said.

'Then it's probably best if you stay here. I'm sure you can remember your way around, and even if you can't, it's not exactly a big house. There's food in the fridge, and there are plenty of towels in the bathroom. I suggest you cook yourself a decent meal and then go and soak in a hot bath. After that, if you want to, you can stay the night and sleep in my spare room. The bed is made up.'

She looked at him, enquiringly, seemingly undecided about the offer. Slater guessed she was probably expecting there had to be a trade-off.

'And no,' he said, 'there are no strings attached. I don't expect anything in return. Look upon it as a favour from an old friend.'

She still didn't seem to be able to make her mind up.

'Or,' he continued, 'you could walk all the way back to your cold, dark house with no running water and nothing to eat and sleep there on your own. It's your choice.'

This seemed to be enough to sway her decision. 'I'll take you up on the food and the bath, if that's okay,' she said. 'But I'm not sure I'll still be here when you get back.'

There was the toot of a car horn outside.

'That's Norm,' Slater said. 'I've got to go. Look, Jenny, I just want to help, and whatever you decide is okay with me, but if you do go before we get back, can you make sure you lock the door on your way out?'

He grabbed a jacket and let himself out of the house. As he began to walk away, he was sure he heard her making sure the door was locked, and he wondered what she was running and hiding from. But he didn't really have time to worry about that right now.

* * *

'So how the hell do we get in?' asked Norman, peering into the gloom.

They had just pulled up outside Jenny Radstock's former house and were sitting in the car waiting for their eyes to adjust to the darkness outside. The downstairs windows had been boarded up to prevent entry although, ironically, this also made it easier for anyone who *did* gain entry to remain unseen from the outside. Jenny, in her guise as Ginger, and Ryan, had obviously used this to their advantage to live in the house and remain hidden during the day.

The rain that had drenched Slater earlier began to fall once again.

'Apparently the board over the kitchen window is held closed by spring clips. Ginger says it can easily be opened from the outside and then pulled back into place once you've gone through the window,' explained Slater.

'You want me to climb through a window?' asked Norman, appalled at the idea. 'Are you kidding?'

'Well, I didn't think I was kidding,' said Slater, 'but obviously when I was thinking, I wasn't thinking, if you see what I mean.'

Norman was confused. 'Is that a yes or a no?' he asked.

Slater sighed. 'Alright, I'll climb through the bloody window on my own,' he said.

'You can open a door for me from the inside,' suggested Norman.

'They changed all the locks, and we don't have a key,' said Slater, sounding irritated. 'And in any case, all the doors are boarded up. How the hell am I going to open one for you?'

'Good point,' conceded Norman. 'You know, when you put it like that, I might as well sit here and wait.'

'Oh no, you don't,' said Slater. 'What if Ryan's in there, takes exception to my arrival, and beats the crap out of me? No, you can come and wait by the window, just in case he gets past me and does a runner. It's his only way out, so you can stop him. And if I am going to need an ambulance, I want to make sure you know when to call for it.'

'But I don't have a coat.'

A wicked grin split Slater's face. 'So you'll get wet,' he said, gleefully.

'But I might catch a cold.'

'For Christ's sake, will you stop bitching?' said Slater. 'If it makes you happy, I'm willing to risk catching a cold, but that means you will have to squeeze through the window and perhaps get your head kicked in by a trained assassin. Do you want to do that?'

It didn't take Norman long to evaluate this proposition, which seemed to involve far more risk than he was willing to face.

'No, you're right,' he agreed. 'It makes much more sense that I catch the cold. I probably wouldn't fit through the window anyway.'

Slater shook his head and pulled his mobile phone from his pocket.

'Okay,' he said, making sure Norman saw him turning his phone off. 'Make sure your phone's off. I don't want to get caught out by an unexpected ringtone.'

Norman found his own mobile phone and made sure Slater watched as he did the same.

'Right, let's go,' said Slater. 'And remember, no noise and no torchlight. We only talk in whispers, right?'

'Got it,' whispered Norman.

They slipped quietly from the car and made their way through the side gate and round to the back of the house. The kitchen window was next to the back door, and just as Ginger had described, there was a hole in one corner just large enough to slip a finger through. Slater pushed a finger through and pulled at the board. With a quiet, satisfying click, he eased it free from the spring clips that held it closed and swung it open. The window behind it was open, and it took just a few seconds for him to climb inside. He went to pull the board closed behind him.

'Hey wait,' hissed Norman. 'If you close that, how will I know when to call the ambulance?'

Slater had actually been joking when he'd mentioned this to Norman in the car, but now he was actually inside the house, enveloped in its deathly quiet stillness, he did feel rather vulnerable, and with good reason. If Ryan was inside, he had all the advantages of the ambusher, as well as all that special forces training in what to do to disable him. He thought maybe Norm was right about leaving the board open.

'Here,' whispered Norman again, reaching his hand through the window. 'Take these.'

Slater took the offering. It was Norm's night vision goggles, a possession he was particularly proud of and rarely let anyone even look at.

'Oh wow! Good thinking, Norm. Thanks mate.'

He slipped the goggles on and peered around. Now he felt a little less uneasy, at least he would be able to *see* Ryan attacking him.

'I'll scream if he jumps on me,' he whispered to Norman, and set off across the kitchen.

* * *

Norman stood close to the window, looking into the kitchen. He couldn't see a thing, of course, as it was much darker inside the boarded-up house than it was outside, but he felt if he focused on his ears to try and hear better, then he just might be able to detect if anything went wrong. It wasn't long before he began to worry. It seemed as if Slater had been gone for hours, but when he glanced at the luminous hands of his wristwatch, he found it hadn't even been five minutes. He stared at the watch, sure it must have stopped, but the second hand was definitely moving.

He wondered if he should go inside. Maybe something had happened and he hadn't heard it. After all, Ryan was a trained specialist; he would probably find it quite easy to ambush and overpower someone without making any noise. He looked at the window again, and then turned his back on it while he considered his options.

If he was being honest about the prospect of getting through that window, who was he kidding? Really, there was just no way, was there? He'd joked about it earlier, but the truth was, he probably *would* get stuck halfway through. He closed his eyes for a moment, and in his head he could see a vision where he had become wedged in the window and they had needed to call the fire service to cut him free. And then the police were alerted and Goodnews and Biddeford arrived to pour scorn on his situation and then charge him with breaking and entering, criminal damage and wasting police time . . .

No, perhaps it would be best if he just waited a bit longer.

Then he felt a hand grab his shoulder, and he was so startled he jumped high enough for his feet to actually leave the ground. He was sure his heart had missed several beats. *Oh, God, it must be Ryan!* He had done in Slater, and now he was going to do the same to him. He let out an involuntary yell.

'Pipe down, you idiot,' hissed Slater, angrily. 'We don't want all the bloody neighbours to hear us.'

But it was too late. An upstairs light was suddenly turned on in the house opposite, then a voice could be heard calling out nearby, and now a dog was barking in another garden.

'Who is that? Is there anyone there?' called a voice from the darkness.

'Quick, let's get out of here,' said Slater, climbing through the window as fast as he could.

He jumped down to the ground, turned, and pushed the board back into place. Whoever had put the hinge and clips in place had done an excellent job, and as it swung quietly into place, he felt a click as the clips did their job. Then he fled from the back garden, down the side path, and out to the front of the house. Norman had managed to find a surprising turn of speed for such a large man who claimed he didn't do running, and he was already in the driver's seat starting the car as Slater jumped into the passenger seat. In truth, Norman had actually started running from the fright he'd had well before the neighbours had shown signs of having been alerted, but he didn't see any reason to explain that to Slater.

As they roared away from Jenny Radstock's former residence, Norman looked in his rear-view mirror and could see more upstairs lights coming on, but they were away now, and he began to relax.

* * *

Five minutes later, they were cruising along just below the speed limit, determined not to attract any attention.

'And you're sure he wasn't in there?' asked Norman.

'No, there was no sign of him, and all the rooms are empty, so there's nowhere to hide. Ginger said he had a rucksack, but there was no sign of any rucksack anywhere. I reckon he must have guessed where she'd gone and decided to do a runner before we got there.'

'Crap!' said Norman, vehemently. 'So we missed him. And I bet he won't go back now. If one of those neighbours calls the cops, you can guarantee the owners will be in there to replace those old boards with metal shutters.'

'Yeah, and the neighbours will be extra vigilant too,' said Slater gloomily.

They drove on in silence for a minute or two before Norm spoke again. 'So, anyway,' he said, 'I'm just a teeny-weeny bit intrigued to know how Ginger knew where you lived.'

'You don't remember whose house that was we were just breaking into?' asked Slater.

'Can you remember every house you've visited in the line of duty?' asked Norman.

'This wasn't long after you first came to Tinton. Remember that first case we worked together?'

'Ruth Thornhill, right?'

'That's the one,' said Slater. 'And remember there was a young barrister who was following the case?'

'A red-haired girl, right? Jenny, something or other. She was using us to get back at her brother-in-law, the guy from the Serious Crime Unit, wasn't she?'

'That was like a bonus for her, a spin-off from our investigation,' said Slater, surprised to find he felt the need to defend her.

'And we were never sure exactly how involved she was with the dead girl's sister,' said Norman.

'They went to school together,' said Slater, defensively. 'There was never any concrete proof she was involved in the murder in any way.'

'Except she might have been the one who suggested it.'

'Again, there was no proof,' said Slater.

'Yeah, well, what's she got to do with this anyway?'

'She's Ginger,' said Slater.

'What?' said Norman in surprise. 'But I didn't recognise her.'

'That's what the hoodie and shades are for,' said Slater. 'She's dyed her hair and cut it really short too. And it's amazing how different you can look with poor nutrition and sod all sleep.'

'But how come she's ended up like this? I thought she was a high-flyer.'

'Yeah, she was,' said Slater. 'I don't know the full story yet, but whatever's happened, it's one hell of a fall. And I'm sure the disguise isn't just so her friends won't recognise her.'

'You think she's on the run?' asked Norman.

Slater shrugged. 'She's definitely trying to hide from something, but I have absolutely no idea what.'

'Changing the subject, did you come up with any ideas about how we get to Sterling?' asked Norman.

'No, sorry,' said Slater. 'Did you?'

'Well, I think I may have. His wife said he was vain, right?'

'She did, yeah, but I got the impression she wasn't exactly painting him in the best light, so I would take anything she said with a pinch of salt.'

'I thought that too, but I doubt we're going to be able to get into that hospital again, so we need to find some way to get him out. So how about we take a gamble and assume she was actually telling the truth, and he *is* vain.'

'Okay, I'm listening,' said Slater.

'Let's suppose he was to be approached by a journalist doing a piece for a magazine about people who are making a big difference, such as creating a new surgical unit. Do you think that might appeal to his vanity?'

'What if his schedule is so tight he can't fit us in for weeks? We need to speak to him as soon as we can. It's even more urgent now Ryan's on the loose.'

Norman grinned. 'The journalist has only just heard about Fabian, and he only has one day left before his deadline.

If Fabian can spare an hour or so, he'll be in. If not, he's missed the boat altogether. He's vain, remember?'

'It's a plan, Norm, and it's better than anything I've got,' said Slater. 'Let's give it a try and see what happens.'

'I'll call him first thing, before he leaves for work,' said Norman. 'I'll let you know what he says.'

* * *

When Norman dropped Slater off a few minutes later, his house was in darkness. He assumed Jenny — or would she prefer it if he called her Ginger? — had gone, so he let himself in and made his way through to the kitchen. It was a lot tidier than he had left it, and when he checked the fridge, he could see she had eaten. So she had washed up behind her. He noticed the washing machine had been put on too, and it appeared to be filled with towels. This meant that at least she'd had a hot bath and something to eat, and he hoped she felt better for it.

He made his way wearily upstairs. The spare bedroom door was slightly ajar, and he knew he hadn't left it like that so he pushed the door open a tiny bit. She was fast asleep in his spare bed, so he quietly pulled the door closed and made his way to his own bedroom where he, too, was soon fast asleep.

CHAPTER FOURTEEN

'I'm sorry, but Ryan had already left before we got there,' Slater explained to Jenny next morning.

She was sitting up in bed, duvet pulled up tight under her chin, clutching the cup of tea he had just brought up for her.

'We think maybe he guessed where you'd gone and decided to do a runner before we got there.'

'I bet he called the church hall,' she said. 'He gets on alright with Chris, the vicar. He would have told him if I was there or not.'

'He's got a mobile phone?' asked Slater in surprise.

'It's a cheap pay-as-you-go phone,' she said, 'I don't know where he got it from.'

'I don't suppose you know the number?'

She aimed a sad little smile in his direction. 'I don't have much use for phone numbers these days.'

'Do you think he would have told Chris where he was going?'

She shook her head. 'No, Ryan wouldn't tell Chris anything. There's no way a vicar would approve of what he was going to do. He believes in keeping things simple and only telling people on a need-to-know basis. He probably said he'd lost me and was I there.'

'There's something else,' said Slater. 'We think the neighbours heard us last night and may have called the police.'

She looked alarmed.

'I don't think it would be wise to go back there,' he added.

She heaved a big sigh. 'What am I going to do now? I suppose that means I'm back on the street.'

'Stay here,' he said.

'No, I can't do that.'

'Why not?'

'I just don't think it's a good idea,' she said. 'And I can't pay you, not even for food. I don't have any money.'

He snorted his disgust. 'I'm not asking you to pay, for God's sake. You're a friend. I'm inviting you to stay.'

She wasn't convinced.

'Look,' he said. 'I don't need to be Sherlock Holmes to know you're in some sort of trouble, and you're hiding from someone. Why don't you stay here for a few days, build up your strength, and catch up on all that sleep you've been missing? Then, when you're feeling better, you can decide what you want to do.'

'But it's only a small house. I'll just be in the way.'

'Rubbish,' he said. 'If you really think that, stay up here in your room.'

'I don't know,' she said.

'Well, think about it. I'm going out in a minute. I don't know how long I'll be gone.'

'What shall I do while you're out?'

'You can stay there and sleep all day if you want. Just be aware someone will come round at about ten o'clock. Her name's Jane, she works with me and Norm. She'll be here for a couple of hours, that's all. I've left her a note to say you're here, so neither of you should get a nasty shock.'

'She won't tell anyone I'm here, will she?' she asked, alarmed.

'You really are in hiding, aren't you? But don't worry, Jane knows how to be discreet. She won't tell a soul.'

'I'm really not sure you should be getting involved with my problems,' she began.

'Look,' Slater said with a smile, 'I don't know why you need to hide, but whatever the reason, this is as good a place as any to lie low for a while. It's warm, there's plenty of food, and I'm on your side. Have you got anywhere better to go?'

'Well, I suppose when you put it like that, no I haven't. But I don't want to be a burden.'

'Just do me a favour and get some rest,' he said. 'We can talk about all this later.'

* * *

Just as Norman had suspected, Fabian Sterling's vanity had made it impossible for him to refuse the offer of an opportunity to be interviewed for the article he claimed to be writing, and bang on 9.30 a.m. as arranged, he was brought over to their table in the rather posh coffee bar at the White Hart Hotel.

'I think this sort of setting is a much more relaxed atmosphere for an interview, don't you?' said Norman, shaking Sterling's hand and inviting him to settle into the seat opposite him.

He introduced Slater as his photographer and co-writer, made sure the interviewee had the coffee of his choice, switched on his recorder, and then suggested Sterling start by telling them all about his project to create a surgical unit at Heston Park.

It wasn't long before both Norman and Slater became fully aware of just how accurate Clara Sterling's assessment of her husband's vanity had been. If anything, she had probably understated it. It took slightly less than ten minutes before Slater tired of Sterling's Mr Super Cool vanity and decided to put a spanner in the works.

'Can I ask why you were chosen to head this project?' he asked.

'Err, I'm sorry?' said Sterling.

'There must be hundreds, maybe even thousands, of very able surgeons in the country who would love to take on a project like this,' said Slater, 'so why did they pick you?'

'I suppose I must have impressed most at the interview,' said Sterling, proudly.

Slater raised his eyebrows. 'Oh,' he said, 'there was an interview. I didn't know that. So, it didn't have anything to do with Stan Coulter insisting it had to be you, then?'

Sterling looked at Slater. This was supposed to be an interview about what an amazing person he was. This line of questioning was something quite unexpected, and he clearly wasn't prepared for it.

'Coulter is bankrolling the project, isn't he?' persisted Slater. 'And a man like him doesn't pay for something like this unless he gets to decide who's in and who's out. So why you?'

Sterling licked his lips and looked from Slater to Norman.

'You see, the thing is, Fabian,' began Norman. He gave Sterling a humourless grin. 'You don't mind if I call you Fabian, do you?'

Sterling nodded dumbly.

'The thing is, Fabian, we've been doing a little research into your background, and what we found, well, it kinda makes you unlikely to be number one candidate for any job, never mind one like this.'

'Oh, God,' said Sterling, in dismay, the super-cool facade slipping rapidly away. 'You're not going to drag that all up again and print it, are you? Why can't you people just let it go? I was cleared of any negligence. It was just one of those things. It was years ago.'

This time Norman gave him a sympathetic smile. 'Yeah, we know that. But we also know you've been turned down for just about every post you've applied for since that happened, and then, out of the blue, along comes Coulter, and suddenly you're the main man. You can see how that looks, right?'

'What is this?' demanded Sterling. 'What sort of journalist are you? You're just here to dig up the dirt and destroy my career, aren't you?'

'I think you might already be doing that yourself, if you're involved with Coulter,' said Slater.

'I took this job in good faith,' argued Sterling, unconvincingly.

Norman yawned. 'Yeah, right, of course you did,' he said. 'And I'm Weight Watchers' slimmer of the month.'

'Have you carried out any operations in this new theatre, yet?' asked Slater.

Sterling licked his lips nervously and looked away from Slater's stare. 'Of course not, it's not ready, yet.'

Norman sighed. 'Jesus, Fabian, if you don't believe what you're telling us, how d'you expect us to believe it?' he asked.

'Come on, Fabian,' urged Slater. 'Think about what you're getting into here. It's not too late to do the right thing.'

'Who are you people? What do you want?' asked Sterling, panic beginning to sound in his voice.

'Do you read the local paper?' asked Norman.

'What's that got to do with anything?'

'A couple of weeks ago, a homeless guy died in a rubbish skip. He was sleeping in there and some nice person set fire to it. The police say it was an accident, although it beats me how anyone could accidentally set fire to a rubbish skip in the middle of the night. Anyway, the important thing is, we say it was murder, and we're in the process of proving it.'

'I don't see what this has to do with me.'

'Bear with me,' said Norman, 'I'm just coming to that. You see, the weird thing is, this guy had a kidney missing, and it was only a day or two after the operation when he died.'

He watched Sterling's face as the colour drained slowly from it. 'Oh my God,' he whispered, raising his hands to cover his eyes.

'I don't think he's going to be much help to you,' said Slater, in disgust.

'Oh dear, Fabian,' said Norman, mock concern in his voice, 'you look a little faint. I'm sorry, do you get queasy talking about these things? Was it the bit about being burnt alive or having a kidney whipped out? Having such a weak stomach must make it very difficult to do your work as a surgeon.'

Sterling seemed to have crumpled into his seat, so they gave him a couple of minutes to pull himself together. When he finally looked ready to talk, his face was ashen.

'I didn't kill anyone,' he said. 'You have to believe that.'

'We don't have to believe anything,' said Slater. 'You might not have killed the guy, but removing one of his kidneys and then kicking him out onto the street wouldn't have done anything to help him survive, would it? We know for a fact he wouldn't have been in that skip if he hadn't been feeling so ill.'

'We think we know what's been happening,' said Norman, 'but it would be good if you told us your side of the story, and then we'll see how it matches what we know.'

'I had no choice,' Sterling said, desperately. 'Coulter told me he'd kill my wife if I didn't do as he said.'

Slater and Norman shared a look.

'Just start at the beginning,' said Norman. 'You can save your excuses for later.'

'When Coulter offered me the job, I thought it was a gift from heaven,' said Sterling. 'It was an opportunity to get away from my past and start again. I could circumvent the system that was holding me back and show them what I could really do given a chance.'

'And it never occurred to you that it was a bit strange that no one else was even interviewed?' asked Norman.

'With my wife urging me to take the job, I never even thought about why I'd been offered it. I jumped at the chance.'

'And, of course, you had personal reasons for wanting to start again,' suggested Slater.

Sterling looked at him sharply, colour now returning to his cheeks.

'We interviewed your wife,' said Norman. 'She told us what had happened in Hereford. Did you know this was the same guy?'

Just as the colour had begun to fill his face with anger, Sterling's face suddenly turned deathly white again, this time with shock.

'That's a powerful motive for murder,' said Slater. 'Your wife's ex-lover coming back on the scene after you'd moved away to start over.'

'I didn't kill him,' insisted Sterling. 'I didn't have any idea who he was.'

'You didn't?' asked Slater.

'Coulter told me this guy had fought with his other son in Afghanistan, the one who died. He said he was a blood match and that he had offered to donate a kidney.'

'So you carried out the operation to remove the kidney in your new operating theatre?' asked Norman, his voice rising in disgust.

'He was a willing donor,' pleaded Sterling. 'And my wife's life was at risk. What else could I do?'

'Call the police?' suggested Slater.

'I'll let you into a little secret,' said Norman. 'Your wife is in no more danger than I am. She certainly gave us the impression she enjoys her relationship with Coulter.'

'What relationship?' demanded Sterling. 'She has no relationship with that man.'

'Well, you can believe what you want. But I think you'll find we're right.'

'She can't be involved in this,' said Sterling, in disbelief. 'She loves me. She wouldn't stoop this low.'

'You are one seriously self-centred guy, aren't you?' said Slater. 'Do you really think she loves you? Are you blind, or is just that you have your head so far up your own arse you can't see what's right under your nose?'

'You have to understand — Stan Coulter is a people-user,' explained Norman. 'I don't think your wife has any idea how he's been using threats against her to manipulate you, but he started an affair with her a long, long time ago. He had found out about you and your history, and he used her to learn even more about you, and he's so convincing she even believes he cares for her.

'Then, once he learned what he wanted to know, he started using you. He's kept the affair going because it suits his purpose. She's not going to tell you what's really going on, and good old Stan makes you believe he's watching her, ready to kill her whenever he wants. I bet he's even told you stuff to convince you he's watching her, right? But it's all stuff she's told him when they've been in bed together. You've been used, Fabian.'

Sterling looked like a boxer on the ropes, totally punch-drunk. 'What's going to happen now? Are you going to report me to the police?'

'Well, we're not going to pat you on the head and send you home with a sweetie, are we?' said Slater.

'What's Coulter going to do about his son?' asked Norman.

'Apparently there's another guy out there somewhere who really *is* a blood match. Coulter says he's done a deal with him to buy one of his kidneys. I'm expected to use it for a transplant to save his son's life.'

'You're supposed to be a bloody doctor,' said Slater. 'Don't you have a code of ethics?'

'When you think your wife's life is in danger, you do whatever you have to do,' said Sterling.

'But her life's not in danger!'

'I didn't know that before, did I? I'm certainly not doing the damned operation now! His son can bloody well die for all I care.'

'No wait,' said Norman. 'You said Coulter had done a deal with a guy to buy a kidney?'

'That's what he told me,' said Sterling, 'but then he told me the first guy was a blood match, so who knows if this is true or not. Thank God I tested it before I cut his son open.'

'It would have been better if you'd tested before you cut Morgan open,' observed Norman. 'He'd probably still be alive.'

'You're in deep shit, you know that, don't you,' said Slater. 'Coulter will deny everything and leave you to carry the can.'

Sterling nodded, his face a picture of misery. 'I'll go to prison, won't I?'

'I'd be bloody surprised if you didn't,' said Slater. 'But there might be a way you can get a lesser sentence. You'd like to get even with Coulter, wouldn't you?'

Sterling suddenly looked interested. 'What do I have to do?'

'You carry on as if nothing has happened, but you keep in touch with us and let us know what's happening. As soon as this guy with the kidney for sale appears, you let us know and we get the police to grab everyone. It's the only chance we have to get Coulter.'

'I'll do it,' said Sterling.

'You've got to be a good actor,' said Norman. 'You can't let your wife know what you know.'

'Yes, I understand that, but if it means I can get even with that bastard Coulter, I'll do it.'

* * *

'Are we doing the right thing?' Slater asked Norman, when Sterling had gone.

'Do we have a choice?' asked Norman. 'If it means we get a chance at Coulter, it's got to be worth the risk, hasn't it?'

'So, are we thinking Coulter is responsible for Morgan's death, just to shut him up?'

'You could point the finger at Sterling for the same reason, plus the additional reason Morgan had been his wife's first affair,' said Norman. 'If anything, his motive is more powerful, but I don't think he's a killer. He hasn't got it in him.'

'And do we think Coulter bumped off Doddsy? If so, what's his motive for that? And don't forget Biddeford said he'd been hit by a car, not beaten up.'

'What if they just ran him down to catch him? What if it was a kidnapping that went wrong? They thought Doddsy was Ryan so they ran him down, intending to disable him so they could steal his kidneys. They removed his sleeves to check the blood group tattoo, and when they couldn't find it, they knew they had the wrong guy. From there, it could be they decided to kill him so he couldn't tell, or maybe they tried to beat Ryan's whereabouts out of him but they went too far. Does that work?'

'I can't see why anyone else would want to kill him,' said Slater. 'And if it was a case of mistaken identity it suggests they don't actually know what Ryan looks like. Is that likely if this story of Sterling's is true? If Ryan is going to sell a kidney to Coulter, I find it hard to believe they haven't met!'

'What if Ryan doesn't trust Coulter?' suggested Norman. 'Maybe he contacted him to make a deal but insisted Coulter supplied him with a mobile phone so they could talk without meeting?'

'But would he really want to sell a kidney?' asked Slater, doubtfully. 'Does that seem likely?'

Norman placed his hands over his face and rubbed hard. 'Shit! I don't know,' he said. 'I know people can lead normal lives with one kidney, but it is a bit drastic, isn't it? Especially if you're putting your life into the hands of a surgeon who's not got the greatest reputation.'

'I'm not convinced,' said Slater. 'Ginger was certain Ryan was going into battle, not bartering one of his organs.'

'I'd like to go and ask Coulter. But if we do he'll know someone's talked, and he'll soon work out who it was.'

'This would be a whole lot easier if we could find Ryan and get him on board,' said Slater.

'Maybe we should stake out Coulter's place,' said Norman. 'Perhaps we'll get lucky and find him before he does something stupid.'

'Let's finish this coffee first,' said Slater, pouring himself another one from the pot.

'Talking of Ginger,' said Norman, thoughtfully. 'What happened to her last night?'

'She slept in my spare room. I didn't know what else to suggest what with her being so jumpy anyway, and the police probably being at her own place after we broke in.'

Norman raised his eyebrows, but didn't comment. 'I hope you warned her Jane was coming round this morning.'

'Of course I did,' said Slater, 'and I left a note for Jane. Hopefully neither will get a shock when they discover there's someone else in the house. I'd better ring just to make sure they're both okay.'

He fished his mobile phone from his pocket. At first he thought it was dead, but then he remembered he'd switched it off just before last night's break in, and he had forgotten to switch it back on. He pressed the button and waited. As the phone came to life, he found he had three voice messages. He decided to call home first.

'Jane says they're both fine,' he said to Norman a minute or so later. 'It sounds like they're getting on like a house on fire.'

He turned his attention back to the phone and those voice messages. A little voice was nagging away, deep inside his head, but he couldn't quite make out what it was telling him. He thought maybe he'd forgotten something, but he couldn't quite put his finger on what it was.

'Oh, crap!' he said as the screen opened and revealed the source of the messages. Now he remembered what that little voice was trying to tell him. What a pity it hadn't told him last night.

'What's up?' asked Norman.

'I was supposed to be on a date last night,' said a dismayed Slater.

'And you forgot?' asked Norman. 'Seriously? Jesus, you'll be in it right up to your neck. Tell her you were working. She ought to understand. It happens all the time. It's part of the job.'

'Yeah,' said Slater, slowly. 'Except I don't have that job any more, remember?'

'Ah, right.'

'And she doesn't actually know I'm working with you, and we're not even supposed to be working this case.'

'And you think she's behind the decision not to investigate it, and Steve Biddeford's just telling us what she's telling him?'

'It's possible, isn't it?' admitted Slater. 'After all, she is his boss.'

Slater was looking at his phone as if he was expecting it to bite him at any moment.

'It's no good just looking at it,' said Norman. 'And you can't ignore it, either. You'd better find out what she has to say.'

Reluctantly, Slater pushed a button and lifted the phone to his ear.

The first call was timed at 21.06. As he already knew, it was Marion Goodnews. Her voice was quite calm and collected.

'Hello? It's me. I came round just as we arranged. Did you forget I was coming? All your lights are on but you don't seem to be here. And your landline isn't working. Has something happened? Can you let me know what's going on?'

The second call was timed at 21.10. This time her voice was showing one or two signs of stress.

'I'm in my car right outside your house, and I know you're in there because I just saw the curtains twitch. I don't understand why you won't let me in. Is it something I've said, or something I've done? Please talk to me.'

The last call was timed at 21.14. This time her voice had gone up a full octave. It would be fair to say she was raging. He could almost feel the venom she was spitting into the phone.

'Now I get it! You've got another woman in there, haven't you? I've just seen her face at the window. What's the matter with me? Aren't I good enough? I can't wait to hear how you're going to explain this, you cheating bastard! How dare you do this to me? And don't think you can hide away and avoid me. I will have an answer, you absolute shit!' There was another minute's worth of message, which wasn't easy to decipher, but Slater got the impression it was series of two-word insults, nearly every one beginning with 'f'.

Norman had been watching Slater's face as he listened to the calls. His colleague was the second person to turn white in front of him this morning, and he seemed to almost flinch at the end.

'And his face turned a whiter shade of pale,' he misquoted. 'That looks like some pile of shit you have to clear up.'

'The silly cow thinks I cheated on her,' said Slater.

'Why would she think that?'

'Ginger must have looked out of the window when she rang the bell, and Marion looked up and saw her.'

'So you can hardly blame her, can you?' said Norman. 'Jesus, Dave, is this déjà vu or what? Haven't you been here before, when Cindy came home and found Darling cooking your breakfast? Don't you ever learn?'

Slater gawped at him. Norman was right; he couldn't really blame her for thinking the worst, and yes, he *had* been here before.

'I've got to hand it to you,' said Norman, 'you certainly like to live on the edge when it comes to relationships. I can't believe you manage to keep on getting yourself into such awkward situations. Do you do it on purpose? Or maybe you just stop thinking with your head where women are concerned?'

'You know it's not that,' said Slater. 'I didn't do anything with Darling, and I haven't done anything with Ginger. I'm bloody innocent.'

'Well, good luck with trying to prove that to your girlfriend,' said Norman. 'I'm glad it's not me who's going to have to explain it to her.'

* * *

It was five thirty. Since the interview with Sterling, they had spent most of the day lying under a hedge spying on Coulter's house, but there was no sign of Coulter, his heavies, or even his car and, so far, there had been no sign of Ryan either.

'This is a waste of time,' said Slater. 'All that's happening is I'm getting cramp.'

'Yeah, you're right,' agreed Norman. 'How about we make our way back to the car?'

Ten minutes later they were back in the car.

'Any ideas?' asked Norman.

'The phone in the church hall,' said Slater. 'I suppose it's pretty ancient.'

'Actually, it's not. When Chris and Diane moved in, the hall was in a pretty crappy state. They wanted it to be refurbished, only they were told there was no money for anything like that. But Diane's cute. She figured if she could get someone from the council to come along and condemn the building, it would be unusable and they would have to close it. Of course there was a public outcry when that happened, and then suddenly the church comes up with the money to refurbish the place. That's why the kitchen's as good as it is. I'm pretty sure the phone's new too.'

'We've missed a trick, then,' said Slater. 'Ginger reckons Ryan probably called the church hall last night to see if she was there. Now, if it's a modern phone it could be you can check the caller list—'

'And his number should be on there, right?' finished Norman. He started the engine and grinned at Slater. 'Not only do you make a pretty good backup driver, and a useful source of ready cash, but you also sometimes have the odd good idea.'

'Does this mean I'm an indispensable part of this team?' asked Slater.

'Indispensable? Heck, no, I wouldn't go that far,' said Norman, as he pulled away and headed for St Anne's church.

* * *

'You're early,' said Diane, as she swung the vicarage door open and found Slater and Norman on her step.

'Yeah,' said Norman. 'We were just down the road. It didn't seem worth going all the way home and then coming back. I hope you don't mind?'

'Not at all,' she said. 'I'm glad of the help. Chris has been out since early this morning and I don't know when he'll be back. I thought I was going to have to do it all on my own tonight.'

'If you let us have the key, we can go on over to the hall and get things started,' suggested Norman.

'That would be great,' she said. 'I'll be over myself in a few minutes, but if you can get things going it'll save me so much time.'

They walked the short distance from the vicarage to the church hall and let themselves in.

'Okay, I'll bring this place to life,' said Slater, flicking on each one of the bank of light switches. 'You check the phone.'

As Slater made his way down the hall closing curtains, Norman made his way into the tiny office where the phone was located. They were in luck; it was a relatively new digital phone with a small screen. He quickly opened up the menu and found the caller list. Ryan must have called during the evening, after Ginger had gone to Slater's house, so he figured there shouldn't be too many numbers to check.

In fact, there was only one call that had come in yesterday evening, and he could tell by the number it was from a mobile phone. It had to be Ryan's. He took out his own mobile phone and quickly added Ryan's number to his contact list. He pressed the call button on his phone as he walked across to join Slater in the kitchen, and the number began to ring, but it just kept on ringing and ringing.

'Okay?' asked Slater.

'I found it easily enough,' said Norman, 'but there's no answer. I'll just have to keep trying every half hour or so.'

'Maybe he'll only answer if he sees Coulter's number on the screen.'

'He's got one of my cards,' said Norman. 'You never know, maybe he'll realise it's me calling.'

Slater thought of his own phone and the messages he still hadn't responded to. He realised he didn't have a clue how he was going to explain it to her, and if he was really honest, he wasn't sure he really cared what she thought. He immediately felt guilty and thought that sounded very callous, but the guilt didn't last long, and he thought maybe that told him everything he needed to know. Whatever, he didn't have time for that now. He had a mountain of vegetables to prepare. They were doing dinner for twenty.

Diane arrived and fired up the cooker, and within twenty minutes the kitchen began to fill with mouth-watering aromas.

'It must be a pain when Chris isn't around. Does it happen often?' said Slater, trying to make conversation.

'He's out comforting another family,' she said, adding irreverently, 'seeing off the dying.'

'Does he do that a lot?'

'No, not really,' she said. 'I think it's a thing of the past. Usually it's the following day, after they're gone, but there have been a couple recently where he's been called out to see them off at night. He got a call about this one last night. He spent half the night there until the person died, and then went back this morning. It's all part of the job.'

'Yeah, I suppose it must be,' he said.

* * *

The evening was as busy as always, but the dinner Diane prepared was worth working and waiting for. It was just coming up to ten o'clock by the time they had finished eating and clearing up. There was still no sign of Chris, so the boys walked Diane home before making their way back to Slater's car. It was just as Slater plipped the locks that Norman's mobile phone began to ring. He fished it from his pocket and stared at the screen, hoping it would be Ryan calling back at last, but to his dismay, the display said it was Steve Biddeford.

What the hell does he want? thought Norman as he raised the phone to his ear.

'Yo?'

'Is that you, Norm?' asked Biddeford's surprised voice in his ear.

'Who d'you expect to be answering my number?'

'I thought it seemed vaguely familiar, but I didn't realise it was your number,' said Biddeford.

'Well, it is,' said Norman. 'What do you want, calling this late?'

'It's a bit of an interesting situation,' said Biddeford. 'I think I need you to come in and answer some questions.'

'What questions?'

'A member of the public was walking his dog this evening when he heard a phone ringing. Thinking someone must have lost it, he followed the sound. It led him to a man's body. The phone was in the pocket of the coat the man was wearing when he died. The thing is, your number is the one that was calling him, and we found a cheap business card with your number on it in his pocket.'

'Ah, shit,' said Norman. 'Not Ryan!'

'So you do know this man?'

'Quite good-looking, scruffy beard, short dark hair, brown eyes, wearing blue jeans and a combat jacket?' asked Norman.

'Yeah, that sounds like him. Mind if I ask how you know him?'

Norman sighed — a big, weary sigh. 'Where are you?' he asked.

'This is a crime scene,' said Biddeford. 'I can't let you near—'

'I don't think you need to tell me the law,' said Norman, patiently. 'I'm not asking you to let me examine the scene. If you let me come down and identify the body, I'll answer your questions.'

'I dunno,' said Biddeford, doubtfully.

'Okay, suit yourself,' said Norman, abruptly. 'You'll just have to come and find me if you want to talk to me.'

'No, wait!' said Biddeford. 'Alright, you can come over. We're on the bypass, in the lay-by—'

'Where you found the last homeless guy?' guessed Norman.

'Err, yeah,' admitted Biddeford, reluctantly.

'We'll be there in ten minutes.'

Norman ended the call, slumped back against the car, and looked up at the sky.

'What is it?' asked Slater. 'I heard you say Ryan's name. Have they arrested him?'

'Worse,' said Norman. 'He's become the latest corpse.'

'Oh, no, not another one. Where this time?'

'Same place they found Doddsy.'

'Come on, let's get out there and see what's what,' said Slater.

* * *

The lay-by was teaming with police and scene-of-crime vehicles when they arrived. Floodlights seemed to have been erected in every possible place. They had to park way past the scene and walk back. Then there was a heated discussion with a PC who, quite rightly, wasn't prepared to let anyone onto the crime scene who didn't have the proper ID. Norman's insistence that DS Biddeford had requested his attendance made no difference.

'I don't care who you are. DS Biddeford hasn't told me, and until he does, your name's not on this list, so hard luck,' was the response.

Finally, Norman's persistence began to make an impression.

'Why don't I call him and ask him?' said the PC, with a smug grin, clearly quite convinced he was going to have the satisfaction of telling Norman what he could do or, even better, arresting him for obstruction. He turned away from them and spoke into his radio. When he turned back, he didn't seem quite so sure of himself.

'He says you've got to wait here,' he said, reluctantly. 'Someone will be down in a couple of minutes.'

It wasn't until Biddeford's partner, DC Naomi Darling, finally arrived in person that he actually stood back and let them through. The pixie-like Darling, a mere slip of a girl not much more than five feet tall, had a big smile on her face when she saw them.

'Wow! Real live humans,' she said. 'I wasn't expecting to come across any of those tonight. All I've seen so far is a dead body, a grumpy doctor, an arsehole of a DS and a whole load of knobhead PCs.'

This remark, accompanied by a baleful glare, was directed at the scowling PC, who didn't look too impressed that this young woman out-ranked him and was more than happy to glare back at her.

'They're still giving you hassle, then?' asked Norman, as she led them away from the PC.

'Bunch of wankers,' she said. 'They keep trying to make my life a misery, but so far I've managed to outwit them all. I suppose they don't like the idea of a girl who can look after herself.'

Slater had worked with Darling briefly, and he knew she wasn't someone to trifle with. She might be tiny, and weigh hardly anything, but there were two huge thugs who could testify to just how tough she was. Anyone trying to mess with her was asking for trouble. It wasn't just her hair that was spiky.

'DS Crabby Git says to meet him over there,' said Darling quietly, pointing to one of the pop-up tents that had been hastily erected in the lay-by where they could see a figure waiting for them.

'Where's the body?' asked Norman, when they reached Biddeford.

'The doctor's looking him over at the moment,' he said, 'but it looks like he's been dead for hours, possibly even since yesterday. When did you last see him?'

'We haven't seen him for a couple of days,' said Norman, 'but we know he was alive early yesterday evening.'

'At least now I suppose you'll admit there's something going on,' said Slater. 'This is the third homeless guy to die. Don't you think that's a bit of a coincidence?'

'It's not me you need to convince,' Biddeford said. 'I said after the second one it can't be a coincidence, but I've been told I'm wrong. I reckon this time, though, she's going to have to take notice. This one's had his sleeves cut off, just like the last one.'

'Jeez,' said Norman. 'That definitely can't be a coincidence.'

Slater felt a stab of disappointment. He assumed when Biddeford said 'she' he had to mean his boss, DCI Goodnews. He hoped he was wrong, but who else was there?

Biddeford had produced a clear plastic bag with one of Norman's homemade business cards inside. He showed it to Norman.

'We found this in his pocket. I don't suppose you know what it means?'

'Yeah,' said Norman. 'That's our business card. I gave it to him.'

Biddeford looked quickly down at the business card, but he wasn't quick enough to hide the smirk that crossed his face.

'*S & N Investigations & Security*,' he read from the card. He looked from Norman to Slater and back again. 'Are you serious?'

'Go ahead and laugh,' said Norman. 'We'll see who's laughing when we go to the press with the story of what's really been going on here, and how the police don't give a shit because the victims are all homeless.'

'He who laughs last, laughs longest,' said Slater. 'Don't forget that.'

'Hey, look,' said Biddeford. 'Don't blame me. I just do what the boss tells me.'

'If you had any balls, you'd do what was right, regardless of what the boss says,' said Slater.

Biddeford was easily riled by such a pointed remark, just as Slater had intended.

'And I suppose you'd be happy to work behind her back and argue with her?'

'If I thought I was right and a case was being dismissed without proper investigation, yes I would,' said Slater.

Biddeford knew what Slater said was the truth, but before he could think of anything to say, a movement caught his eye. He looked over their shoulders, saw a figure approaching behind them and blanched.

'Well, here you go,' he said to Slater. 'If you want to argue with her, be my guest. She's just turned up.'

Slater whirled round. Sure enough, DCI Marion Goodnews was striding purposefully in their direction, and as she approached, he could feel his face turning red.

If she had seen Slater and Norman, Goodnews showed no sign of recognition as she walked up to Biddeford. She made a point of ignoring them and even made sure to turn her back on them before she addressed him.

'Good evening, Sergeant, what have we got?' she asked.

'Evening, boss,' said Biddeford, clearly self-conscious in front of Slater and Norman. 'Body over the back there.' He pointed beyond the trees that lined the back of the lay-by. 'Male, in his late thirties. He's been stabbed in the back. Apparently his name is Ryan, and he's another one of Tinton's homeless community.'

'You're sure he's been stabbed?'

'Yes, boss.'

'No way this could be an accident?'

Biddeford shook his head. 'Not unless he stabbed himself in the back and then threw the knife away.'

'Don't try to be clever just because you have an audience,' she warned him. She indicated Slater and Norman with her thumb. 'What are these two doing out here anyway?'

'Err, the dead man had this in his pocket,' said Biddeford, passing her the card in the plastic bag.

She bent her head to look at the card. 'S & N? Do we have any idea what that stands for?'

'That's our business card,' said Slater, indignantly.

She wheeled round to face them. There was a smile fixed on her face, but it belied the fiery glow in her eyes. She looked at Slater as if he was something she wanted to wipe off her shoe. It was as much contempt as Slater had ever seen on a face.

'Oh, I see,' she sneered. 'S & N, of course, Sloppy and Numpty.'

Despite her anger and scorn, Slater almost laughed at the insult, and he had to struggle to keep a straight face. He thought she really was very good when she got going, although he would have preferred it if she had been directing it at someone else.

'What the hell are you doing on my crime scene?' she demanded.

'Actually, boss, I asked them to come,' confessed Biddeford. 'There was a mobile phone in the victim's pocket, and Norman was the last person to call it. And then I found the card. I thought maybe they could help—'

She had turned back to face him as he started to speak, and now she interrupted him.

'Yes, thank you, Sergeant. Next time you want to invite two non-police officers onto one of my crime scenes, perhaps you'll be good enough to ask me first.'

Biddeford hung his head. 'Yes, boss,' he said. 'Sorry.'

'Give the guy a break,' said Norman. 'He did the right thing calling that number. I offered to come and identify the body and help in any way I could. I wasn't intending to poke around the crime scene.'

She aimed a scowl in his direction.

'Well, in that case,' she said, 'you won't be disappointed to know I'm not letting you anywhere near it, will you?'

'It looks like they're bringing the body out,' said Darling, who had been a fascinated observer since Goodnews had arrived.

Goodnews turned to Norman. 'Would you come with me? You can have a look at his face as they bring him out.'

'Sure,' said Norman, just about resisting the urge to say what he really thought.

Slater took a pace forward and she shot him a look that made him stop dead in his tracks. 'Oh no,' she warned him. 'Not you. You can wait here. I'll deal with you later.'

She called the PC who had been so happy to detain them earlier. 'Make sure he stays right here,' she said.

'Yes, ma'am,' said the PC, giving Slater an evil grin.

Now Goodnews turned her attention to Darling. 'DC Darling,' she said, 'I'm sure you and Mr Slater must have lots to talk about, but don't you have work to do?'

'Err, yes, boss,' she said.

'Well then, go and do it!'

Slater watched Darling scurry reluctantly back in the direction of the crime scene, and then turned his gaze to follow his fiery-tempered girlfriend — no, he thought, make that ex-girlfriend — lead Norman and Biddeford over to intercept the gurney carrying the body.

'I don't know what you've done to piss her off,' said the PC, quietly, 'but whatever it is, I suggest you keep a tight hold of your balls, cos it looks as if she intends to have them for breakfast.'

'You think?' said Slater.

'So what have you done?'

'You really don't want to know.'

'Oh, I do,' said the grinning PC, 'and I promise I won't tell a soul if you tell me.'

'Yeah, right,' said Slater. 'Like I'm that stupid.'

* * *

It was almost twenty minutes before Slater saw Goodnews heading back in his direction. There was a no sign of Norman or Biddeford. He guessed they had been sent off somewhere so Biddeford could take a statement.

'Here we go,' said the PC quietly, another evil grin creasing his face as she approached. 'I'm going to enjoy this.'

'Right, Constable, thank you,' she said as she arrived. 'You can go now.'

The disappointment could clearly be seen all over his face.

'I know, it's a shame, isn't it?' she said, 'You were so looking forward to listening in, weren't you?'

The PC tried to look innocent.

'We both know I'm right,' she said. 'I heard you say so as I walked over, didn't I?'

'Err, well, what I actually said—'

'I don't care what you actually said,' she snapped. 'Just make yourself scarce. Now!'

The crestfallen PC wandered away. Goodnews waited until he was out of earshot, and then gave Slater an icy, humourless smile.

'Now then,' she said. 'While Mr Norman does his civic duty and gives DS Biddeford his statement about the dead man, you can give me your statement about what happened last night. And I don't want any bullshit.'

Slater shifted uncomfortably from foot to foot. He wasn't sure exactly how he should handle this situation. When the same sort of thing had happened with his former girlfriend, Cindy, he had avoided the issue by chickening out of going to see her. One thing was for sure: avoiding a showdown this time was no longer an option.

'Well, say something, for God's sake,' she demanded.

'To be honest, I don't know where to start, and I don't think you'll believe me anyway,' he said, lamely.

'Well, I suggest you try me,' she said, 'because right now, I've only got my side of the story to go on, and it doesn't look very good.'

'Look, I'm really sorry I stood you up, but you know what it's like. Something came up and I had to rush off.'

'Something came up,' she repeated. 'That something wouldn't have anything to do with the girl in your house, would it?'

'It was nothing to do with her. I had to go out.'

'And you didn't think to call me?'

'I've said I'm sorry,' he argued. 'How more many times do you want me to say it?'

Slater realised anyone watching would easily be able to see what was going on, with her arms waving around animatedly and his arms folded in self-defence. It was rather like being back at school getting a bollocking from the headmistress, and frankly he had just about had enough of being made to feel like that this week.

'We had arranged a date—' began Goodnews.

'No, actually,' he said. 'I think you'll find *you* had arranged a date. You didn't ask me, you told me.'

'I don't recall hearing you refuse.'

'I don't recall being offered the bloody chance.'

'Don't you swear at me,' she snapped, indignantly.

'Ha! That sounds good after some of the names you called me down the phone,' he countered.

'So, who is this girl?'

Slater sighed. This was going to be the really tricky bit. 'She's an old friend who needed somewhere to sleep for the night,' he said.

'And you didn't think to tell me?'

'It was all a bit last-minute. She's alone, and she's frightened, that's why she wouldn't answer the door. I wasn't even at home when you came round.'

'So where were you?'

'I told you, I was with Norm. You see, it doesn't matter what I tell you, you just don't listen!'

'Oh great! So you'd rather be out with your numpty mate than wait in for me? My my, don't you know how to make a girl feel good?'

Slater didn't say anything. He was in a dilemma. Okay, he had committed the cardinal sin of forgetting she was coming round, but as far as he was concerned, apart from that, he had done nothing wrong, and he resented having to justify himself to her.

Of course, he could explain it all away quite easily, but that would mean telling her all about the case, and what was really stopping him from telling her about that was the information, gleaned from Darling's comments not half an hour ago, that Goodnews was directing the police investigation. Or perhaps non-investigation would be more appropriate. She really was the one who was telling them to stay away. Biddeford was merely a mouthpiece.

And then he realised something that probably told him all he needed to know. If it had really mattered to him, would he have forgotten she was coming round that night?

His thoughts were interrupted as he realised she was speaking again.

'I feel totally let down by you. Why didn't you call me and tell me what was going on?'

'But that's just it, Marion. It's all about you and your precious career, isn't it?'

'How do you work that one out? I listened to your problems the other night, didn't I?'

'Well, yeah,' he admitted, 'but only because I brought the subject up. You haven't asked me anything without prompting.'

'Like what?'

'Well, like what I'm going to do for a job.'

'I've just found that out, haven't I?' she said, derisively. 'Sloppy and Numpty, private investigators.'

'Yeah, go on,' he said, 'let's hear all the scornful remarks now and get it over with. You would have known about it a damned sight sooner if only you had thought to ask.'

'But you don't ask me about my day,' she said.

'Yes, I do, or at least I did, but once I realised you were never going to tell me anything, I thought, What's the point? Whenever I ask, all you ever say is it's police business and you can't discuss it with me.'

'But I can't!'

'Of course you bloody can! I've dealt with police business half my life. Why would I suddenly start telling everyone about it now? Christ, if you can't trust me to keep my mouth shut, who can you trust?'

'I don't trust anyone,' she said. 'I can't afford to.'

'Well, there you go. You finally reveal the root cause of this whole problem. You don't trust me.' He shook his head. 'Dear, oh dear, oh dear. If you can't trust me, Marion, we have no future as a couple. In fact, if you can't trust anyone you'll never have a normal relationship.'

This appeared to be a truth that stung her when he said it, and her face quickly reddened. Suddenly she was the one struggling to know what to say.

'So, what *do* you want me to say?' she asked, stupidly.

'Jesus, Marion, it's supposed to be spontaneous. But then nothing ever is with you, is it? Even the sex has to be exactly the way you want it.'

This comment seemed to shock her back to her senses. 'Are you saying you don't enjoy it?' she asked, coolly.

'No, I'm not saying that at all. I'm just saying everything has to follow your plan. What about what I want? All I ever hear is what you want. It's always "do this, Dave, do that, Dave, put it in now, Dave, faster, faster, slower, slower". It's like you're directing a porn film. You don't want a boyfriend, you want a bloody sex machine.'

'It would probably keep going longer and be more satisfying,' she said, spitefully, instantly wishing she could take the words back.

He looked at her sadly. 'Is that how you want this to go? So we end up taking cheap shots at each other? Well, I'm sorry to disappoint you, yet again, but I'm not going to keep *this* going long enough to satisfy you, either. If all you're going to do is get bitchy, I've nothing more to say. I just can't be arsed.'

'I didn't mean it like that,' she said, hastily.

'How else could you have meant it?'

'You don't know how lucky you are,' she said, desperately. 'There are plenty of men who'd be glad to climb into bed with me.'

'Yeah, I'm sure there are,' he said, 'and that's the rest of the problem. You just want to have your frustration humped away by some Neanderthal sex slave, and I want something more.'

'I could find another man tomorrow if I wanted.'

'I'm sure you could,' he said, 'but we both know it won't last, because the man you're really looking for hasn't been created yet. That's why you're on your own now, and if you don't change, that's all you will ever be.'

He turned on his heel and headed off towards his car.

'Hey, wait a minute,' she fumed. 'You come back here. We're not finished yet.'

'I think you'll find we are,' he called back to her. 'Goodbye, Marion.'

He couldn't catch the exact words she was spitting after him, but he was pretty sure they were mostly expletives.

* * *

Half an hour later, Norman returned to Slater's car and found his friend waiting for him.

'Are you okay?' he asked.

'Yeah,' said Slater, starting the car. 'I'm fine.'

'Lover's tiff, huh?'

'Something like that.'

'You wanna talk about it?'

'There's nothing to talk about, mate.'

'Okay,' said Norman, who could take a hint.

They had been driving for a couple of minutes before Slater broke the silence. 'So? What did you tell them?'

'As little as possible,' said Norman.

Slater raised an eyebrow and glanced at Norman. 'But we've almost solved the case for them,' he said.

'Yeah, we have,' agreed Norman, 'but as far as Goodnews is concerned, there is no case. Why should we tell them what we know and let them step in and take over? We're the ones who've done all the work.'

'So what did you learn?' asked Slater.

'About the murder? Only that Ryan's probably been dead since last night, but you already heard that, same as I did. What I *did* learn is that Biddeford is like some sort of puppet, just doing what your girlfriend tells him.'

'That's what I thought,' said Slater, ignoring the 'girlfriend' reference.

'I know you like her,' said Norman, 'but is it just me, or did she treat everyone like shit out there tonight?'

'No, it isn't just you,' agreed Slater. 'She didn't exactly cover herself in glory, did she? What else did you learn?'

Norman seemed to take this second hint and moved off the topic of Goodnews. 'Biddeford knows there's a case to investigate, but he's too scared of her to do anything about it. Naomi Darling would do it, but I got the impression Biddeford's doing his best to make sure she can't outshine him. The net result is there's nothing happening.'

'So it's down to us, then,' said Slater. 'Are we alright with that?'

'Hell yeah, no one else is going to do it.'

'Tomorrow morning, then,' said Slater. 'I think it's time we had another chat with Stan Coulter.'

CHAPTER FIFTEEN

They were in a spacious conservatory at the back of Coulter's house in the hospital grounds. Slater and Norman had hoped to catch Coulter off guard, but even though they had arrived at ten in the morning without warning, he seemed perfectly comfortable with their intrusion, and once he'd been made aware they were at his front door, he had personally escorted them through the house. Now they were sitting in comfortable chairs opposite the main man himself, who was sitting at a large leather-topped desk, waiting for coffee to arrive. To Coulter's left, there was a computer monitor, at which he glanced from time to time.

'So, what can I do for you two boys?' he asked pleasantly.

'The game's up, Coulter. We've figured out what you've been up to, and why,' said Norman.

Coulter looked intrigued. 'I'm flattered you seem to think there's some big deal going down. But I'm afraid I haven't really got time to get involved. All I'm interested in right now is trying to find a cure for my son's illness.'

'Yeah, exactly,' said Norman. 'That's what this is all about, isn't it?'

'Now look,' said Coulter, 'there must be hundreds, probably thousands, of other parents in similar situations to mine. Have you been poking your nose into their business too?'

'The thing is, none of the other parents are going around murdering people in the process,' said Norman.

Coulter steepled his fingers and then leaned forward to rest his chin on them as he considered Norman.

'Have you lost all your marbles, now?' he asked. 'I haven't a clue what you're talking about. All I've done is try to find a kidney donor for my son. Where do you get this idea from that I've been going around murdering people? I told you before, you can't just kill the nearest person and pinch their kidneys. It doesn't work like that. These things have to be carefully matched. That's especially the case with my son because he's got a very rare blood group.'

'Transplants are supposed to be regulated,' said Slater.

Coulter gave him a sympathetic smile. 'Look, son. Regulations are for losers. I've never been a great believer in them myself, that's why I'm successful. Besides, when it's family, you do whatever it takes.'

'Like blackmail and murder,' said Norman.

'You know, to be honest, I've never liked you, Norm,' said Coulter, 'but I've always thought you were a pretty good copper. Not brilliant, but dogged and professional, you know? But I have to tell you, mate, you're barking up the wrong tree if you think I've murdered anyone. Maybe it's time you got it into that thick head of yours that you're past your sell-by date. You should accept it's time to retire now and take up golf or something.'

The coffee arrived at this point and they sat silently as the maid placed the tray on Coulter's desk. Once she had left the room, Coulter spoke again.

'I've got to admit, I do find the idea that you think I'm involved in some sort of murder conspiracy quite intriguing,' he said. 'So I'll tell you what I'm willing to do. I'm not busy this morning, and I could do with a good laugh, so why don't I pour us all a nice cup of coffee, and then you can tell me exactly what you think you've figured out and who it is you think I've murdered.'

While Coulter poured the coffees, Slater took the opportunity to snatch a look at Norman. His partner looked unruffled, but Slater was getting a little concerned by Coulter's attitude and demeanour. This really wasn't quite how he had imagined the morning would go.

'Now then,' said Coulter, as he sat back with his coffee. 'Do go ahead, Norm. Let's hear it. I'm all ears.'

'You're blackmailing Clara Sterling,' said Norman. 'You started an affair with her so you could find out all about her husband. You needed a surgeon you could manipulate into doing a transplant outside the regulations, and Fabian Sterling fit the bill. When Clara realised what you were up to, and tried to stop the affair, you threatened to tell her husband. Then you bought him by offering him a job he couldn't refuse, and then kept him under control by telling him you'd kill his wife if he didn't do what you said.'

'That's very good,' said Coulter. 'Apart from all the bits that aren't true. Did Clara tell you I was blackmailing her?' He shook his head. 'That's the only thing wrong with that woman. She'd be damned near perfect, but she will not take responsibility for her own actions. Don't you find that annoying? I didn't have to blackmail her, Norm. She was only too willing to have an affair. And you've got it the wrong way round. I didn't know her husband was a surgeon until after the affair started.'

'You targeted her because her husband was a surgeon,' insisted Norman.

'No, mate, I targeted her because I fancied her, and I recognised her as the type of woman who would be easy to get into bed. And I promise you, I don't need blackmail to keep the affair going. She can't get enough of it, and d'you know why? She loves it because I tell her what she wants to hear, and I give her the attention she craves. Her husband neglects her, you see, because he's so busy looking in the mirror at his own reflection he can't see how lucky he is. Still, his loss is my gain, eh?'

He took a sip of coffee before continuing.

'Finding out her husband was a surgeon was a stroke of luck, and when she told me what had happened to him, well, it was too good an opportunity to miss. I mean, my own pet surgeon. Who wouldn't want one, when you have a sick son whose only hope, long term, is a transplant? All I had to do then was find a hospital that had ambition and needed a donor with bottomless pockets.'

'But you control him by threatening his wife,' said Norman. 'That's hardly having a pet surgeon, is it?'

'Do I bollocks,' said Coulter, scornfully. 'He knew exactly why I wanted him in that hospital from day one. He couldn't give a damn about his wife. He works for me because I pay him a fortune. He's as bad as her when it comes to taking responsibility for his actions.'

'So let me get this straight,' said Slater. 'You admit Sterling works for you, but you deny blackmailing him.'

Coulter looked at Slater and then at Norman. 'He's a sharp one, isn't he, Norm?' Then he turned back to Slater. 'Yes, I admit it. He works for me because I pay him about fifty times what he would normally get, and I screw his wife because she likes it. I have no hold on either of them. They're here because they want to be. And I'm building a surgical facility here so my boy can have his transplant. Satisfied now?'

Slater didn't say anything, but he admitted to himself he was far from satisfied. If Coulter was telling the truth about this . . . But then, men like Coulter lied as a way of life, didn't they? Then again, he didn't *look* as if he was lying . . .

'Let's move on, shall we?' said Norman. 'What about Morgan, the guy who died in the blazing skip. I suppose you're going to tell me that was nothing to do with you?'

Coulter sighed. 'We've been through this before,' he said, patiently. 'I told you last time I had no reason to kill the guy.'

'Maybe you wanted to stop him talking,' said Norman.

'Look,' said Coulter, the patience not quite so evident in his voice this time. 'The guy contacted me and said he was with my son Bobby in Afghanistan. He told me he had the same blood group and he wanted to donate a kidney. He said he felt guilty about Bobby's death and donating would make him feel better. You don't look a gift horse in the mouth, do you? How was I supposed to know he was telling me a load of shit? I knew there was another lad with the same blood group as Bobby, so it made sense.'

'You could have had that checked before you took his kidney,' suggested Slater.

'Yeah, well that's the doctor's job, not mine,' said Coulter. 'I didn't know he wouldn't check until it was too late.'

'Isn't that the sort of thing that got him into trouble in the first place?' asked Norman.

'Yes, but I thought he'd learned his bloody lesson. He was lucky he didn't kill anyone. I felt like killing him when I found out what he'd done, but what would be the chance of finding another surgeon now?'

'Jesus,' said Slater. 'You do realise there's a good chance he'll kill your son if he does a transplant, don't you?'

'Look,' said Coulter, desperately, 'my son's going to die anyway if I don't do something soon. I could go through the proper channels, but then he'd die while he was on the waiting list. I've lost one son, I don't want to sit and watch another one die when I've got the money to save him. You'd do the same!'

By some sort of unspoken agreement, this seemed to be the appropriate time for them all to take a sip of their coffee. Coulter placed his cup and saucer on the desk.

'Let me show you something,' he said. He reached for the monitor on his desk and slowly turned it round far enough for them to be able to see the screen. The image was that of a young man lying comatose in a hospital bed.

'You see that?' asked Coulter, sadly. 'That's a live feed from the room of my youngest son, Terry. He's more or less comatose all the time now. Another few weeks and he'll die if

I don't find him a donor. Do you really think I'm interested in anything else right now?'

He left the monitor facing them for a few moments, and then turned it, almost reverently, back to its original position so only he could see it.

'All this makes no difference,' said Norman. 'You still have a great motive to kill Morgan.'

Coulter sighed. 'I'm sure you've got a good motive to kill some people, but you haven't done it, have you? Sterling has a much better motive than me, maybe you should take a closer look at him.'

'So this guy who has the matching blood group. Have you been looking for him?' asked Slater.

'What do you think? Of course I have.'

'Yeah, we know,' said Norman. 'You sent your two heavies down to St Anne's church hall.'

'They told me you guys had wanted to start a fight,' said Coulter, 'but there was no need for that. I only sent the boys down there because I heard they fed the homeless people down there. I just wanted to see if they could identify the guy I was looking for.'

'They were supposed to drag him back here, weren't they? So you help yourself to one of his kidneys?' asked Norman.

'If they saw him they were just supposed to give him a mobile phone with my number programmed into it. They were to tell him I would pay him a lot of money for a kidney. The phone was so he could call me and negotiate.'

'And did he?' asked Norman.

'Surely he would have more sense than to trust someone like you and a bogus surgeon,' said Slater.

'You really think so?' asked Coulter. 'Don't be so naive. Everyone has their price.'

'So you were actively looking for this guy?' asked Norman. 'How would you know if it was the right one this time?'

'Tattoo on the upper arm. Lots of the SAS lads have their blood group tattooed there.'

'What about the guy you killed and dumped in a lay-by on the bypass at Tinton?' asked Norman. 'What happened there? I guess you thought he was your guy, but just to make sure, you hacked his sleeves off. Then, when you found no tattoos, your goons beat the shit out of him in frustration. Or were they trying to find out where the real guy was and they just got a little bit too rough?'

'When was this?' asked Coulter.

'The night after your heavies came to the church hall.'

'I wasn't looking by then. The guy I was looking for — Ryan — had already called me that morning. I told you — that's why we gave him the mobile phone.'

'So your guys got a phone to him that night we saw them?' asked Slater.

'He was outside when they left.'

'But why would he take the phone from them?'

'I don't know,' said Coulter. 'Maybe Morgan told him how much I was prepared to pay for the right kidney. Like I said, everyone has a price. I'm just waiting for him to let me know when he's coming in. He was supposed to be here yesterday but there's been a delay for some reason.'

'Maybe he got cold feet and changed his mind,' suggested Norman.

'No, I don't think so,' said Coulter, confidently. 'He's a warrior, a man of honour. He'll be here.'

Slater exchanged a glance with Norman. If Coulter knew Ryan was dead, he was a very good actor. He had been blowing holes in their theory right from the start, and if he really didn't know Ryan was dead, that theory was about to sink without trace.

'Err, I wouldn't be too confident about him turning up, Stan,' said Norman.

'Of course he'll turn up. He's special forces. He was my son Bobby's best mate. He'll turn up.'

Coulter's confidence suddenly seemed to disappear as he took in the two faces opposite him. 'What? You know something, don't you?' he asked, beginning to panic. 'What's happened? Where is he?'

'Are you sure you don't know?' asked Norman.

Coulter was close to hysteria now, and he jumped to his feet. 'Of course I don't bloody know!' He banged on the desk with his fists. 'You tell me where he is!'

'He's dead, Stan,' said Norman, quietly.

'Dead? He can't be dead! He promised me he was coming!' Coulter sank back down into his chair, but then he had an idea. 'But if he's dead, we can still have a kidney, we can have both of them! We need to be quick though, they don't last long.'

'It's too late,' said Slater. 'He died about thirty-six hours ago now.'

'Why didn't you tell me sooner?' asked Coulter, hysterically. 'We could have done something.'

'He had already been dead twenty-four hours when he was found,' said Norman. 'There was nothing that could be done.'

Coulter was distraught. 'Who did this?' he demanded. 'Someone's condemned my son to death because of this. Who did it? I'm gonna kill 'em.'

'His sleeves had been cut off, just like the last guy,' said Norman. 'We thought it must have been you checking his blood group.'

'Me? You think I killed him? Why would I kill the only man who could save my son's life?'

'We figured he'd gone back on his word and you'd hunted him down.'

'We had a deal. He was going to make a million quid. It was what he wanted to start a new life. Even if it was true and he had backed out, why would I kill him?'

'You were trying to grab him so you could knock him out and steal a kidney,' suggested Slater, 'but it went wrong and he died.'

Coulter was purple with rage now, and he was screaming. 'If we'd killed him we would have brought the body back here and taken both kidneys, wouldn't we, you bloody idiot?'

Alerted by all the noise, Coulter's two heavies had rushed to the conservatory and the door suddenly burst open as they arrived.

'Are you okay, boss?'

'Get these two idiots out of here,' snarled Coulter.

* * *

'How did we get that so wrong?' asked Norman, as Slater drove away from Coulter's house.

'You believed him, too?'

'I don't think you could fake all that grief,' said Norman, 'and like he said, why the hell would he kill Ryan and leave the kidneys?'

'So you think we got it all wrong?'

'I think we got it wrong about the murderer,' admitted Norman.

'So what's going on then?' asked Slater.

'I thought Coulter was the key to this. I was convinced, but now I'm not sure. If it's not about finding a kidney for his son, what the hell is it about? I mean, what other reason could anyone have for cutting the sleeves off their victims?'

The drove on in silence for a short while before Slater spoke.

'Maybe we're just looking at it the wrong way round. What if someone was trying to stop Coulter's son having a transplant?'

Norman thought about this new idea.

'I dunno,' he said. 'How would that work? If you wanted to stop the transplant, why not just tell the authorities? Or if you want to kill people, why not kill the surgeon? No surgeon, no transplant, right?'

'But there's always another surgeon, isn't there?' argued Slater. 'And could you be sure the authorities would act? I get the impression Coulter would be used to dealing with that sort of stuff, and he's probably got a plan B anyway. No, when the patient has a rare blood group, the odds of finding a donor are miniscule. It's a miracle they found one in the first place. What better way to wreck the plan than kill the donor?'

'But what's the motive?' asked Norman.

'To make Coulter suffer,' said Slater, 'and I think it worked, don't you?'

Norman thought about this a bit longer. 'Shit,' he said, finally. 'If we've got to start working our way through a list of the people who would want to get even with Coulter, we've got one hell of a long job in front of us. There must be hundreds . . .'

* * *

It was after one o'clock when they got back to Slater's house, and Jane Jolly was still there.

'Are you okay?' asked Norman. 'You're supposed to finish at twelve.'

'I'm fine,' she said. 'I've been waiting for you two to get back.'

'How's Jenny?' asked Slater. 'She was pretty upset when I told her about Ryan this morning.'

'She's fine. We had a long chat earlier. I think she needed someone to talk to. She's been through a lot, poor girl. Ryan was just the latest in a long run of misfortune.'

'That's what I thought,' said Slater, 'but I've been waiting until she's ready to talk. I didn't want to force her to tell me, you know?'

'I think you'll find she will talk to you, if you give her time, but she doesn't want to be a burden,' said Jolly.

'She isn't a burden.'

'Then you should make sure she understands that,' said Jolly. 'She does trust you, she's just not ready to tell you, yet.'

'Where is she now?' he asked.

'Upstairs, sleeping. She's going to need a lot of it.'

'Do you think I should go up?'

'No, she's fine, leave her there for now. I've got something you need to see. I was doing some online research for myself this morning, and I came across something quite interesting. I printed it out for you, one copy each.'

She gave each of them six printed pages. 'Here you are,' she said. 'You settle down and read these. I'll make you a cup of tea before I go.'

CHAPTER SIXTEEN

It was just before seven p.m. when Slater, Norman and a small slip of a girl with spiky hair walked into the church hall.

'What's this, another volunteer?' asked Diane as they walked into the kitchen.

'This is Naomi,' said Norman. 'She wanted to know what we do here, so I thought there's no better way of finding out than by actually getting your hands dirty, right?'

Chris looked up from his vegetable-chopping. 'Hi Naomi, you're very welcome. Any friend of Norm's is a friend of ours.'

'Come on in, Naomi,' said Diane. 'There's plenty to do. Are you any good at peeling potatoes?'

'Sure,' said Naomi. 'Where do I start?'

* * *

It was nine thirty by the time all the guests had gone and the five remaining workers sat down to eat.

'That was such terrible news about Ryan,' said Diane. 'Does anyone know what happened?'

'Apparently he was stabbed in the back and then dumped in the same lay-by where they found Doddsy,' said Norman. 'Only Doddsy's body was left in the road where he was easy to spot. Ryan's body was hidden away behind the trees at the back of the lay-by.'

'I don't understand,' said Chris. 'Is that relevant? What do the police say?'

'Oh they won't actually tell us anything,' said Norman, 'but it looks like they think it's just some random killing. They don't seem to give a damn about homeless people, so I doubt they're going to make much of an effort to find out what really happened.'

'So they don't think it's the same person responsible?' asked Chris.

'They think Morgan's death was an accident of his own making, and Doddsy was a hit-and-run,' said Slater.

'What about Ryan's death?' asked Diane.

'Random killing,' said Norman.

'They're not linking Ryan's death with Doddsy's?' asked Chris.

'Why would they?' asked Slater.

'Err, well, they were found in the same place,' said Chris. 'What did you mean about the body being hidden? Surely that's what any murderer would do with a body, isn't it?'

'Not necessarily,' said Norman. 'It's often the case that the murderer just wants to flee the scene and get as far away as possible. Dumping Ryan and Doddsy out in the lay-by smacks of planning.'

'I thought you said Doddsy was a hit-and-run accident,' said Diane.

'The police are saying it's a hit-and-run. We think he was run down alright, but it was no accident. And it didn't happen in the lay-by. He was run down somewhere else and then dumped in the lay-by.'

'It's a bit of a coincidence, two bodies being found there,' said Chris.

'That's not the only coincidence,' said Slater.

'You mean the sleeves?'

'Oh, you know about that?' asked Norman.

'It was on the radio earlier,' said Chris, hastily, 'in a news report.'

Slater and Norman exchanged a glance and there was an awkward silence, broken by Diane. 'What do you think of these two detectives, Naomi? Don't you think they're clever, working to solve a case on their own.'

Naomi smiled. 'Yes,' she said, 'it's a pity the police won't take the deaths as seriously. I'm sure someone thinks they've got away with three murders.'

'You really think so?' asked Chris.

'Oh yes,' she said. 'Someone *thinks* they've got away with it.'

'Gosh, I wonder who it is?' said Diane.

'It can be the most unlikely people,' said Norman.

'I suppose if it was Agatha Christie, it would be the butler?' suggested Chris.

'Yeah,' said Norman, 'or maybe the vicar?'

Chris dropped his knife, but quickly picked it up and tried to carry on as if nothing had happened. It seemed he had become all fingers and thumbs, so he placed his knife and fork on his plate.

'No,' said Diane, laughing. 'It can't be the vicar, he's a paragon of virtue . . .'

She stopped speaking as she realised no one else was laughing. She looked at her husband, but he was staring down at his plate. 'Chris? What's the matter? What—'

'Shall we tell her, Chris?' asked Slater. 'Or do you want to?'

Diane looked shocked, but still her husband stared down at his plate.

'Have you ever met his mother?' Norman asked Diane.

'No, she died of cancer when he was very young,' she said. 'I never got the chance to meet her.'

'She did die when he was very young, but she didn't die of cancer,' explained Norman. 'She was an innocent victim who was gunned down in a bank raid. She just happened to be in the wrong place at the wrong time. That was thirty-five years ago. The gang that raided the bank were caught and put away for armed robbery, but the woman who they killed had left a son, and for a fortnight he sat and watched his mother on a life support machine until she eventually passed away.'

He looked across at Chris. 'That must have been really hard, to lose your mum that young. What were you then, five?'

'Six,' whispered Chris. 'I was six when she died.'

'The guy who had the sawn-off shotgun was called Coulter,' continued Norman. 'He had a son called Stanley. Stan was part of his father's gang, and he assumed control when his father was put away. He had big ideas, and he now makes a very tidy living from some very dodgy dealings, but he's clever enough to keep just out of reach of the law.

'Stan Coulter had three sons. One joined the army and was killed in Afghanistan, one's his right-hand man, and the youngest is in a private hospital just a few miles away from here. He's got a terminal kidney condition. His only hope is a transplant, and because he has a rare blood group, his only real hope was a guy called Ryan.'

Diane looked at Slater at the mention of Ryan's name.

'Yeah, that Ryan,' confirmed Slater. 'He had the same blood group, so the chances were he would have been a near-perfect tissue match for a transplant. He was going to do it, too, except Chris got to him before they could perform the operation. The thing with organs like kidneys is that they don't survive for long in a dead body. Starved of oxygen, they soon die and become useless. Because Ryan's body had been hidden, he'd been dead twenty-four hours before he was found. It was plenty of time to make sure the kidneys were no use to anyone.'

Diane looked from face to face, looking baffled. 'But this is crazy. Chris wouldn't do anything like this. Tell them, Chris!'

But Chris said nothing. He just continued to stare at his plate.

'But he's never out of my sight,' she said.

'What about those parishioners he's been visiting at night?' asked Norman. 'You said one family called the night Ryan died. We checked your phone for incoming calls. The only call was from Ryan.'

She still couldn't make sense of what they were saying. 'Yes, but—'

'Have any of those dead people had funerals, Diane?' asked Slater. 'Naomi checked recent local deaths. Apart from an elderly Sikh, the only deaths have been Morgan, Doddsy and Ryan. Chris was seeing off the dead, but not in the way you thought.'

'But why would he kill Morgan and Doddsy, if Ryan was the one?'

'I think Morgan was an accident,' said Slater, 'but only in the sense that he shouldn't have been in the skip. That was Ryan's skip, where he slept. He only let Morgan stay there that night because he was so ill he needed shelter.'

'Yeah, Morgan died for nothing,' said Norman. 'Just like Chris's mum. He was in the wrong place at the wrong time.'

'But why Doddsy?'

'It took us a while to figure that one,' said Slater. 'But then we thought about how jealous Chris was when Doddsy flirted with you. We think he was a bit of an opportunist victim. With us looking at SAS and army links to Morgan's death, it was easy to fit Doddsy in. The sleeves were cut off to add to the suspicion this was about blood group tattoos.

'Chris was actually setting us a trail that led to Stan Coulter, and we followed it all the way. It was only when we confronted Coulter that we realised it didn't add up. That's when we had a little bit of luck. We have a lady who's part of our team. She's had some bad luck that's really tested her faith and she's been looking for someone to talk to. We suggested Chris. The thing is, Jane's not one to rush in without checking someone out first. She looked up Chris online. She's *really* thorough. She found the story about his mother's murder and Coulter's father being the shooter.'

'After that, we saw everything in a whole new light,' Norman finished, 'and suddenly things started to add up. Like how Chris is always out comforting someone when these guys die.'

'And you'd have to be the killer to know about the sleeves,' said Slater. 'Someone at Tinton Police Station thought like us, and although she couldn't do much, she made sure that little detail was never revealed publicly.'

'Now he's going to have to watch his son fade away, just like I watched my mother die,' spat Chris, suddenly awakened from his trance.

'But you killed three people,' said Diane. 'How could you do that? What did they ever do to you?'

'Do you think it was easy?' he said. 'Killing innocent people? I'm a vicar, for God's sake. I feed the homeless. I care for them because no one else seems to even notice them.'

'And of course, if they're not noticed, they're not missed if someone murders them, are they?' said Slater.

'Of course they'll be missed. I miss them, you miss them. I really didn't want to hurt them; they were my friends.' Chris drummed his fingers furiously on the table. 'But I had to. They were a means to an end.'

'I think I'd better make that call now,' said Naomi. She got up from the table and walked a discreet distance away and used her mobile phone.

Diane looked puzzled.

'I'm sorry, Diane,' said Norman. 'I couldn't tell you earlier. Naomi is a detective from Tinton Police Station. She's actually the only one there who was interested in investigating these murders, but she's had her hands tied up until now. She's just calling for a car to come and take Chris away. She's recorded everything here, and we're going to give her all our evidence. I'm really sorry.'

CHAPTER SEVENTEEN

It was after midnight. Chris Moore was now safely locked away in a cell at Tinton Police Station, and Naomi Darling was busy writing a report of her investigation into the murder of three homeless men. Slater and Norman had sat with Diane until her mother had arrived to look after her and now Norman was driving Slater home.

'I guess that was a result in the end,' said Slater.

'I suppose,' agreed Norman. 'But maybe there wouldn't have been so many bodies if your girlfriend had ordered a proper investigation in the first place.'

'Yeah, you're right.'

'I am?' asked Norman, surprised.

Slater sighed. 'I want to make something clear,' he said. 'She is not my girlfriend, right? Yes, I have slept with her, but in hindsight that was a mistake. I've realised now she's not someone I could have any sort of meaningful relationship with.'

Norman looked at Slater. He had a brief 'told you so' moment, but thought better of voicing it. 'Is this what's been on your mind since you got back?'

'What d'you mean?'

'Well, something's been eating you,' said Norman. 'It's either got to be about her, or something happened while you were away.'

'Why do you say that?' asked Slater.

'You went away for two weeks in Thailand, extended it to three weeks, and yet, since you got back, you've had nothing to say about it.' Norman peered at him suspiciously.

'What do you want me to say?'

'Well, bearing in mind you asked me to go with you, I thought you might want to tell me what I missed,' said Norman. 'For instance, was the weather good?'

'The weather was fantastic. Warm sunshine every day. How do you think I got this suntan?'

'Well, from what you've told me so far, you might have spent three weeks on a sunbed down the road. I don't think you should rely on the Thai Tourist Board beating a path to your door looking for you to write their next guidebook. From what you've shared so far, I can only assume it was so unremarkable, I didn't miss anything and I made the right decision to stay here.'

Slater sighed. 'Actually I've got loads to share. It's just that I don't know where to start.'

Norman raised an eyebrow and glanced at Slater. 'Look, if you need to talk something through, I'm here, right? Isn't that what friends are for?'

'Yeah, but like I said, I don't know where to start—'

'So start anywhere. We can piece it together afterwards, if we need to.'

Slater heaved another sigh.

'Look,' said Norman. 'You've been deathly quiet about your holiday ever since you got back, so something is obviously bothering you about it.'

'Yeah, but—'

'Can you honestly tell me you're *not* preoccupied with whatever this problem is?'

'Err, well, no, I guess not,' admitted Slater, reluctantly.

'So it would be a good idea to talk about what's bothering you to help clear the fog. It can't hurt, can it? It's not as if I'm going to go broadcasting what you tell me.'

'I suppose not.'

'Right, so start talking.'

Slater sighed yet again. 'Okay,' he said, at last. 'How much do you know about your past?'

'I'm not sure exactly what you mean by that. As far as I know, there aren't any skeletons in my background.'

'When I was twelve,' began Slater, 'my dad walked out and left me and my mum.'

'Ah!' said Norman. 'I see what you mean. It's not something I'm familiar with. My parents are still together even now.'

'I was always told he had left us for another woman,' said Slater, 'and that my mum had to work her arse off to keep a roof over our heads and raise me.'

'That must have been tough,' said Norman, looking as if he wanted to say more but didn't know what.

'Yeah, that's what I believed,' said Slater. 'Up until a couple of weeks ago.'

'Why? What happened a couple of weeks ago?'

'I met my dad, out in Thailand.'

'What, you just bumped into him?'

'Well, no. He's been writing to ask me to go for months. I kept putting him off because I wasn't sure I wanted to meet him. I used work as an excuse, you know? But then when I quit, I didn't have that excuse any more and I was at a loose end, so I thought okay, why not?'

'So going to Thailand wasn't a spur-of-the-moment decision at all?' asked Norman.

'Not right out of the blue, no. It just seemed like a good time to go and meet my past, what with quitting the job and turning forty.'

'This is beginning to sound like mid-life crisis time,' said Norman.

Slater grinned. 'I suppose it is something like that, but don't panic. I'm not going to rush off and buy a flashy sports car and start trawling nightclubs for a twenty-year-old girlfriend.'

'I'm glad to hear it,' said Norman. 'No self-respecting twenty-year-old's going to go for an old fart like you anyway. Your hair's beginning to thin, and you don't have anywhere near enough money.'

'Rubbish,' said Slater. 'They'd be queueing up, mate.'

Norman laughed. 'In your dreams, maybe.'

They were outside Slater's house now. There was a light glowing behind the curtains in one of the bedroom windows, and as Norman switched the engine off he noticed the curtains twitch.

'Is Ginger still here?' he asked, gazing up at the window. 'Or do we call her Jenny now?'

Slater followed his gaze. 'Whatever you might think of her, she helped get both our careers back on the rails. Right now she's in trouble, so I think it's only right I should try to help her.'

'What trouble is she in?'

'I don't know yet,' admitted Slater, 'we haven't got that far.'

They continued to gaze up at the window.

'Anyway,' said Norman, 'you were telling me about your father.'

'Yeah,' said Slater. 'Look, I know it's late, and you're probably tired, but do you want to come in for a coffee?'

Norman knew when someone needed to talk. 'Yeah, why not?'

* * *

'He's seventy now,' said Slater, once they were settled inside. 'He's married to a Thai woman the same age as me. They have a bar in a town called Chiang Mai. It's tourist hotspot, a real gold mine.'

'And you didn't know any of this?' asked Norman.

'Not until he wrote to me a few months back.'

'So why did he suddenly want to find you if he walked out all those years ago?' asked Norman. 'Has his conscience suddenly started playing him up?'

'Well, that's the thing,' said Slater. 'It turns out he used to write to me when I was still a boy. He used to send cards for my birthday and Christmas, and he sent letters every month. He kept it up for five years, and then he stopped because I had never written back.'

'And you didn't write back because you felt he had betrayed you?'

'Oh no,' said Slater, matter-of-factly, 'I didn't write back because I didn't know where he was, and I didn't know he was writing to me. My mum made sure I never saw a single one of those letters or cards. She never mentioned all the money he used to send her every month either.'

'But I thought you said she was working her arse off to keep a roof over your head?'

'That's what she told me,' replied Slater. 'As far as I knew she was just about making ends meet, but it looks as though we were actually quite comfortable.'

'But why would she do that?' Norman sounded puzzled. 'Why pretend? And surely it should have been up to you to decide if you kept in touch with your own father?'

'Yeah, you would have thought so, wouldn't you?' said Slater. 'As for pretending, the only thing I can think is she was scared that he might tell me what had really happened to make him leave like that.'

'Ah,' said Norman, sadly. 'I think I see where this is going. So what you were told at the time wasn't exactly the truth, right?'

'Not even close,' said Slater, grimly. 'It turns out it was my mother who was playing away from home — with my dad's best mate. That's why he left the area. He couldn't stay near them once he had found out what was going on. He didn't want to leave me, but he thought I would be better off with my mother, and despite what had happened, he made sure she had enough money coming in every month to keep the house and to look after me.'

'So you've just found out your dad wasn't the villain you always believed he was. Holy shit!'

'Yeah,' agreed Slater. 'Holy shit is right.'

'So what happens now? Are you going to spend some time with him?'

'There is no time,' said Slater, grimly.

Somewhere in Norman's head, a penny dropped with a resounding crash. 'Oh crap. So that funeral you went to recently . . .'

'Yeah. My dad.'

Norman wondered just how crass and stupid he must be not to have realised. Now it all made sense. No wonder Slater had suddenly taken off to Thailand.

'Jesus, Dave,' he said, finally. 'I'm so sorry. I had no idea.'

'It's okay,' said Slater. 'How could you know? You're not a mind reader, and I didn't tell anyone.'

'Yeah, but I feel so bad . . .' Norman squirmed in his seat and felt distinctly uncomfortable. Slater glanced over at him.

'You have nothing to feel bad about, Norm,' he said. 'Honestly. I went to Thailand because my dad's wife wrote to me and told me he was dying. She told me what had really happened back then. She even sent me copies of old bank statements that proved he had been sending money to my mother.'

'What? He kept them all that time?'

'No, she kept them. I don't think Dad knew she'd done it. She had always intended to get them to me somehow, but she had guessed my mother never passed anything on to me. When my dad finally found my address, she hoped I would come to see him, but when I didn't write back she decided to take charge and send them to me. I'm glad she did.'

'Is this why you quit your job?'

'No way,' said Slater. 'I'd already quit when I got her letter. That's why I took off so suddenly.'

'Did you get there in time?' asked Norman.

'Yeah. We had a few days before he went.'

'That must have been good to see him, but pretty harrowing at the same time.'

'I don't think I'd recommend it to anyone.' Slater rubbed his jaw. 'Not seeing my dad for all that time and then finding out he's dying was bad enough, but then to find out he was actually the good guy and not the villain was a bit of a choker, I can tell you.'

'I can't imagine how you're feeling,' said Norman.

'Right now I'm feeling just a bit cheated,' said Slater, grimly. 'For twenty-eight bloody years.'

'I don't know how you deal with something like that,' said Norman. 'I've had some crappy times in my life, but that one takes the biscuit, that's for sure.'

'Having a Thai step-mother helps, believe it or not,' said Slater. 'She's a psychologist, would you believe? The last week I was out there she taught me a lot about how to deal with my anger and how this might have been affecting my life.'

'How does that work?'

'Well, for instance, I'm not good at accepting authority, am I?'

'You admit that? You never have before.'

'But now I understand why,' said Slater. 'My father represented authority when I was young, and to my mind he had let me down. Consequently, as I grew older I transferred that resentment to all authority figures.'

'Yeah, I can see that,' said Norman. 'I've always wondered why you were so quick to argue. It's a pity you didn't know that stuff a few years ago, you might not have got into so much trouble along the way.'

Slater grinned a rueful grin. 'I learned another painful truth as well. It was a lot harder to admit, but it's probably right.'

'What's that?'

'I can be pretty childish sometimes, right?'

'I think petulant is a good word,' said Norman.

'Which means childish and sulky, doesn't it?'

'Well, yeah, I guess so,' admitted Norman, reluctantly.

'It's alright, Norm. It's true. I admit it. I can be very childish at times, but now I understand why that was. Hopefully I can now unlearn that behaviour and start to grow up.'

'Wow, these are pretty big steps you've taken. Can you introduce me to this lady? Maybe she can help sort me out!'

'Sunny,' said Slater. 'Her name's Sunny, and she is a ray of sunshine. I can see why my dad loved her. You'd love her, too. Anyway, there's more. She reckons my inability to have a relationship that lasts is because I'm scared of committing to something that might end up breaking up, like my parents.'

'I've heard of that one before,' said Norman. 'It's quite common among kids whose parents split up, isn't it? You press the self-destruct button before it gets too far, right?'

'That's more or less how it works.'

'And you're okay with all this stuff?'

'I know it's a bit more complex than I make it sound, but it all makes sense to me.'

'So what happens now?' asked Norman. 'What happens with you?'

'Well, now I understand how some of the things I don't like about myself have developed, and I know why they happened,' said Slater. 'But more importantly I now know the "why" that drove them was misplaced. On that basis I'm rather hoping I can start to change those bits. Does that make sense?'

Norman looked at Slater with a big smile on his face. 'Whoa! Are you telling me you're going to make something positive out of this whole situation?'

Slater smiled back. 'Haven't you always told me I should look for the silver lining?'

'Yeah, but I never actually thought you were listening and would take it on board!'

'Maybe those seeds you were planting just needed a bit of Thai sunshine to help them grow,' said Slater.

Norman looked at his watch. 'I should get going. Are you gonna be okay? I can stay if you want to keep on talking.'

'No, you're alright,' said Slater. 'I've had a couple of weeks to get used to the idea, so I'm past the "going mental" stage.'

'If you're sure,' said Norman.

'I'm sure,' said Slater. 'How about I come over tomorrow and you can buy me lunch. At least if we're in the pub where you live, you can't say you left your money at home.'

CHAPTER EIGHTEEN

Next morning Slater slept in. He hadn't intended to, but he had forgotten to set his alarm clock. It was the gentle hand shaking his shoulder that woke him.

'Mmmnnn,' he groaned.

'Hey, wake up,' said a female voice. 'I'm doing breakfast. You've got ten minutes.'

For a moment he couldn't make sense of the voice, but then it suddenly came back to him. Ginger, or should it be Jenny? This was something he was going to have to ask.

* * *

'I guessed you must like bacon and eggs, or you wouldn't have them in the fridge,' she said as he walked into the kitchen. 'Go and sit at the table, I'll bring it through in a minute.'

He did as he had been directed. The table had been laid for two, and there was a mug of steaming tea at each place. The postman had been and Jenny had placed the two letters at the end of the table furthest from the kitchen. He sat down and picked up the letters. The first one was obviously junk, but the second had obviously come from overseas and looked official.

'Here you go,' she called, as she came through from the kitchen carrying two plates bearing toast, bacon and eggs.

He looked up as she called out. She was still wearing the same old clothes, albeit washed but still tatty. Her demeanour was different this morning, though. The tiredness still showed — he thought that would probably take weeks to change — but she didn't look anywhere near as stressed.

'You don't have to do this, you know,' he said.

'Actually, I think I do,' she said, placing his breakfast in front of him. 'If I'm going to stay here for a few days, the least I can do is cook a few meals and keep the place tidy.'

She set her own breakfast down, settled opposite him, and looked him in the eye.

'You're not here as a housekeeper,' he said.

'No, but I have to pay my way somehow, and I don't have any money. I'm not going to be able to accept your hospitality if you don't let me give something back. How do you think that would make me feel?'

He chewed on a mouthful of bacon as he considered. 'Okay,' he agreed. 'I think I can understand that, but I don't want you to feel you have to pay your way—'

'I want to, and I *do* have to,' she said. 'End of story.'

He looked at her and smiled. 'Now that's more like the Jenny I remember. And I have to say, you look a lot better today.'

She laughed and a smile lit up her face. 'That'll be having access to a proper bathroom, and hot water, and soap.'

They ate in silence for a few seconds, then she spoke again. 'What are you doing today?'

'Nothing special,' he said. 'I said I'd meet Norm for lunch, but that's all. What about you, do you have any plans?'

'There is something I'd like to do, if it's alright with you.'

'Go on.' He nodded encouragingly at her.

'I was talking to Jane,' she said. 'She says I should talk to you. She thinks you need to hear what's been happening to me and how I came to end up like this.'

'And are you ready to talk?'

'Yes,' she said. 'I've had enough of being pushed around and persecuted, but I don't know what I can do to fight back. I know I can trust you, so I think talking to you would be a good way to start.'

* * *

It was gone three by the time Slater made it to the pub. Norman was not looking best pleased.

'What time do you call this?' he complained. 'I'm starving.'

'Yeah, I'm sorry about that,' said Slater.

'You're probably going to be even more sorry at some point,' said Norman. 'And me too. Naomi called me earlier. Apparently DCI Goodnews is not best pleased that a humble DC has taken the plaudits for solving a triple murder case and made her look stupid in the process. She's also not impressed the case was solved with the assistance of what she calls "two black sheep numpties".'

'She'll get over it,' said Slater, unconcerned.

'I wouldn't bank on that,' said Norman.

'We'll cross that bridge when we get to it,' said Slater, excitedly. 'I've got much more important things to tell you.'

'Why, what's happened?'

Slater fished a letter from his pocket and handed it to Norman. 'Here, this came for me this morning. Read it.'

'But it says "private and confidential".'

Slater tutted. 'Just read it. It's important to you as well as to me.'

Norman looked puzzled but opened the envelope, slipped the letter from inside and began to read it, his mouth falling further open as he read down the page.

'Is this for real?' he asked. 'He had all this money and he left it to you? But what about his wife? She isn't going to contest this, is she?'

'It was her idea,' said Slater. 'She gets the bar, which is a gold mine, remember, and I get the money. In the long run she's probably better off this way.'

'There's enough here to—'

'Clear my mortgage, invest in our business, and still have plenty over,' finished Slater. 'Now I've got money to live on if it takes us a while to get going.'

Norman laughed an 'I-can't-quite-believe-this' laugh. 'Wow! We'd better order champagne. Oh, and there's another thing. I think I might just have found us some offices.'

'Where's that?'

'They have some old stables out the back of the pub here, and they're looking to do them up and rent them out. It would suit us down to the ground. We can take a look after lunch and you'll see what I mean.'

'It's all systems go then,' said Slater. 'And there's something else. You need to listen to Jenny Radstock's story. I'm pretty sure you'll feel the same way I did when she told me all about it this morning.'

Norman beamed. 'I think S & N Investigations & Security is almost ready for business, don't you?' he said, holding out a hand.

Slater held out his own and they shook, grinning at each other.

Norman looked around. 'Now, where's my lunch?'

THE END

THE JOFFE BOOKS STORY

We began in 2014 when Jasper agreed to publish his mum's much-rejected romance novel and it became a bestseller.

Since then we've grown into the largest independent publisher in the UK. We're extremely proud to publish some of the very best writers in the world, including Joy Ellis, Faith Martin, Caro Ramsay, Helen Forrester, Simon Brett and Robert Goddard. Everyone at Joffe Books loves reading and we never forget that it all begins with the magic of an author telling a story.

We are proud to publish talented first-time authors, as well as established writers whose books we love introducing to a new generation of readers.

We won Trade Publisher of the Year at the Independent Publishing Awards in 2023. We have been shortlisted for Independent Publisher of the Year at the British Book Awards for the last four years, and were shortlisted for the Diversity and Inclusivity Award at the 2022 Independent Publishing Awards. In 2023 we were shortlisted for Publisher of the Year at the RNA Industry Awards.

We built this company with your help, and we love to hear from you, so please email us about absolutely anything bookish at: feedback@joffebooks.com.

If you want to receive free books every Friday and hear about all our new releases, join our mailing list here: www.joffebooks.com/contact.

And when you tell your friends about us, just remember: it's pronounced Joffe as in coffee or toffee!

ALSO BY P.F. FORD

SLATER AND NORMAN MYSTERIES

Book 1: DEATH BY CARPET
Book 2: DEATH BY PLANE
Book 3: DEATH BY NIGHT
Book 4: DEATH BY KITCHEN SINK
Book 5: DEATH BY TELEPHONE BOX
Book 6: DEATH IN WILD BOAR WOODS
Book 7: DEATH IN THE RIVER
Book 8: DEATH IN A SKIP

THE WEST WALES MURDER MYSTERIES

Prequel: A DATE WITH DEATH
Book 1: A BODY ON THE BEACH
Book 2: A BODY OUT AT SEA
Book 3: A BODY DOWN THE LANE
Book 4: A BODY AT THE FARMHOUSE
Book 5: A BODY IN THE COTTAGE

Printed in Dunstable, United Kingdom

70013354R00139